THE MASTER EXECUTIONER

BY LOREN D. ESTLEMAN FROM TOM DOHERTY ASSOCIATES

CITY OF WIDOWS

THE HIGH ROCKS

BILLY GASHADE

STAMPING GROUND

ACES & EIGHTS

JOURNEY OF THE DEAD

JITTERBUG

THE MASTER EXECUTIONER

MURDOCK'S LAW

THE ROCKY MOUNTAIN MOVING
PICTURE ASSOCIATION

THUNDER CITY

WHITE DESERT

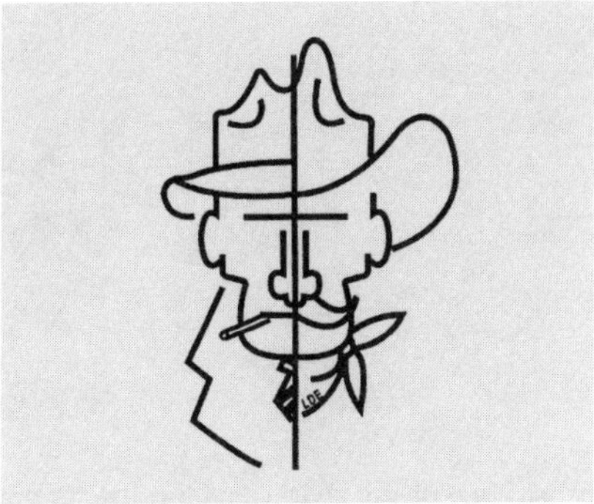

THE MASTER EXECUTIONER

LOREN D. ESTLEMAN

A TOM DOHERTY ASSOCIATES BOOK
NEW YORK

This is a work of fiction. All the characters and events portrayed in this novel are either fictitious or are used fictitiously.

THE MASTER EXECUTIONER

This book is printed on acid-free paper.

A Forge Book
Published by Tom Doherty Associates, LLC
175 Fifth Avenue
New York, NY 10010

www.tor.com

Forge® is a registered trademark of Tom Doherty Associates, LLC.

Library of Congress Cataloging-in-Publication Data

Estleman, Loren D.
The master executioner / Loren D. Estleman.—1st ed.
p. cm.
"A Tom Doherty Associates book."
ISBN 0-312-86970-3
1. Executions and executioners—Fiction. I. Title.

PS3555.S84 M3 2001
813'.54—dc21 2001023181

First Edition: June 2001

Printed in the United States of America

0 9 8 7 6 5 4 3 2 1

For Dylan Ray Brown;
a dark bouquet for a bright future

ACKNOWLEDGMENT

Thanks to Don Coldsmith, an excellent writer of historical fiction and a physician of the compassionate old school, for invaluable clinical information relating to spinal trauma—and for settling the two-hundred-year-old controversy of subaural vs. occipital.

To undertake executions for the master executioner is like hewing wood for the master carpenter.

Whoever undertakes to hew wood for the master carpenter rarely escapes injuring his own hands.

—LAO-TZU, CA. 604–531 B.C.

Part One

GALLOWS BIRD

gallows bird (găl/ōz bûrd), *n.* One who deserves to be hanged. *Slang.*

hemp (hĕmp), *n.* A tall, annual moraceous herb, *Cannabis sativa*, native in Asia, but cultivated in many parts of the world. 2. The tough fiber of this plant, used for making coarse fabrics, ropes, etc. The seeds are used as food for caged birds.

hempen (hĕmp/ĕn), *adj.* 1. Of, pertaining to, or like, hemp. 2. Of or pertaining to a hangman's noose; as, *a hempen circle*, collar, necktie, etc.; *a hempen fever. Slang.*

hemp/string (-strĭng), *n.* A hemp cord; hence, *Slang*, one who deserves hanging; a gallows bird.

—*WEBSTER'S NEW INTERNATIONAL DICTIONARY*, SECOND EDITION

Galena, Idaho, June 1897

It occurred to Anders Nilsen that if it weren't for having to wait at the train station he would be quite contented to remain both a deputy sheriff and a Methodist.

His particular sect frowned upon all the standard vices, including the use of tobacco, and although from the smell of it he doubted he would ever appreciate the taste of smoke upon his tongue, he thought the thousand little gestures involved with lighting a pipe or a cigar or a cigarette, keeping it burning, and disposing of the ash might make him look less the fool while awaiting the whistle's first reedy blast.

Reading a book or a newspaper didn't answer. There was seldom a space to sit on the benches, and anyway the words and letters had a way of coming out backwards whenever he tried to concentrate. His attempts to strike up a conversation with a fellow vigilant were usually unsatisfactory; even law-abiding individuals felt uncomfortable in the presence of a man wearing a star and responded in monosyllables. And so to avoid pacing the platform and attracting unwanted attention he was forced to lean against a post and find something to do with his hands.

The fact that of late he had begun to form certain opinions

about criminal punishment only made the wait on this occasion less pleasant than usual.

He did, however, take pride in his powers of observation. When the big new oil burner thudded up the tracks at last and the first passengers allowed themselves to be helped down by a red-faced conductor with magnificent white imperials, Nilsen amused himself by guessing their occupations based on their dress and comportment. The woman in the coarse woolen wrap and plain hat tied under her chin with a scarf had to be a schoolteacher, for what other unescorted female would take such pains to prevent her ankles from showing on the steps? The shiny black bowler and loud plaid inverness of the fellow behind marked him as a drummer even if he hadn't been lugging a sample case as heavy and bulky as a Wells Fargo box. Here was a butcher in his trademark straw boater and great belly. The disgruntled-looking older couple sold hardware, and barely enough to cover the rent on the shop. The farmer was as obvious in his suit, too short in the cuffs and ten years out of style, as if he'd left on his brogans and overalls; he scanned the platform with weather-faded eyes for a porter or someone to reassure him that the new plow—harrow? manure spreader?—he'd bought in Pocatello would indeed be delivered.

"Excuse me. I think you are waiting for me."

Nilsen shifted his attention from the farmer to the man who had addressed him. Clearly he was a banker, thickset with spectacles and a well-trimmed gray beard in a charcoal suit with the faintest of stripes, quietly tailored and beginning to show genteel wear. His hat, fawn-colored with a narrow rolled brim and silk band, was set squarely on his head and he carried a black leather Gladstone bag, scuffed at the corners but hand-rubbed to a soft shine.

"I'm afraid you're mistaken." Nilsen spread his coat a little to show the star. "I'm meeting a man named Stone."

"Oscar Stone. Yes. Pleased to make your acquaintance."

He gave his hand to the man's dry, firm grasp in confusion. "Mr. Stone. Of course. Pleased. I thought—"

"I would be tall and thin like a scarecrow, dressed all in black. That is the general expectation. I am sorry to disappoint you. You must have me as I am, you see." The tight smile in the gray beard acknowledged the existence of humor without partaking in it.

The deputy realized he was still shaking the old man's hand. Embarrassed, he let go abruptly—and became even more embarrassed that Stone might think he had acted out of revulsion. His gaze fell to the black bag. "Is that all your luggage? I'll carry it. You must be exhausted. I suppose you travel with your own, er—" He felt his face grow hot. He kept hurling himself against the shore of the man's damn implacability.

"Shirts and underthings, yes. I am not at all tired. The train did all the work. I have a trunk. You will want a porter to help with that."

The trunk was old-fashioned, long and deep and black, with painted metal corners, four leather straps buckled tight, and a brass padlock as big as a horseshoe. The contents shifted with a clank when Nilsen and the black porter lifted the trunk onto the hand cart. It was heavy enough to contain a body. The deputy had not expected it to contain anything metal. It made him curious; but there was something about Stone that discouraged questions, although he was certain that any he asked would be answered without hesitation. The newcomer handed the porter a banknote and asked him to see that the trunk and his bag were delivered to the Czarina Catherine Hotel.

"Sheriff Connaught reserved a room for you at the Railroad Arms," Nilsen said.

"Please thank him for me, with my apologies. I am getting on in years and have come to depend upon my comforts. The Catherine and I are very old friends."

"You've been here before?"

"In 'seventy-nine, yes. The Mike Rudahaugh business. You don't know it? Before your time, I suppose. A successful effort. The sheriff's name was McAndrews. Unpleasant man."

"The governor threw Charlie McAndrews out of office ten years back. He beat a prisoner to death. The man turned out to be innocent. I'm in favor of jail over execution myself. You can always undo a wrong if the man you wronged is still alive."

"Yes. Well, that is the responsibility of the courts, isn't it? If it's a question of a man's life perhaps they will be more careful." Stone dusted his palms. "Is the Sugar Bowl still in operation? I'm famished. I never visit dining cars. The menu is limited and the swaying upsets my digestion."

"It's still the best place to eat in town. I'll take you. The sheriff lent me his trap."

Among the checked tablecloths, homely still lifes, and chuckling crockery in the restaurant, Stone became animated. He looked around, eyes bright behind his spectacles, like an eastern tourist hoping to spot a frontier legend tying into a chicken-fried steak. "It has not changed. How reassuring. So much else has, you see. I stopped in Denver and did not recognize it."

He'd surprised Nilsen by ordering a bowl of tomato soup and a loaf of bread, warm from the oven and moist as a sponge, with buttered beans. The Sugar Bowl was known for its steaks and roast turkey. Stone ate fastidiously but with obvious enjoyment. The deputy contented himself with coffee and a slice of bread. Stone's appetite had for some reason deprived him of his own.

When the check came, Nilsen took it. Stone made no protest. He drank his water, wiped the corners of his mouth, and flung his napkin onto the table. "Let us go talk to your Sheriff Connaught."

Milt Connaught had the reputation of an emotionless man, which was what had elected him. Tall and chiseled, the son of a Scots farmer who had broken his health and his legacy on the prairie, he was admired for his resolution and calm impartiality. He was no vicious McAndrews, but neither was he a mollycoddler. In twelve years in law enforcement, four as chief deputy, he had not once been questioned about the propriety of his arrests or his treatment of the prisoners in his charge.

Few were aware of how much his stoicism cost him in human suffering. He endured ulcers and insomnia, went through an envelope of headache powders a day, and was separated from his wife, who had gone to visit relatives in Joplin a month ago and had not written since. He carried a miniature tintype of her in his watch case.

When Nilsen entered the office with Oscar Stone, Connaught rose from behind his desk and shook the visitor's hand. He thought there was something foreign about the comfortable-looking fellow in banker's clothes; German, perhaps, although there was no trace of an accent in his precise speech.

"We don't usually bring someone in from outside," the sheriff said. "In the past it was the head turnkey's job, but there's talk of moving the capital here. That means promotions all around, and no one wants to get stuck in a position with no future. I hope you don't mind my being blunt."

"A dead-end job, yes." Stone's smile held no warmth. "I got it in the first place because no one else would volunteer. Nothing has changed."

"You'll want to meet the man, I suppose. He's a bad one. He took a farmer apart with a Stevens ten-gauge four miles outside town and raped his widow and slit her throat. He came for a cash box that was supposed to be hidden in the house but he never found it. It probably never existed. There always seems to be a cash box involved but I've never heard of anybody ever finding one."

"Even bandits live on hope. Has he been weighed?"

He found the paper on his desk. "One hundred sixty-three and a half. We used the scales at Berger's feed store."

Stone rubbed the side of his nose. "I don't doubt Mr. Berger's honesty, but shop scales are not always accurate. They must be tested frequently and adjusted. Would he mind if I inspected them? I brought my own plates."

"I'll put it to him as delicately as I can. He's the kind to take offense."

"I'm sure he'll understand once the importance is explained. I once saw a man's head snapped clean off his shoulders because the fellow in charge misjudged the drop."

Anders Nilsen went pale. Connaught told him to see about having Stone's plates unpacked and brought around to Berger's. Nilsen went out with the key to the padlock. The sheriff liked the young man and thought him reliable, but he had too many convictions. If he stayed long enough to outlive his idealism he'd be a good deputy.

"If I put it to Berger that way, he'll agree. It would mean you suspect his scales are cheating him more than his customers."

"You are a diplomat, Sheriff. Unlike your predecessor."

"You mean McAndrews. There's a new century coming, no room for the likes of him. You may be retiring yourself soon. I heard they're installing an electric chair in Boise."

The gentle bearded face assumed an expression of extreme distaste. "I witnessed an execution by electricity two years ago in San Francisco. Barbaric. Flames shot out of the poor devil's head. It will be a dark day for civilization when such a thing replaces a short drop and a clean break."

"That's progress. The county bought me one of these new gas-powered self-loading rifles. It's sure as hell fast, but I don't know that it's a better weapon than my old Winchester."

"Thank you for reminding me. I assume there is a local ordinance against carrying firearms."

"Within the city limits. Marshal Henry will be enforcing it tomorrow."

"Splendid. Please ask him to close the saloons as well. If he chooses not to, I request that the prisoner be given a bottle of whiskey tonight. I will pay for it."

"What in thunder for?"

"It's a matter of respect. If the man must die before drunks, he should not be sober."

"That makes sense."

"Naturally I would prefer that everyone present abstain. Execution is serious business. In any case, hanging a man who is drunk or out of his mind presents complications. I cannot be held responsible for the outcome if he resists while I am trying to adjust the knot."

Something about Stone's unblinking calm brought a graphic image to Connaught's mind. Attending hangings was by far the least favorite part of his job, but he felt himself fortunate that he had never witnessed a badly botched one.

"The saloons will be closed. Do you want to see the prisoner now?"

"Please."

Morse Potter's surname wasn't Potter. At the age of six months he'd been rescued from the water barrel of a pilgrim wagon after his parents were killed by raiders. No one knew what the family was called, and so he was named for the field where the remains were buried.

When he was fourteen he'd used a hay knife to eviscerate the widowed farmer who reared him, stolen a mule and the wedding ring that belonged to the farmer's late wife, and left that country; he'd been on the run ever since. Running cost money. He had been unable to make that clear to either the clodbuster outside town or his slack-jawed woman, and that was why he was sitting in this cell instead of washing his feet in the Pacific.

"Stand up."

He didn't move or even raise his eyes. He sat on his cot with one boot off, trying to get a thumbnail under the head of a spike imbedded in the heel. He intended to use the spike as a weapon when they came to take him outside, or on himself if that didn't work. One good thrust under the corner of his jaw would spoil the show for everyone.

"Stand up or I'll have you hauled up by your ears." The sheriff sounded more tired than angry.

Potter stood, still holding the boot. Through the flat metal grid that circumscribed his world he saw that there was a third man present, a doctor or a watchmaker from his clothes and spectacles.

"Ask him to put on his boot."

"What's the matter, Parson, you don't like the stink?"

The watchmaker spoke before the sheriff could open his mouth. "I need an approximate measurement of your height, to make sure I use the proper length of rope. I don't want you to strangle."

He gathered in his grin. "You're the hangman."

"I am. If you would?"

He stooped and tugged on the boot.

"Stand straight, please." The eyes were steady behind the sparkling lenses. "Five feet ten, I should judge, including the two-inch heels. I think one sixty-three and a half was somewhat parsimonious. One sixty-seven would be closer. We shall know once the scales are tested. Are you fully prepared, Mr. Potter?"

"Prepared for what, eternity? You a Christian neck breaker?"

"Eternity lies outside my jurisdiction. What I mean to ask is, are you resigned to the fact that your life is ended?"

"What in hell business is it of yours?"

"Carrying out a sentence is an altogether different proposition when the man is stoic. In Cheyenne last year I was forced to stand by while the condemned was dragged up the steps, struggling and pleading. It was a most unpleasant business and could have been prevented with a simple injection of morphine."

"I ain't no coward."

"I am pleased to hear that." He turned toward the sheriff. "Do you observe the custom of a last meal?"

Connaught nodded, watching Potter. "He ordered steak and eggs and a pot of coffee. He'll be eating it in the morning."

"A healthy appetite is an excellent sign. Thank you for your time, Mr. Potter."

"I'll see you in hell."

"That is your privilege, of course." The two men left the cell area. Potter spat a white gob that flattened against the thick door connecting to the office.

Stone approved of the gallows and scaffold, a permanent structure, built behind the courthouse of seasoned redwood, mortised and tenoned and treated with pitch against weather. The trap swung smoothly on a pivot, released when a lever was manipulated with a foot. It fell open with a thump and the hundredweight sandbag tied at the end of the rope shot through the opening and stopped with a thud and not too much bounce.

He was less satisfied with the rope, a stiff scratchy one of new yellow hemp.

"The phrase 'to hang with a new rope' is based on a misapprehension," he told Connaught. "It needs to be stretched and lubricated until it is as supple as full-grain leather. A noose that has been properly oiled will slide swiftly through the knot and provide the snap that is required."

"I'll put Nilsen right on it."

"That won't be necessary. I brought my own."

The sheriff stroked his jaw. It was blue-shadowed and his calloused fingertips made a scratching sound like a sanding block. "Do you enjoy your work, Mr. Stone?"

"Do you enjoy yours, Sheriff Connaught?"

"Some parts. Not this one."

Stone leaned a hand against the scaffold railing and used his handkerchief to polish the toe of his shoe where the lever had scuffed it. "When a man falls four feet and swings to a rest as peacefully as that sandbag, there is no greater satisfaction."

"You mean because he's paid for his crime?"

"His crime? No. I am not a follower of the Old Testament.

Whatever his deed, no man deserves to choke to death slowly or have his head torn from his shoulders like a chicken. I am a simple craftsman, like the fellow who built this scaffold. The sweetest sound to me is the clean sharp crack of a neck breaking precisely at the second cervical vertebra."

They went from there to Berger's feed store, where under the glowering eye of the bald-headed proprietor Deputy Nilsen had removed the iron balance plates from the canvas sack in which Stone had placed them before packing his trunk. Each was embossed with its poundage clearly enough to be read easily by the meatpackers in the Chicago plant from which they'd been acquired. Stone tested the scales personally, adding and removing plates to and from the treadle as indicated and grunting when the scales proved to have been weighing three and a half pounds light, as suspected. He told the storekeeper how to make the simple adjustment, returned the plates to the sack, and went out with the sheriff while Berger was figuring out on a piece of paper how many free pounds of feed he had let walk out the door since the last time the scales were tested.

"He's forgetting how many free pounds he bought the same way," Connaught said.

"It is the German temperament. I am Bavarian on my father's side and have seen it before."

He rode in the sheriff's trap to the Czarina Catherine, where he assured Connaught everything would be in readiness by noon of the following day.

"What time should I send Nilsen around to get you?"

"Thank you, I shall walk. I prefer to stretch my muscles before work."

The lobby of the hotel was as handsome as he remembered, paneled in red oak with pink marble on the desk where he registered, but he was not yet reassured. Out there, where things changed so rapidly and no tradition was older than ten years, the reputation of an establishment depended less upon the establishment itself than upon the character of whoever owned it at present. He was a veteran of western stopping places and knew that a clerk in a stiff white collar did not necessarily mean a clean chamber pot in the room.

He accepted his key, shaking his head at the clerk's offer to summon a bellman to carry his canvas sack of weights. He'd noted the curious expression on the young man's long, pockmarked face, concluded from it that the reason for his visit was known to the staff, and chose not to expose himself to more gawking and possibly morbid questioning on the part of additional personnel. In most situations he was content to let others go on thinking from his appearance that he belonged to one of the more common professions. He only discussed his work at his own choosing.

His room to his relief was clean and comfortable, although not large, and located an inconvenient distance from the second-floor landing; all the prime space was already reserved for those who had come in to see the execution. He did not know how he felt about performing his work in public. The farther east he traveled, the more people he encountered who thought it barbaric that a man's death should be treated as a spectacle. He understood their distaste, but he also agreed with the late Judge Parker of Arkansas that a hanging carried out in private, as if it were some shameful act, was uncomfortably close to a lynching.

Oscar Stone hated lynchings. The possible injustice of the practice did not concern him so much as the shocking ignorance of those who would tie a bit of ragged rope around a man's neck and walk a horse out from under him, leaving him to twist and jerk and turn black in the face and stick out his tongue in a ghastly parody of death. He despised the untidiness, and he felt pity for the condemned. He himself did not judge a man by his crimes. Insofar as he gave the matter any thought at all, it was his belief that murderers and rapists were born missing something vital and should be no more despised for this misfortune than a man with one leg or an infant with its heart on the wrong side. It was Stone's job, once the man was judged and sentenced, to remove him as an inconvenience both to society and to the man himself. Since it took only a little more effort and a certain amount of knowledge to do the thing quickly and without physical suffering, there was no excuse for doing it any other way.

The abominable electric chair he considered a throwback to the days of inquisition and torture. To send a jolt of galvanic current through a man and boil him in his own juices was no improvement over pouring molten lead into his eyes and ears. It was hideous to witness, created an indescribable stench, and would certainly result in transferring execution from the exhibition grounds to some black dungeon, bringing to pass the worst of Parker's fears. There was no more science in the thing than scalding a hog. Any fool could throw a switch.

He removed his hat and suitcoat and unpacked his satchel, laying out his shirts, collars, socks, and underclothes in the drawers of the rosewood bureau and arranging his shaving things on top. The lid of his trunk had been left open after the sack containing his balance plates had been removed, and now he took out the oilcloth bundle that filled the rest of the space, untied and spread it out on the bed, and inspected each of the four ropes coiled in a figure-eight inside. They were as flexible as silken sashes and nearly as smooth; their braided lengths, saturated with oil, slid like satin through his hands, which were even more thickly calloused than the sheriff's from years of bending and kneading various grades of hemp, thousands of miles of Indian (the best), American (the worst), and Chinese (inconsistent, but superior when not grown in times of drought or fire or bandit raids), but sensitive to the slightest break in the fibers. He found one in the first rope he selected and frowned at it, testing and separating the frayed ends with the ball of his thumb, then laid the rope aside. He had used it only four times. It was becoming increasingly difficult to find the hand-plaited variety he preferred. Machine-made ropes were not equal to the sudden and repeated strain he asked of them.

At length he decided upon one he had used eight times but had been reluctant to use again for fear he was expecting too much. The fibers were intact, and when he worked in a fresh application of oil they accepted it without resistance. Years of search and trial had led him to sewing machine oil as a lubricant; it was light and consistent and had a pleasing utilitarian scent. It dyed the hemp a golden saffron that he liked to think removed some of death's harsh sting. When that was done he wiped the excess from his hands and wound the rope into the traditional thirteen coils—one for each stripe in the flag, and for each of the original colonies. He slapped the tight hard tube against his palm to make sure it held. Then he returned the rest of the ropes to the trunk, rewrapped the one he'd prepared in the oilcloth, and put it in his satchel. In his vest and shirtsleeves he sat up in the comfortable leather armchair reading his travel-worn copy of Marvel's *Reveries of a Bachelor* for thirty minutes before retiring.

The next morning was sunny and mild, and he did not mind the weight of the satchel as he walked the six blocks to the courthouse, where a crowd had already gathered behind it to pick the best spots. A deputy he had not met determined his identity and opened the gate in the low picket fence that surrounded the execution grounds to let him in. The old rope had been removed from the gallows by order of the sheriff, and a stepladder provided. In his shirtsleeves, Stone threaded the replacement through the staples and over the pulleys, allowing the noose to dangle five feet below the gallows arm and fixing the other end with a sailor's knot to a steel ring sunk in a concrete base buried in the earth beneath the scaffold. Anders Nilsen, sweating and fidgeting in a ready-made suit and celluloid collar and stiff new Stetson, helped him secure the noose to the hundredweight sandbag, then stood back as the hangman tripped the lever. The bag dropped without bouncing.

Together they hauled it back up to the platform and the deputy carried the bag inside the courthouse while Stone readjusted the noose and reset the trap.

All this was hot work, requiring concentration. Folding his coat over one arm. Stone descended the steps and went into a private room in the courthouse to freshen up, washing his face and hands and neck with soap and water from a basin, putting on a fresh collar and cuffs from the satchel, and combing his hair and beard. He attended to these details with the same care he brought to his ropes and balance plates, a matter of respect for the gravity of the proceedings.

While he was adjusting his necktie, a commotion took place upstairs in the cell area. Someone shouted, something struck the floor above hard enough to dislodge a powder of plaster from the ceiling onto his coat where he had hung it over the back of a chair. Then silence. He shook the coat, brushed off the rest of the dust with his hands, and was putting his arms in the sleeves when Sheriff Connaught entered, red in the face but otherwise calm. Stone approved of repose in a public servant.

"Potter tried killing himself," Connaught said.

Stone scowled at his reflection in the tin mirror above the basin. "How?"

"He got hold of a two-inch spike, I don't know where. He jabbed Nilsen with it while he was putting on the manacles to take him downstairs. It was just a prick, but when Nilsen grabbed for it Potter stuck himself in the neck. He's bleeding all over. Doc Pullen's up there. He was on hand to sign the certificate after the hanging."

"I won't hang a man who is half dead. It looks improper."

"That depends on whether the doc can stop the bleeding. We'll postpone if we have to."

"I'm expected in Fort Smith next week. If it can't be done by tomorrow I'll have to come back."

Connaught went out. Stone sat down on the chair and smoked

a cigar. It was a vice he customarily denied himself until his work was done, but he'd left his book in the hotel room and he hated being idle. He pressed out the stub in the bowl of a scarred smoking stand just as the sheriff returned.

"We'll go on. It was a sticking-plaster fix. He missed the artery."

"Good."

The execution took place twenty minutes behind schedule. Stone was standing on the platform, listening to the leather-throated vendor hawking his pretzels among the crowd, when the back door opened and Sheriff Connaught came out carrying a shotgun. A fat minister followed in a dusty coat, reading from a Bible—*"Yea, though I walk . . ."*—and behind him clanked the prisoner with manacles on his wrists and ankles, braced by Anders Nilsen and another deputy. Potter appeared calmer than Nilsen, who had a bandage wound around his left wrist. Dr. Pullen, small and sallow, with glossy handlebars like a bartender's, brought up the rear carrying his black bag.

Potter had nothing to say. As Stone slipped the noose over his head, he saw his own reflection in the man's eyes, twin death masks in that familiar glaze of defiance and hate. He placed the coils beneath the left ear, noting with satisfaction that the rope did not abrade the circle of white plaster pasted to the tender flesh under the jaw. He removed the black cotton hood from the side pocket of his coat and slid it over Potter's head. He no longer tried to imagine the blackness inside. The hood billowed in and out with the man's quickening breath—the first sign of fear he had shown, quite natural.

He adjusted the coils one last time—meaninglessly, an old habit—then stepped back off the trap, placed his foot beside the lever, and looked at the sheriff. Connaught hesitated. His throat worked once. Then he lowered his head a tenth of an inch. Stone kicked the lever. The hinge squeaked, the trap thumped. The black hood dropped out of his vision. The rope caught with a quivering twang, a gentle bass note heard only by Stone, drowned out for all others by a bang like a pistol report and under it the splintering crackle across the second cervical vertebra. The rope creaked, rotating a half turn to the left.

The crowd exhaled all at once. A woman whimpered. Another voice whispered a hoarse prayer.

Dr. Pullen waited below the scaffold while the body was lowered to the ground and the noose was removed. Through the square opening Stone watched as Pullen bent over the prisoner, feeling for a pulse. The doctor straightened, looked down at his open pocket watch, and pronounced death at 12:21 *post meridian.* Stone shook Connaught's hand and walked down the steps while Nilsen and the other deputy lifted Morse Potter's body into the white pine coffin waiting on the ground, bound for a nearby buckboard and then Potter's Field. He would return later for his rope.

For luncheon he ordered a very large salad with bread and a glass of lemonade. He never ate breakfast the day of a hanging and was ravenous. Although the restaurant was filled with people talking about the thing they'd witnessed, he had a table to himself. No one came to share it. When his salad came, the leaves white and crisp and beaded with moisture in a great polished wooden bowl, he inspected it carefully, then with a frown removed a shred of chicken with his fork and laid it on the edge of his bread plate. He hadn't eaten meat in twenty-four years.

Part Two

THE HANGMAN'S CHOICE

White shall not neutralize black, nor good
Compensate bad in man, absolve him so;
Life's business being just the terrible choice.

—ROBERT BROWNING

There's small choice in rotten apples.

—WILLIAM SHAKESPEARE

ONE

His brother was the better killer.

At twelve, Oscar was the more accomplished shooter of the pair. His reflexes were faster, and invariably his old side-by-side boomed half a second ahead of Jacob's newer single-barrel, sending a woodcock plummeting in a vertical drop as sudden and satisfying as the one his later subjects would take through the trap. From that point on he deferred to fifteen-year-old Jacob.

When neither the pellets nor the fall managed to kill the unfortunate bird, it became necessary to wring its neck. Oscar was seldom immediately successful; he would hesitate a split second, or fail to exert the force necessary, and the creature's heart would continue to flutter and one of its elliptical eyes would catch his with an expression of accusation and pain, disturbingly human. Jacob would then seize the bird by its head and snap its neck with a single one-handed twirl, like a muleskinner cracking his whip. On those occasions when two birds fell close together and Jacob got to them first, he would do both at once, whirling them above his head with a flourish Oscar thought unnecessary, showing off. The younger Stone disapproved, but he had come to dread that look of silent condemnation between bird and boy so much that he purposely lagged behind in order that Jacob might be first on the scene. They were both aware that Oscar's slowness was deliberate, but the knowledge was never spoken, and so remained a thing of shame between them.

That was in the late Pennsylvania fall, when their father's potatoes were dug and the hay was in the barn. The next year, Jacob ran away to join the Bucktails, to be counted among the fifty thousand dead at Gettysburg, three years later and less than twenty miles from the stone house where he was born. Their father was gone soon after, buried at forty-seven along with his broken dreams of a son in the medical profession. Ernst Stein himself had wanted to be a doctor like his father in Munich, but had never managed more than two dozen words in English, and Oscar, who could not end the misery of an unthinking bird, had by his comportment in general demonstrated an equal lack of potential to relieve human suffering. He buried his father on a hillside next to his mother, dead eight years of a neglected infection, and three siblings who had expired in swaddling, placed the farm for sale with the bank in York, and joined the 150th Pennsylvania there. The recruiting sergeant, a veteran since First Manassas with one empty sleeve pinned to his shoulder, never looked up from his sheet to verify Oscar's age; the bloody draw at Gettysburg had rammed a hole through the Federal reserves and the recruiters were filling it with old men and children and scarecrows from the fields.

He served for twenty months, including five weeks when he was laid up with a shattered shinbone after falling from a flatbed car on the tracks outside Chattanooga. He was on his feet too soon, so that the bones knitted poorly, and for the rest of his life limped whenever he was tired or forgot himself. The reason he got up was the 150th was pulling out for Atlanta and he didn't want to be left behind by men he'd marched, slept, and eaten with since training. War was less hideous when faced in familiar company.

He missed out anyway. He was hobbling along the Atlanta road on a crutch he'd cut from a forked limb when he heard hoofbeats coming fast behind him and without turning to look withdrew into

the trees at the side of the road. The area was crawling with Confederate cavalry and bands of guerrillas and ragged deserters who preyed upon stragglers from both armies.

"You! Soldier! What is your regiment?"

The demand was bawled in the honking bray of the East Coast Northerner and belonged to a corpulent major in a blue uniform corded with gold braid, aboard a fat gray round-muscled horse, a rarity among the gaunt mounts living off that burned-over land. He wore a felt hat with the brim pinned up on one side and a white plume curling out behind. The dozen men he had with him were mounted equally well, in uniforms less elaborate. All were armed with Henry repeaters—the first Oscar had seen, although he had heard all about them from envious fellow troops weary of recharging their muzzle loaders in the sting of battle—and all were aiming at him.

Oscar remained in the shadows, supporting himself against a tree with his Springfield rifle in both hands. But he gave the major the information he wanted.

"The One-fifty is halfway to Savannah by now," said the major. "You'll never catch them. I've a saddle needs filling. Can you ride?"

"Yes, sir." In fact he had been astraddle a horse rarely; his father would not have his plow horses used for any purpose other than the work to which they'd been broken. However, he was not so anxious to rejoin his regiment he would pass up an opportunity to relieve his injured leg of its burden.

"Name and rank."

"Oscar Stone, private."

"Squarehead?"

"No, sir, I am American."

"It matters not. Harney."

One of the men at the rear moved out of line and trotted to the front, leading a riderless gray.

"Mount up, Private," said the major. "You're one of Collingwood's Raiders now."

In 1861, John Quincy Adams Collingwood had closed the bank he owned in Rhode Island, had uniforms made for himself and those of his staff who volunteered to follow him, and struck off south to make war on the Confederacy, armed with new Henry rifles ordered to his specifications from the Volcanic Repeating Arms Company in New Haven, Connecticut. He'd had the foresight to invite along a journalist from the Providence paper, who coined the name "Collingwood's Raiders" and wired back dispatches reporting details of daring skirmishes with the rebel army and enemy courthouses captured. In reality the band wandered along the broad swath carved by the Army of the Potomac, picking off stranded wretches in threadbare gray uniforms and billeting in hotels and mortar-blasted plantation houses while patrols scoured the country around for edible crops and livestock. Below Mason-Dixon the major was best known for his table, maintained by his personal chef from his estate in Newport, and the cases of pre-Revolution wine he managed to scrounge from abandoned cellars already picked over by the hundreds of troops who had preceded him. This he did by seeking out the slaves of the departed owners and paying them to tell where the stores had been hidden to await their return; whereupon he would declare those slaves emancipated and leave them to savor the sweet fruit of freedom in the drafty and roofless cabins where he'd made their acquaintance. Regular officers who came to dine with him and proclaim the excellence of the claret were only too happy to report his humanitarian actions to their superiors, who mentioned them in dispatches when there were no new victories to declare. "An army travels on its stomach," as the major was fond of quoting his hero, Napoleon, and his had been growing since Fort Henry. The assistance of a lieutenant was required to hoist him into the saddle, and most days he suffered from gout, which he excused to visitors who found him with his foot elevated and bound as the recurring misery of a saber wound contracted at Fredericksburg.

All this notwithstanding, the Raiders had not found the war to

be one gastronomic and vinial excursion through the ruins of the Old South. They had been involved in some running fights with Confederate cavalry, and had lost one man to a sniper on the Atlanta road the day before they encountered Oscar. This was the owner of the horse he now rode.

As the newest member of the company, Oscar spent his camp time washing Major Collingwood's Irish linen tablecloth and napkins and polishing his silver. He contemplated leaving to resume his search for the 150th, but did not think his leg was up to a long journey on foot, and did not want to take the gray and risk being shot for a horse thief. He might be shot either way, if he were captured and the major decided to treat him as a deserter. And so he remained, following the path of Lincoln's army with the others and sneaking out of his bedroll evenings to soothe the burning in his red, chapped hands by smearing them with river mud, until South Georgia Crossing.

A village had existed there when the ferry had still been running across the river, but then state engineers had built a covered bridge and when there was no longer money to be made from passage, the population had moved on. Only a boarded-up schoolhouse and a scattering of cabins still stood along with the remains of the dock to mark the spot where a community had thrived. Major Collingwood moved his gear into the schoolhouse for the night while the others sought quarters in those buildings whose roofs had not yet fallen in, or wherever else offered shelter from the rain, which had begun in the morning as a light drizzle and had settled into a steady downpour by late afternoon. As was their custom, they removed what provisions they needed that night and packed the rest in an oilcloth. They then gathered the corners together, tied them, and hauled the waterproof bundle into the upper branches of a sycamore to protect it from bears.

A rifle report awoke Oscar shortly before dawn. The rain had stopped. Leaving his shelter on the sloping bank beneath the bridge, he approached the glowing globe of a lantern and found most of the command, some in stocking feet with their braces dangling, standing around the sycamore. The oilcloth bundle was gone; a frayed scrap of rope dangled beneath the limb where it had hung.

"There. I knew I hit one of the sons of bitches." Sergeant Harney, fully dressed and wreathed in smoke and the rotten egg stench of spent powder, pointed with his Henry at a dark spot on the ground that glittered in the lantern light.

"Here's another," sang out Private Wheelock. He was crouched a few yards away holding a flaming match near the earth.

Major Collingwood joined them, tucking in his shirttail, as they began to follow the trail of bloodstains, led by Harney with his lantern. The trail ended at a shallow ford downriver. The horses were brought, after which they crossed and discovered more blood on the other side. As dawn broke they found the fugitives seated beneath a twisted old apple tree, around the oilcloth spread out on the ground as at a picnic. One of them was winding a length of dirty rag around the even dirtier bare foot of another, while the rest were too busy gorging themselves on half a roasted chicken and a leg of mutton to hear the riders approaching. Their dirty, emaciated faces showed no surprise when they were surrounded, only exhaustion.

There were four, including an old man of sixty and a boy not much older than twelve. The others were young men, but their unshorn hair, whiskers, and hollow cheeks and eyes made them ancient. One of these was the man with the wounded foot. The group's clothes were a motley mix of faded homespun and Union castoff. Only the old man retained a morsel of the Confederate uniform: a gray kepi, unspeakably filthy, with a broken peak. The boy and the injured man were barefoot. When questioned, the old man revealed that the three adults were all that remained of the Tallapoosa Volunteers, an Alabama company that had been fighting since Fort Sumter. The boy had been with them only six weeks.

The prisoners were disarmed—it was a pitiful arsenal made up of one good Navy Colt, a squirrel rifle of 1812 vintage, a shotgun, and a LaMatte pistol whose action was so loose it would have had to be fired with both hands just to keep it from flying apart—and placed under guard while a conference took place.

"The articles of war are clear in cases such as this," said the major. "Enemy soldiers found in friendly dress are to be hanged as spies."

Wheelock was argumentative. "It's just old rags. They haven't enough between them to make up a complete uniform."

"The articles say nothing about completeness. In any case, we can't keep them. They will slow us down, and there is no telling when we'll come upon a regiment that will be willing to take them into custody."

Oscar said, "They're just vagabonds. They were only after food."

"Food is life," said the major. "Where do we draw the line before we starve? Gentlemen, let us vote."

The vote was eight to six in favor of execution. The prisoners were driven on foot—the injured man leaning upon the man who had bandaged him—to the covered bridge, which had taken several mortar rounds in some forgotten skirmish, leaving most of one side open with shreds of shattered siding dangling from the timbers. Ropes were produced, and the four were lined up on the open edge with nooses around their necks and the other ends slung up over a stringer. Nobody knew how to tie a proper hangman's knot, and so a square hitch was used. The man with the wounded foot cursed from the pain, the other young man spat insults and struggled when his hands were bound behind him, but Private Bending struck him alongside the head with the buttstock of his Henry, dazing him until he was securely trussed. The old man was silent. The boy cried, snuffling snot and whimpering, and his knees buckled, but Corporal Loesser hauled him up by the seat of his britches while Harney secured the noose. Oscar stood out of the way with a lump of ice in the pit of his stomach and watched.

When the last of the ropes was tied fast and the men who tied them had climbed down, Major Collingwood told Harney to get on with it. The sergeant strode the length of the bridge, pausing just long enough to give each man a one-handed shove from behind.

One neck broke, Oscar thought, possibly two; those of the young men. He heard a sharp crack, and in any case, neither of them moved beyond the jerks and twitches of healthy muscles unwilling to surrender their motor functions without a fight. The old man was all bones, a husk, and lacked the weight necessary to snap the spine, and his body writhed and twisted and his throat rattled. The boy's example, however, would stay with Oscar long after he'd forgotten how the old man had died. The young body is built to survive; once it has conquered the many pernicious childhood afflictions, it resists unnatural death in its every grain. So violent were the convulsions that Oscar thought the boy was consciously trying to regain his foothold on the bridge while the fluid cooked in his throat and his tongue slid out and his face went from scarlet to purple to deepest black. Later, an army orderly who was studying to practice medicine would tell Oscar that a body deprived of oxygen begins to expire within three minutes. He did not believe it. In his memory, the boy struggled for the better part of an hour before he swung at last in a balletic half revolution to the left, his legs drawn up beneath him to form an elongated question mark four feet above the South Georgia River.

Seeking for some place to rest other than that congested profile, Oscar's gaze slid to the boy's hands. Below the coarse rope that lashed his wrists they were swollen, with red streaks against the white where the thick veins and arteries had hemorrhaged. The fingers were as fat as sausages.

The prisoners' bowels had released, and the reek sent Oscar to the grassy bank opposite the Raiders' camp to be sick. But he had eaten nothing and could bring nothing up. He stopped trying and sat down with his forehead resting against his knees. The wet grass soaked through his trousers, chilling him. For the rest of his life, the feel of damp clothes against his skin would bring back the war, and with it the sight of the boy's hands, like scarecrow's gloves stained and stuffed with straw.

TWO

"Well, Jacob, I hope you had the chance to wring some rebel necks."

Darkness was sliding over the dead at Gettysburg. There had been plenty of sun when Oscar reached the cemetery, but he had wandered among the markers two hours before he found his brother's, nestled between a sergeant named Hilltop and a private whose Polish name took longer to read than it did to forget, and nearly exhausted the perimeters of the tiny marker: English, German, and Pole laid out according to a sameness and equality they had not known in life. The vastness of the burial ground, its thousands of pale markers laid out in even rows like stitching, made him feel smaller than he had any time during the war and filled him with a bottomless sense of alienation. He had thought his service would bring him closer in some way to Jacob, but it only succeeded in widening the gulf that separated them. The mean little skirmishes in which he had taken part did not seem to have belonged to the same war. He had not seen troops massed in formation on a sunlit field, each corps and regiment identified by bright scraps of color fluttering from staffs, had never heard the ringing of bugles calling out the many and various harsh melodies of assembly and charge and retreat, differing from one army to the next and from one body of infantry and cavalry to the next according to where they had been trained and which commanders led them. His war had not been a brilliant and terrible clash between the defenders of the Union and the champions of states' rights, but a ragged series of low and filthy scuffles involving musket fire from trees and across fences and small gaunt desperate bands slashing at one another with bayonets and sabers and shooting each other point-blank in the face.

Even after he had taken his leave at last of Collingwood's Raiders and rejoined the 150th, he had found himself fighting among strangers whose faces he barely recognized and whose names he had forgotten, each intent upon destroying as much enemy flesh as possible for no other principle than the will to come out alive. Rain fell on much of the fighting, churning the torn earth into gray slime and soaking him to the skin; when the sun came out, it brought forth the stink of blood and shit and reminded him of four corpses in rags hanging from a blasted bridge.

The visit had been a mistake. He had only made it because Gettysburg lay in the path to York, where his bank was holding the proceeds of the sale of his father's farm. He had walked most of the way, snagging rides where he could on hay carts and honey wagons where he lay among the mold and manure resting his throbbing leg. The war had been over for nearly a month, and yet a grateful Union had made no arrangements to bring its weary children home. They trudged along roads gutted by caissons and limped across fields made barren by fire and pocked with craters, the stretches between treacherous with unexploded mortar shells. He had come upon so many corpses torn apart for putting a foot in the wrong place he no longer saw them.

The countryside near home was unscarred. That night he slept in the open, in a field smelling sweetly of ripe wheat. He lay on his back with his hands behind his head, looking at the stars and making plans. He'd been raised as a farmer but had no intention of working the land; it was labor that broke the back and the heart as well when the weather proved venal, and he had seen the toll it took on his father's health. He had no training for the higher professions. The thought of chaining himself to a desk in some institution of learning after nearly two years of war seemed to him soul-destroying. He knew, too, that he had the temperament for neither medicine nor the law, and that his patience with human frailty would not extend far enough for him to teach, assuming he could acquire information sufficient to share.

His thoughts, like those of the rest of his shattered and fused-together nation, turned toward the West. Many had gone in that direction when the Homestead Act passed; many more would follow now that peace was restored. Chiefly they were soldiers like him who had walked from York to Savannah and back, Northerners no longer content to stake themselves to the places where they were born and Southerners who had no homes to which they could return. He himself could see nothing more alluring in turning over a spadeful of Kansas soil than in the Pennsylvania variety, but those who did would be dependent upon others, merchants and craftsmen and itinerant peddlers, for materials and work that would free them to live out their dreams. Oscar had helped his father and brother rebuild their barn after a windstorm had toppled it the spring he turned eleven; he had learned a great deal in a short time about routing and beveling and fitting pegs and joints and had found the clean sharp scent of fresh sawdust intoxicating. Farmers needed towns to supply them. Towns needed buildings, and buildings had to be built. Carpentry was an ancient and honorable calling, associated with the Lord. It paid well, and it did not involve death.

With the money from the farm sale deposited in an account in his name in the bank in York, he took a room in town, asked some questions of the natives, and apprenticed himself at length to a cabinetmaker named Pickerel. The first project Oscar assisted him with was the construction of a coffin.

The deceased was a doctor who had delivered nearly one quarter of the local population and served five terms as county coroner; upon his passing his likeness had appeared in the newspaper with ribbons containing the dates of his birth and death and a border of angels blowing trumpets. He was widely respected, the family was comfortably well off, and an eternal vessel of the first quality was required within twenty-four hours. The boards, selected from a shipment of fine Central American mahogany that Pickerel had been hoarding for just such a customer, had been measured and cut, and had only to be fitted, sanded, and varnished, after which the lining would be attached by a local upholsterer.

Oscar made his first mistake five minutes after he put on his apron, when he asked where the nails were kept.

Pickerel was a stout man of fifty with a superabundance of black hair. It grew without order or reason from his scalp, overhung his eyes in a thatch, covered the bottom half of his face as impenetrably thick as Georgia underbrush, and furred his forearms and the backs of his hands so coarsely that from a distance he appeared to be wearing bearskin gauntlets. From deep within this verdancy issued the roaring declaration that not one nail had ever reposed within his shop or ever would; that nails were for securing iron shoes to horses' hooves and nothing else; that wood and iron were natural enemies (wood attracted moisture, moisture rusted iron, rust stained wood) and could not be married without inviting disaster; finally, that any young man who suggested the use of nails in carpentry had better disabuse himself of the notion at once or else consider apprenticing himself to a blacksmith. Oscar applied the advice generally and henceforth forebore from opening his mouth unless directly addressed.

The assembly and finish work proceeded smoothly. Oscar respected tools, was patient with his hands, and did not complain when his fingers cramped and his muscles howled for lack of rest. Pickerel did not seem to require it and the young man was aware that whatever other part of the project the cabinetmaker was working on, his attention remained fixed on what Oscar was doing, measuring as with a level or a T-square whether exhaustion or youthful hubris—weaknesses equally low in his regard—was affecting his performance. The older man's hands were strong, his forearms as large as some men's thighs, and his eyesight was sharp, unlike his apprentice's, which had required corrective lenses for years. Pickerel exhaled an impatient gust whenever Oscar had to pause and produce a handkerchief to wipe the fog of sweat from his spectacles.

But the planing and sanding went well, and even before the varnish was applied, the dark reddish wood felt like satin to the touch. After the varnish had dried overnight, Oscar reported to work at dawn and began the painstaking, backbreaking process of hand-rubbing the glossy finish until it gave off a soft glow, as if from its own inner source of light. Pickerel's inspection was thorough; he walked around the coffin, stopping to peer at it from every angle, once resting his cheek on the beveled lid and closing one eye to sight down its length like a sharpshooter aiming a rifle, and even squatted between the sawhorses that held it up to examine the bottom. He rose with a grunt, which was as close to a compliment as it seemed he ever gave. Oscar, for whom mere survival had been reward enough for his actions for two years, warmed with satisfaction.

They had just time to clean up and change into morning coats for the doctor's family who came to view the coffin. The widow, small and shrunken in weeds and a heavy veil, was supported between her sons, themselves approaching middle age in vests and gray gaiters. Accompanying them was a solemn, flaxen-haired girl of about sixteen. This was the daughter of one of the sons and the doctor's only grandchild. She wore her hair loose behind her back after the fashion of females not yet of marriageable age, beneath a wide-brimmed straw hat with a black band and matching ribbon, and her gray dress was undecorated, a plain placket concealing even the buttons. Oscar, who had not shared a room with a female of his own generation since before the war, admired her slender hands clasped before her in white cotton gloves and the length of her neck. Throughout the inspection her eyes remained cast down or upon the coffin and never made contact with his. He felt, however, that she was aware of him.

The coffin was approved and the family took its leave. Later that morning, laborers from the undertaking parlor came to claim it. Oscar was by that time at work on another project, turning a table leg upon a treadle-operated lathe, and had no interest in the removal of this evidence of his first successful attempt at cabinetmaking; throughout his life he would refuse to linger over the details of an assignment once his part in it was finished, allowing himself only a moment of contentment over a thing properly done before directing his attention to the next. It was the German temperament, mixed with a strong dose of the Puritan, but at Pickerel's it was not at all unpleasant. He found the clean, fresh pine and powerful turpentine smells bracing, the golden haze of sawdust that filled the sunbeams as full of promise as the dawn at Appomattox, and felt no need to dwell upon what had passed, with one exception: Ever and again his thoughts returned to the solemn-faced girl in the straw hat.

Her name was Gretchen Smollett. Her father, who had left medical school after his first year, was a pharmacist, grinding prescriptions behind an elevated counter in a shop he owned eight blocks from Pickerel's. He did not recognize Oscar when the apprentice went there to purchase headache powders for his employer, but became familiar with him over succeeding visits—Pickerel was susceptible to the spirit fumes in the shop and was sometimes forced to spend days at home nursing a headache while Oscar dealt with customers, kept the books, and acted as his own master—and exchanged many pleasantries. It was clear he liked the polite young man. Even so, six weeks elapsed before Oscar found the courage to present himself at Smollett's home and request permission to see his daughter socially.

He did not spend the time wringing his hands. First he drew

some funds from his account and commissioned a suit of clothes from one of the city's finer tailoring shops, attending three fittings before both he and the stout bald man who measured him were satisfied with the hang. Then he went to a print shop and ordered 250 calling cards bearing just his name in engraved script upon pebbled ivory stock. Finally he chose a Sunday morning when he knew the family was at church to pull the bell at the front door of the modest brick house and leave a card with the sharp-featured maid who answered. When upon the next day he visited the pharmacy to place his regular order, no mention was made of his call, although Smollett was pleasant as always and gave no indication that anything had happened to alter their cordial but disinterested relationship. Oscar expected no more, and certainly no less.

He let two more days pass, then appeared at the house wearing his new suit and a pearl-gray bowler he had purchased at the same haberdashery where Smollett acquired his hats. The maid took this, along with the roses he had brought from a florist and conducted him to a parlor hung with flocking and paintings of flowers in oval frames, where the pharmacist received him warmly. Oscar shook Smollett's hand and declined a cigar, sensing that to indulge in the habit might count against his character. Smollett began the conversation by expressing his reservations about whether his daughter was of an age to receive male visitors. Oscar replied that he understood and was willing to abide by his decision. The pharmacist nodded in approval and asked him what his intentions were.

"Marriage, sir. If Gretchen and I are pleased with each other's company, and if she will have me and you approve of the match."

"But you have seen her only once, and the two of you did not speak."

"That's true. But I know her family's reputation, and even on that short acquaintance I could see that she was well brought up."

Smollett pulled on his cigar; he had no prospective father-in-law to impress. "You served in the war against the Rebellion, I understand."

"Yes, sir, with the Hundred and Fiftieth Pennsylvania Volunteers."

"My wife's brother served with the Seventy-fifth. He was killed at Gettysburg."

"I lost a brother there as well."

"A criminal waste. I hope you don't intend fighting in any more wars. I won't have Gretchen a widow when she is barely a woman."

"I'm finished with war." He spoke firmly.

"How old are you, Mr. Stone?"

"Eighteen, sir."

Smollett lifted his brows. They were darker than his hair, and heavy; his father's likeness in the newspaper had contained the same feature. "You lied about your age when you joined. I can see why it wasn't questioned. You seem older. What is your education?"

"I left school after eighth grade to work on my father's farm."

"You speak well for a man with so little schooling."

"My mother taught me to read from Shakespeare. I still read a great deal."

"Is it your intention to make your living as a carpenter?"

"Yes, sir, it is."

"There are many carpenters in York. I don't suppose it pays very well."

"There are fewer out West, where their work is in greater demand. That's where I will go after I've served my apprenticeship."

"What part of the West? Ohio?"

"Kansas."

"Good God! It's a desert!"

"Hardly, sir. It's cattle country. The world needs meat, and when the railroads come through it will become a major shipping point. They will need stock pens and barns, and hotels and houses to shelter the buyers and workers. Craftsmen of every kind will be in short supply."

Smollett smoked the better part of his cigar in silence. At length he put it out. "I will be in communication with you shortly, Mr. Stone. In the meantime, I hope you will give this adventure of yours a great deal of consideration. I won't risk my daughter's life among savages."

Oscar rose. "I've already given it a great deal of consideration, sir. My decision is made."

"In that case you may have my answer now."

"I think I already have it. Thank you for seeing me, Mr. Smollett."

For the next several weeks, Oscar and Pickerel were busy filling an order placed by a retired professor of history from Philadelphia for six book presses, routing and fitting the black walnut and fighting with the glazier, who arrived drunk and remained in that condition despite all attempts by master and apprentice to locate and destroy the bottles he had smuggled in and squirreled away in various niches. When the man's leaded panes continually failed to fit the doors Pickerel and Oscar had built, the cabinetmaker threatened him with a hammer. Oscar stepped between them and the glass man wobbled his way out the door.

"That was a mistake," Pickerel said. "His customers won't thank you."

"We'll find someone else."

"We haven't the time. You'll have to do it yourself."

"But I'm a carpenter."

"I'm the only carpenter here. Look here, if you take your time with a thing, you can't help but do well. Do well every time and you're a craftsman. Do it with *respect*, and you may one day become a master. Without it you're just a man with tools. Anyone can own tools. Look at that ass who just left."

Oscar had observed the glazier at work. He took his time, did not break any panes, and took reasonably well to the unfamiliar skill, although not to his own satisfaction; after all these weeks he was still somewhat distracted by his failure with the pharmacist. *There* was another thing he thought could have been done better, but he did not know how. Perhaps he was just a man with tools.

He was alone in the shop, routing one of the doors for hinges, when Smollett's maid appeared in a bonnet and cape, bearing an invitation from her master. Mr. Stone's presence was requested at a social gathering at the Smollett home Friday evening next. Her master had instructed her to add that Miss Gretchen would be in attendance.

THREE

Oscar's tailor, an unflappable Russian who had seen his father beaten for refusing to remove his hat when Napoleon's coach passed at Tilsit, altered a suit of evening clothes to the young man's fit in one astonishing day, and so Oscar's appearance was one thing that did not trouble him during four hours of tea and biscuits and stultifying conversation about Southern Reconstruction in the close drawing room at the Smolletts'. He saw again the pharmacist's brother, a senior law clerk in a firm that specialized in real property transfers, made the acquaintance of Mrs. Smollett, a pale quiet woman with dark circles under her eyes who appeared to be several years older than her husband, and was introduced to Gretchen, after which they talked for some time on a bench upholstered in scratchy mohair. She wore a becoming slate-blue dress that brought out the color in her eyes, the inevitable white gloves, satin pumps, and a very large bow in her hair that looked as if it might carry her aloft in a strong wind. He did not remember what they talked about, that night or later, and supposed it to be of little consequence, as meaningless as the drab affair that had been assembled merely to place them in the same room. He did notice she had a low, pleasing voice, and that when she forgot herself and looked him in the eye without embarrassment, the way a man would, he was more intrigued than disconcerted, somewhat to his surprise.

On their second meeting he took her riding in a hired trap. He spoke of his plan to practice carpentry in Kansas, watching her out of the corner of his eye for signs of disapproval as he drove. She gave none, saying nothing and looking at scenery she had seen a thousand times, with one hand holding her flowered hat in place. He concluded that she'd been forewarned by her father.

He attended church with the family, sitting next to Gretchen and sharing a hymnal with her when they rose to sing. Her sweet contralto stirred him in ways he had not anticipated when he had selected her as a suitable candidate to share his new life.

Two months passed in this fashion. In December, when snow was on the ground he came to take Gretchen skating. Smollett greeted him at the door instead of the maid and asked to speak with him in the parlor. On this occasion, when a cigar was offered, Oscar accepted.

"I've spoken with my brother," the pharmacist began. "There is a place for a junior clerk in the firm where he works. He's agreed to recommend you to the head of the firm if you will in turn agree to give up this wilderness scheme and settle down in York with my daughter. My brother expects to be offered a partnership next year, and then there will be an opening for a senior clerk. I think you have the character and the ability to fill it."

"I haven't any training."

"That will be provided. Steadiness and intelligence are all that is required."

Oscar took a long pull on his cigar, placed it in a brass tray, and stood. "Please thank your brother for the offer, Mr. Smollett. I cannot consider it."

"You mean you will not."

"They are the same thing."

Smollett's dark brows drew together. "Even if it means giving up my daughter's hand?"

"I'm sorry, sir. I had the dream before I knew the daughter."

"Sit down."

"Standing or sitting, the answer is the same."

"Sit down, confound it."

Oscar sat down.

Smollett rotated his cigar rapidly, puffing up a thick veil that concealed his expression, and eventually most of the features of the room. After two minutes he leaned forward and pressed out the cigar beside his guest's. His face was a vague oval. "What made you decide upon my daughter to accompany you on this insane adventure?"

"She is healthy and young. I suspect she will bear many children."

"Well, thank God for that. I was afraid you were going to tell me you were in love."

Oscar had not considered the matter until that moment. He supposed he loved Gretchen, at that. He thought it a positive sign, after the war, that he could still manage to astonish himself.

"Your mind is set."

"Yes, sir, it is."

"She is my only child. Her mother will not bear the separation."

"She can visit us, sir. You both can, and we can come back to visit. In a few years' time the railroads will reduce the journey from weeks to days."

"By then you both will have been eaten by bears or scalped by savages."

"If I thought that were a likelihood I would go alone."

"You *will* go alone."

Oscar sat with his hands folded politely in his lap and let his cigar smoke itself out.

The mantel clock chimed, echoing like a ship's bells in dense fog. Smollett leaned back then and tugged at the bell rope hanging beside his armchair. The maid entered, curtsied, and coughed.

"Alma, bring the cognac and two glasses. Mr. Stone and I have a betrothal to celebrate."

The wedding was set for May. Oscar arranged with the Russian for a suit of formal clothes and kept out of the way while Gretchen and her mother discussed invitations with the same printer who was responsible for Oscar's calling cards and planned the details of the ceremony. This was not difficult. Pickerel had accepted a commission to provide desks and seats for a schoolhouse in rural Red Lion, and he and Oscar worked throughout the winter crafting the one-piece items from yellow oak. Whatever diversions the project offered in the beginning, by the third desk the work had become redundant and mindless, with seventeen desks still to be built. So the cold months passed, one day marching stiff-legged into the next, while Oscar's thoughts drifted ahead to Kansas and the fresh challenges that awaited him in the West.

The desks were ready for shipment in April. Because the shop was crowded with the stacked merchandise, work was impossible, and Pickerel gave Oscar a week off to rest and prepare for his wedding. But he had no preparations to make, and Gretchen was too busy with her own and had no time for him. He visited the shop daily to talk carpentry with the proprietor. On the day of the wedding, he found the shop clear of desks and Pickerel seated on the stool before his bench, glowering at a chisel in his hand. Representatives from Red Lion had paid him early that morning and loaded the shipment aboard two wagons.

"This is the first tool I ever bought," Pickerel said. "It's twice as old as you."

The chisel looked it. The corners were worn round and only a few shreds of red paint remained on the handle, itself shiny with wear. Oscar wondered if the cabinetmaker was going to make a ceremonial presentation.

"It must be a very good chisel."

"It's the worst thing in the shop. The fellow who sold it to me said it was made of high-carbon steel, hard as a diamond. I can bend it in my hands." When he turned it, Oscar saw that the shaft curved slightly. "People are still using some of the pieces I made with it. I hope I never see one again."

The young man smiled. "You told me it's a poor carpenter who blames his tools."

"Blames, yes." He flipped it onto the bench. "When you use the best equipment, you have no excuse for doing second-rate work. Excuses are a luxury for blunderers. A master never leaves himself a reason to fail."

"I'll remember that."

"If you do, you'll be the first who does. There will be nothing more I can teach you."

"Are you coming to the wedding?"

Pickerel held up his hands, large and scarred, blotchy from acids and stained dark with extract of walnut, years of it on top of calluses as thick as dog pads. "Can you see these poking out of white cuffs? You can tell me about it later, but only if one or both of you trips on the way down the aisle. Flawless weddings put me to sleep. I've had twenty chisels since I bought that first one, all of them twenty times better. Guess which one I think of when I think of a chisel."

"I wish you'd change your mind."

"You can always wish, except when you're working."

Silence settled like sawdust. Oscar stirred it by drawing out his new gold pocket watch—an early wedding gift from his future father-in-law—and popping open the face. He was expected at the church in twelve minutes. "What are we working on next?"

"I have to make a new dado for the courthouse. Worms and weather have done for the old one."

"I'll be in first thing Monday."

"I don't know why. I said there's nothing more I can teach you."

"But I'm no master."

"God makes masters. I only make carpenters, and few enough of those. If I had the time I'd make a cabinetmaker out of you, but that takes years, and it's foolish to discuss years with young men. Go to Kansas and show them how it's done. If you stay here you'll end up turning out school desks."

Oscar smiled. "I may have to use some nails."

Pickerel's bearded face bunched like a fist. "Do it. Don't talk about it."

"Thank you, sir." He couldn't think of anything else to say.

"Don't. And don't cut any more glass, either, unless you're prepared to give up carpentry. A jack-of-all-trades is just a blunderer with versatility."

A hired phaeton, its white ribbons wilting in the misty spring rain, was drawn up before the church, where a sour-faced driver in an old-fashioned beaver hat waited to whisk the newlyweds to the hired house in the country where they were to spend their first weekend. Oscar, who had a horror of getting wet after South Georgia Crossing, hurried up the steps. Smollett intercepted him at the door and asked him to join him in the minister's office.

The bridegroom accompanied him, apprehensive. Had Smollett enlisted the clergyman to aid him in his campaign to keep the couple in Pennsylvania? He found the determination of the middle-aged demoralizing.

But the minister was not present. There among the theological tracts decaying away on shelves and the general musk of dusty male spinsterhood—stale tobacco, old brandy, and Bay Rum—the pharmacist handed him a thick envelope bound with a black ribbon. Oscar, who thought at first it was money, started to give it back. His savings were enough to stake them to a start on the plains and he did not intend to begin his new life with a debt. Smollett's hands went into his pockets, however, and would not come out to accept it.

"They are letters of introduction, signed by the president of my brother's firm at his request. They will recommend you to speculators in Topeka for whom the firm has handled a number of acquisitions. A bank and a granary and a number of shop buildings are planned. They will need a good carpenter."

"Topeka?"

"It's the capital, as I'm sure you know. At present it's a farming community, but that will change soon enough when the railroad goes through. Surveyors are there now, with the army in place to protect them from hostiles. I take some comfort from that."

Oscar's tongue was in a tangle. He had not gotten so far in his thinking as to pick a town. He had had the dream, but the vision had belonged to a sedentary York merchant who feared for his daughter's future. He managed at last to thank him.

"Thank my brother. He never could refuse Gretchen anything. As for me, I'd be a poor father if I let her starve in the Great American Desert." He took his hands out of his pockets and grasped Oscar's right.

FOUR

On June 12, 1866, the Stones, Oscar and Gretchen, left a grave-faced Smollett supporting his weeping wife on the station platform and started with a lurch for St. Louis. Their luggage, in addition to various carpetbags, included a brass-cornered trunk bearing the name of Gretchen's grandfather, originally used to transport medical instruments, and which now contained counterpanes and clothing; a dress form that had belonged to Mrs. Smollett, pressed upon the daughter along with several bolts of material in the certainty that without them she would soon be reduced to wearing hides; and a three-foot wooden box with a pole handle, piled high with carpentry tools.

Upon arrival in the sprawling city of chimneys and bridges, the couple took a room in the railroad hotel and spread copies of half a dozen local newspapers on the bed. It became apparent immediately that they would experience less difficulty than Oscar had imagined in finding an acceptable number of fellow emigrants with whom to continue their journey west; quite the opposite, in fact. In the spring of the first year of peace, so many wagon trains were organizing in St. Louis that the couple was forced to fall with pencils in hand upon the many advertisements recruiting pioneers, circling the happy features and striking out the undesirable ones, as if working a Sunday puzzle. In the face of this crush, Oscar fretted that he had struck too late after all, and would find dozens of carpenters already ensconced in Topeka, engaged in savage competition. Gretchen, whose coolness of character had begun to assert itself at the time of their betrothal, snuffed out this fear by pointing out that however many rivals had preceded him, many more hundreds of customers were on their way every day.

They signed on at last with a train being organized by a wagon master named McNutt. Lately an officer with the Kansas State Militia, Colonel McNutt was a small man of clerkly appearance, shorter than Oscar, with longish hair gathered into a queue beneath the broad flat brim of his black hat and a long black coat buttoned to his chin, which gave him the appearance of a priest. He had in fact taught Sunday school before the war. Beyond the standard requirements of sufficient supplies and provisions, the colonel stipulated that the members of his party refrain from cursing, card-playing, and imbibing of alcoholic beverages for the journey's duration on pain of instant banishment. Oscar, who had no proclivities in any of these areas, agreed, and signed a pledge to that effect. McNutt kept his hands behind his back throughout the discussion and did not offer one, but expressed his pleasure at having an experienced carpenter along, as breakdowns were frequent.

The costs of wagons took Oscar aback. He had allowed for a hundred dollars to cover both vehicle and team, and was appalled to learn that the cheapest wagons sold for eighty dollars. Moreover, he was disappointed with the quality of the less expensive specimens. He settled finally upon a Studebaker built of stout hickory upon an elmwood frame that rang like iron when rapped with a knuckle. The cover was a new one of bleached twill waterproofed with linseed oil, and he approved of the fact that all the holes for the pegs that held the construction together had been burned through with hot irons rather than bored with augers in order to avoid cracking the wood. He paid ninety dollars for the wagon and parted with an additional eighty for two pairs of oxen, which informed opinion had convinced him were superior to mules for endurance, if slower; eight miles per day was the average. Colonel McNutt had added that the animals posed less temptation for Indians, who preferred to steal mules and horses for purposes of riding, and could also be eaten in case the stores ran out; mule meat being disconcertingly tough and notoriously pungent.

When it came to supplies and provisions, Gretchen's counsel was invaluable. The amounts of flour, salted meat, dried fruits and vegetables, beans, and coffee, as well as water to sustain them, were mysteries to a young man who for three years had lived upon forage and restaurant fare. Fortunately, a minimum of grain was needed for the oxen, who were expected to graze their way to Kansas, freeing up funds for the procurement of spare parts for the wagon. After buying up pots, pans, and miscellaneous other utensils, Oscar spent an evening with paper and a pencil and decided that the balance was sufficient to set the couple up in Topeka, with a little set aside for emergencies. The figures were tight enough to cause him to reconsider the cost of his wedding suit, but after giving the matter some thought he concluded that it had been an investment as sound as any he had made since he had first settled upon Kansas, all those months before when he was hiking home from Atlanta; it had gotten him Gretchen, and the value of her partnership had proven itself fifty times over. He found her a cool head and a warm companion. They had discovered together the rewards and awkwardnesses of the physical act of love, begun to learn each other's shortcomings and strengths, and come to terms with the fact that they were two flawed individuals embarked upon an adventure greater and more frightening than a mere two hundred fifty miles of uncivilized country.

The trek was frightening enough, however. Rising before dawn on the day of departure, they were white-faced and excessively polite. They found a measure of calm by reminding each other that the situation was more tense for those in the train who were headed all the way to California and Oregon, and jested that as they neared

Topeka, the couple might have to take turns standing watch to see that Oscar was not abducted to employ his skills in repairing wagons the rest of the way across the country. "Perhaps they'll see I'm not that good," said he, "and we'll both be able to sleep."

"You are that good," she replied gravely.

It was a large procession, made up of sixty wagons arranged in fifteen segments, four wagons to each, with a bearded band of experienced men on horseback herding what appeared to be several thousand cattle and horses at the rear—food for the travelers and a second string of mounts for the herders and the buffalo hunters who rode on ahead. In transit, the wagons were strung out over three quarters of a mile, with the women and children riding on the seats and the men walking beside the teams of oxen, carrying whips and rifles. Oscar shouldered the muzzleloading Springfield he had carried all through the war, freshly cleaned and glistening with oil. The weather was pleasant, the stately pace agreeable, and the distractions were at a minimum, giving him opportunity to dream of success and plan toward its attainment.

By the end of the first week—the first long, relentless, unchanging seven days—he found himself wishing for some disaster, albeit a small one and harmless, to interrupt the monotony. It occurred to him that his Great Risk, what his father-in-law had called "this insane adventure," had in practice shown itself to be no more diverting than making school desks. He had anticipated Indians, wolves, grizzlies, herds of stampeding buffalo. The south bank of the Missouri River had so far given him only noisy flocks of unidentified birds and the occasional jackrabbit. Even his dreams had begun to fail him, as by night he lay beneath the wagon with Gretchen breathing evenly beside him and relived in his sleep the uneventful events of the day past.

On their tenth day out, the warped notes of the signal trumpet belonging to Colonel McNutt drifted back to Oscar's wagon and the train came to a ragged halt. After thirty minutes of unexplained delay, Oscar joined a small group gathered several wagons ahead and inquired after information. His question was interrupted by a comment from a red-bearded Irishman named Grady.

"It can't be an attack. We'd have had some warning."

Willett, a cadaverous West Virginian, shook his head. "All I know is, McNutt's pow-wowing right now with the chief, or whatever he is. Giving the herd away, most like."

It developed that a band of Indians had stopped the train and that the wagon master was meeting with some of their representatives. Willett's prediction that they were after the livestock turned out to be one of the more optimistic. Some of the others thought it was the women they wanted. A former Missouri riverboat pilot who called himself Captain Dick believed the Indians were delaying them until the rest of the tribe arrived, after which there would be a massacre. Rifles were inspected.

A clatter of hooves caused Oscar to thumb back the hammer on his Springfield. The newcomer was no savage, however. R. J. Carmichael, long and brown in an eastern suit of clothes worn shiny in the seat and along the left forearm where he cradled his Hawken rifle, drew rein and leaned down from his saddle to address the group. The former mountain man had served as an Indian scout for the army and had hired on as the expedition's guide. Whatever disappointment he had caused by not reporting for work in romantic buckskins was balanced out by his creased and weathered face and the smell of hickory smoke and spent powder that clung to him.

"Any of you gents palaver Dutch?"

Karl Van Horn spoke up. "My family came from Amsterdam. I didn't learn English until I was ten."

"Not that Dutch, the other Dutch. You. What're you?" He pointed a brown wrinkled finger at Oscar.

"I'm American. My father was German."

"You palaver the lingo?"

"A little."

"Climb aboard. Leave the rifle."

Oscar handed the Springfield to Grady, who offered to look after Gretchen while he was gone. Oscar liked the Irishman; he was traveling with his wife and eight children, including a son who was close to Oscar's age.

"Don't squeeze my ribs so tight. I got a Blackfoot arrowhead in there."

Riding behind Carmichael, Oscar loosened his grip around the guide's trunk and squeezed the piebald mare's sides with his thighs. Even the many months with Collingwood's Raiders had not made a horseman of him. "How is my German going to help?" he asked over the galloping of the hooves.

"Your people have been coming out here since the forties," Carmichael said. "Dutch is the only civilized lingo some of them talk."

They arrived at the front of the procession, where a sheet had been removed from a wagon and stretched across the top of four wooden stakes to create a canopy. In its shade, Colonel McNutt sat cross-legged on the ground facing three men seated similarly. The strangers wore hide leggings, plain red breechclouts, and moccasins decorated with beads and quills; nothing else aside from feathers in their long black hair. Their skin was a deep cherry color, as if burned by the sun.

Grasping Oscar's arm—was he afraid he might escape?—Carmichael ducked under the canopy and directed him to sit beside McNutt while he arranged himself on the other side. Oscar could not tell which of the three men who faced them was the one in authority. They looked to be close in age—early to middle thirties—and wore nothing to indicate to the outsider a designation of rank. Their eyes were red-rimmed from constant exposure to sun and wind, and their faces were in the Oriental cast, made up of bunched ovals with prominent noses and strong chins. They might all have been related. The three studied him with curious interest and what seemed to him recognition. He supposed they were reacting to his Germanic features.

McNutt addressed Oscar without looking away from the Indians. "Stone, isn't it?"

"Stone, yes."

"They're stubborn, Stone. Carmichael says they're Cheyenne so he opened with that, but it might have been Chinese for all they stirred a hair. They would have none of Sioux and Arapaho either. Start by telling them who you are, but don't ask them their names. Indians are superstitious about identifying themselves to strangers."

Oscar thought for a moment. He hadn't spoken German in many years. His father had discouraged it in his house, not wanting his sons to share his encumbrance.

"Mein name ist Oscar Stein." This he directed to the man in the middle, on the theory that the center of a triangle is the strongest part.

The faces brightened. The man in the middle turned his head right and left and said something low in a language that was neither German nor English. The others responded with wordless gutturals. Then all three fell silent and resumed looking at him.

"Tell them you're a carpenter."

He searched for the word. *"Ich bin ein Zimmermann."*

"Zimmermann?" The Indian on the right tasted the unfamiliar term.

"Wald." Oscar looked around, then reached out with a fist and rapped on one of the wooden stakes that supported the wagon sheet.

"Sie sind Wald?" The man on the right appeared puzzled. He reached out suddenly and touched Oscar's knee. When he flinched, the Indian drew back his hand quickly, as if in apology.

Oscar put a smile on his face. He was afraid it looked like a grimace and spoke softly. *"Nein, nein."* He pantomimed holding a nail with one hand and hammering at it with the other, clicking his tongue to imitate the sound of the blows. He couldn't help feeling that he was betraying Pickerel.

All three Indians grinned broadly then. They hadn't a full set of teeth among them.

"*Wo gehen sie?*" asked the man on the right.

"Kansas."

The Indian on the left snorted and leaned across to whisper hoarsely in the ear of the one on the right, who laughed, a short bark, and spoke rapidly in German.

"What did he say?" asked McNutt.

"I couldn't catch it all. Something about going from where there is much wood to where there is little."

"The one on the right's the leader," Carmichael said. "It's like them to throw us off. Confounding white men is their biggest sport."

"Ask them what they want."

"*Wass wollen sie hier?*"

The leader studied Oscar's face. At length he raised a hand and pointed two fingers at his own eyes.

"I think he wants to try on my glasses."

"Let him have them," McNutt said.

He unhooked his gold-rimmed spectacles and held them out. Calloused fingers brushed his hand as the Indian took them. He put them on, clumsily hooking them over one ear and then the other. With his long hair and whiskerless face he looked like an ascetic from the Far East. When he turned his head to show his companions, they looked at him and hooted.

"They don't appear to bother him none," said Carmichael.

Oscar said, "Perhaps he is nearsighted."

When the hooting stopped, the man wearing the spectacles pointed to the Indian next to him and jerked his chin in the direction of the three white men.

"You will give us eight of your cattle for permission to pass through our land," the Indian in the middle told McNutt.

McNutt said, "You speak English."

"I speak German as well, and some Sioux. My first tongue is

what you white men call Cheyenne. Hunting Water prefers to speak for himself, and to make himself understood. Bad mistakes have been made by Cheyenne translators in the past." He looked directly at Carmichael, who stirred.

McNutt touched the guide's knee before he could open his mouth. "Hunting Water is your chief?"

"He speaks for us."

The Indian on the right leaned over and whispered in his ear.

"Hunting Water says he wants to keep the spectacles as well. You are right," he told Oscar. "He cannot see far and has missed many buffalo."

"Can you get along without them?" McNutt asked Oscar.

"I will manage as far as Topeka."

"Tell your chief we can only part with four head of cattle. Most of us are going all the way to the great water in the West."

There was a quick consultation among the Indians in a language Oscar did not know. The man on the left raised his voice sharply, but the leader cut him off. The one in the middle looked at Colonel McNutt.

"Runs the Snake says you can spare eight."

"We might," McNutt said. "We won't."

"That is what Hunting Water said. He said also that if we want eight cattle and you want to give us four, there is a number upon which we all can agree."

McNutt held up six fingers.

The Indian in the middle looked at Hunting Water, who nodded. He then looked at the Indian on the left, who was scowling at the ground between his spread knees. After a moment he nodded, a brief jerk.

Hunting Water grinned at Oscar and spoke in German.

"Now what?" asked McNutt.

"He says he can now see a bird's thing from a mile away."

That was why, three weeks later, Oscar Stone's first glimpse of Kansas was blurred.

FIVE

In Topeka, where those members of the party who were going on stopped to rest and replenish their supplies, Oscar shook hands with Colonel McNutt, who thanked him for his assistance with the Indians and told him to look for him in Portland if he ever ventured that far, and arranged for a room for himself and Gretchen at the Baron Hotel until they could find a permanent residence. The Baron, like the city itself, was in the midst of construction; the couple awoke early in the morning to the pounding of hammers and hee-hawing of saws, crept along one wall of the corridor leading to the lobby stairs in order to avoid the painting and papering taking place on the wall opposite, and breathed sawdust day and night. The smell was like oxygen to Oscar, who associated it with prosperity, but although Gretchen never complained, her eyes watered constantly. He determined to settle them on the older end of town where the signs of growth were not so bumptious as soon as he found employment.

The oculist who fitted him with new glasses had spread a canvas tarpaulin over the floor of his consulting room to keep out the dust from the former feed store below, currently being converted into a dress shop to accommodate the expected influx of wives and daughters when the railroad came, but fibers and shavings still found their way through the spaces between the planks. A fine powder coated everything, including the lenses and instruments kept in drawers. It affected the oculist's lungs as well, and when Oscar's lenses were ground and fitted into new gold frames he was grateful to pay his bill and remove himself from the coughing and hacking.

His ardor for the new life he had planned for so long had by this time leveled off. He'd been to see three of the men for whom his father-in-law had given him letters of introduction, and after reading the *Daily Commonwealth* from front page to back in their outer offices, he'd been admitted only long enough to be told with regret that their carpentry needs were fulfilled for the time being. They inquired after the health of Smollett's brother, shook his hand, and instructed him to tell their secretaries where he could be reached as soon as something opened up. His worst fear—that he'd come too late to take advantage of the construction boom—was realized. The funds remaining from the sale of his father's farm, deposited now in a local bank, would not see the newlyweds through the summer if he didn't find work—or move farther west, where the railroad would not reach until later and the pickings were not yet exhausted. Each day they remained in the hotel chipped away at their capital, reducing the latter option. A decision would have to be made soon.

"If only you had come to me this time last year. We were positively desperate for masters in every craft."

Cornelius Skinner ran the local land office for the Atchison, Topeka, and Santa Fe Railroad. A florid man with a head of elaborate silver-gray hair who wore his suitcoat buttoned only at the top after the western fashion to expose the ornaments of fraternal affiliation on his watch chain, he leaned back in the studded leather chair behind his desk and shook his head at the letter Oscar had given him, as if he could communicate his disappointment to its author. "Yes, an accomplished carpenter in July of 'sixty-five could have punched his own ticket."

"In July of 'sixty-five I was still walking back from Georgia," Oscar pointed out.

"Yes. Well." Skinner laid down the sheet and spread his plump pink hands. The smile on his face was sympathetic.

Oscar leaned forward in his chair. "It doesn't have to be fine work. You must be shorthanded somewhere. The whole city is under construction."

"Smollett speaks highly of your work. I wouldn't insult you."

"Please insult me, Mr. Skinner. I have a wife to support."

The railroad man drummed his polished nails on the blotter. At length he drew a sheet of foolscap from the top drawer of his desk, wrote something on it with a horsehair pen dipped in purple ink, and signed it. He blotted it and sealed it in an envelope.

"Give this to Berensen at the county courthouse. You'll find him working behind the building. He's foreman on a project there. He complained to me just last week he was having trouble keeping men on the job. Some men are superstitious."

"What's he building?"

"A gallows."

A farmer named Emmett Hollingshead had aroused the suspicion of his Shawnee County neighbors six months before when he told them his wife Rachel had gone to visit relatives in Kansas City. When they asked why a woman would undertake such a lengthy trip alone in a hired buckboard in the dead of winter, he confessed that they had had a fight and she had packed her things and left without much thought to the hardship. This at least was plausible; on any evening when the conditions were right, neighbors as far away as half a mile could hear the couple's voices raised in anger, often punctuated by the unmistakable sound of shattering crockery.

Nevertheless, the husband's explanation seemed deficient, and word reached the county sheriff, who sent deputies to visit the Hollingshead farm. The owner greeted them affably and conducted them upon a tour of the house and outbuildings, allowing them to open doors and shine lanterns into dark corners. The wardrobe in the bedroom was empty of feminine clothing, indicating that she had indeed left with all her worldly accoutrements, and he showed them a rectangle of clean floor in an otherwise dusty crawl space where it appeared a large trunk had reposed until recently. These things, together with Hollingshead's calm and cordial demeanor, satisfied the deputies. They reported to their superior that nothing was amiss.

The sheriff, however, was a thorough man, who before moving to Topeka and running for office had served as an army quartermaster sergeant at Fort Harker, responsible for every item that passed through his warehouse. He sent deputies around to all the local livery stables to inquire if any of the owners or their employees had rented a buckboard and team to a woman answering Rachel Hollingshead's description. They replied that they had not. All their animals and equipment were accounted for, and in any case the circumstances of an unescorted female entering into such a transaction were unusual enough that they would have remembered the incident.

Deputies paid another call to Hollingshead, this time in the company of the sheriff with a search warrant issued by the county. A detailed examination of the house uncovered a tintype of the wife's parents hidden in a bureau drawer. Unable to provide a satisfactory explanation as to why she would leave such a sentimental relic behind, the shaken farmer was placed under guard while the party extended its search to the grounds and outbuildings. Rakes were applied to a charred patch of ground behind the house where the snow had melted, excavating scraps of gingham and lace—the remains of dresses and women's underclothing—that had escaped a recent bonfire. Encouraged by this discovery, and remembering that at the time of Rachel Hollingshead's disappearance the area had been experiencing a major cold spell, the sheriff directed his deputies to dismantle a large stack of firewood that had been erected against the west wall of the barn, on the theory that the only patch of unfrozen ground within convenient reach of the house would have resided there. Half an hour after the men began digging, their spades thumped against something which proved to be the lid of the trunk that had been removed from the crawl space inside the house. The trunk contained all that was left of Hollingshead's wife, chopped into manageable sections with the same axe the farmer had used to cut the firewood.

Confronted, the farmer confessed: At the height of an argument with his wife he had stalked outside to work off his rage on the woodpile, only to take the axe to her instead when she pursued him into the yard to continue the fight. Broken to tears, he was arrested and tried for murder and mutilating a body. The lawyer who represented him, a shrewd pleader who had successfully defended a band of track graders the year before for an assault upon a corrupt Kansas Pacific paymaster, argued at the trial that Hollingshead had lashed out blindly to protect his own person, then concealed the corpse in his panic, but the jury had deliberated for only thirty minutes before returning a verdict of guilty. The defendant was sentenced to hang. His was to be the first execution using a proper gallows in the city's history, and the sheriff had arranged for the construction to be carried out under the supervision of the hangman, a professional brought out from Fort Leavenworth at the county's expense.

Berensen, the foreman on the project, was a blonde, blue-eyed Norwegian, powerfully built and with a countenance that might have been pleasing were not the right side of his face mangled from an accident involving a two-man saw that had ended his days as a lumberman. His assessment of the carpenter Skinner had sent him, half his size and wearing spectacles, was clear in his tone when he demanded to know if Oscar had any experience in gallows building.

The young man admitted that he had none.

"Well, it ain't as if it has to stand for long. They'll be taking it down as soon as the thing's done. It won't do for businesses looking to settle in town seeing no neck stretcher standing there just waiting for its next customer. Ever see a man swing?"

"I saw four at once."

"To hell with you. Nobody never hung no four men at one and the same time. You're the fifth milk-face I've had on this job. If I get a day's work out of you before you turn rabbit I'll count myself lucky."

"I've never left work unfinished yet."

Something in Oscar's tone made the Norwegian bite back whatever remark he'd had ready. He fingered his scar for a moment, then drew a folded sheet from his flannel shirt pocket and snapped it open. "Here's the plan, there's the lumber. Just don't cut no timbers so short they can't be used for something else later. Wood don't grow on trees, you know." Pleased with his jest, Berensen went inside the courthouse, leaving Oscar standing next to a stack of fresh-cut pine with the flimsy sheet in his hands.

The plan was simple, drawn on the triangle principle, with the requisite thirteen steps to the scaffold and the L-shaped arm from which the rope would depend looming above. On the other side of the sheet someone had drawn the trap mechanism with rather more knowledge than skill. No attempt had been made to indicate the scale, but a child would have understood at a glance how it operated. It was clear that whoever had made the sketch had merely added it to a plan that had already been worked out, probably by the foreman.

The base was finished, describing a square ten feet across, partially sunk in trenches dug to accommodate it. Oscar approved of the twelve-by-twelve timbers that had been selected—they were as solid as railroad ties—but did not care for the way they were fastened, with square iron spikes driven through the sides of the longer pieces into the butt ends of the shorter. He worried that the weight of the uprights and scaffold would force the anchoring timbers apart and jeopardize the integrity of the entire structure. After contemplating the problem for some time, he decided to notch the ends of the timbers and cut wooden pegs.

He used the wrecking hammer from his toolbox to remove the spikes. This took an hour. He had his saw out to cut the notches when Berensen emerged from the courthouse.

"What in Christ's name are you doing? I thought you'd have the uprights up by now. They're hanging Hollingshead Friday."

"Not if the gallows collapses Thursday night. Who nailed these timbers? He didn't even use new spikes. I broke the rusted head off one pulling it."

"You don't waste new spikes on something that's coming down in a week. What are *you* going to put them together with, sticking plaster?"

Oscar told him his plan.

The foreman swore. "We'll need blasting powder to take it apart! You're building a gallows, not a church. It's a waste of wood and time. Use the damn spikes."

Oscar marked his place on the first timber with a T-square and a flat pencil and began cutting. Berensen snatched his arm, throwing off his stroke. When Oscar looked up, the scars on the foreman's face stood out dead white against the congestion.

"Pack up your tools and get off this lot! There's only one straw boss on this job."

"Why don't you let the lad be? If he does it his way, we might just kill the man we have in mind instead of crushing to death the spectators."

This was a new voice, whiskey-roughened, with an Irish lilt. Neither Oscar nor Berensen had been aware of the presence of a third party standing before the back door of the courthouse. He was tall and thin in a black frock coat that needed brushing and pressing, striped pants gone baggy in the knees, and a high silk hat caved in on one side. He had a little paunch that poked out when he hooked his thumbs in his vest pockets, as he was doing now, and a round knob of a nose that was redder even than the Norwegian's face, white stubble on his chin. A flat glass pint bottle made a sag in his right coat pocket.

"Who the devil are you?" Berensen demanded.

"I'm Rudd."

A grayish pallor slid under the foreman's high color. "Rudd from Leavenworth?"

"Sounds heroic the way you say it." The newcomer took out his pint, uncorked it, and tipped it up and down quickly, as if to measure the amount. He pointed the bottle at Oscar. "I'll warrant you're fixing to rabbet the boards on the scaffold."

Oscar said, "There will be less play in them if I do. If it rains the day of the hanging, there's less chance they'll swell up and cause the trap to stick."

"Can't have that. In 'sixty-three I had to ask a deserter to jump up and down to make it work. He refused, can you imagine it?" He cackled and took another swig. Then he heeled in the cork and returned the bottle to his pocket. "I said in my letter I wanted the construction sound. I said I wanted oak as well. If that arm cracks when he drops through, it will take the snap out of the rope. That will make a fine sight for your new citizens. Ever see a man strangle at the end of a noose?"

"*I* have," Oscar said.

"I promised Skinner I'd bring this in under bid." Berensen's voice had sunk to a murmur. "Oak's up to fifty bucks a ton."

"Spend a little. It's a hanging. You'll make it up in concessions."

Oscar said, "It's seasoned pine. It will hold with a brace."

"I hope you're right, son. What do you think of the trap? It's my own invention. I drew it for your sheriff."

"It's a little complicated. I'd have used a simple linchpin."

"But how would you operate it from up top? A condemned man has the right to stand next to his executioner when the sentence is carried out."

Oscar thought. "I'd bore a hole in the platform and use pulleys."

"Interesting. We'll do it my way, I think. It's worked seventeen times."

Berensen said, "Well, if you're going to do it, don't waste time talking about it. Hollingshead could die of old age waiting to hang." He made a wide circle around Rudd and banged the door shut behind him.

The hangman cackled. "I do believe that's a superstitious man."

"I wouldn't tell him that to his face. He said four men quit on him because they didn't want to do this kind of job." Oscar fitted his saw into the kerf he'd started while Rudd walked around the timbers. He smelled strongly of sour mash.

Rudd stooped to pick up one of the discarded spikes. "I'll bet a nugget to a hunk of granite that squarehead was fixing to bill the county for new nails. You'd best take a good look at that lumber."

"I did. It isn't the best, but it's solid."

"Sure these timbers will support the dead load?" The hangman pushed at one with a heel. He wore old-fashioned high-topped shoes with hooks for the laces, heavily blacked to cover the scars on the toes.

"They're older than these others. They were used for something before. That's what's good about them." Oscar finished the lengthwise cut and leaned down to blow out the sawdust. "They're almost as hard as stone, but they've learned to give a little, like good steel. I know wood."

"You know more than that. You know stresses. Who taught you?"

"A man named Pickerel, in Pennsylvania. I hate to think what he'd say if he knew what I was doing with what I learned."

"Why, because you're building a gallows? There's no shame in a thing done correctly. You said you've seen a man strangled by a noose. The one that did that ought not to raise his eyes to another human being without burning inside. A short drop and a loud bang, and a nuisance to society swept away in a piece of a second; there's a thing to boast about, and it couldn't be done without a good gallows. Let nail bangers like that squarehead you're working for shuffle along looking at the ground. He's no better than a strangler." He uncorked his bottle and swigged, as if to seal the verdict.

Oscar finished making the horizontal cut. "You sound a bit like Pickerel."

"There's few enough of us in the work. I could tell you stories that would shrivel your inwards: one-legged men jerking like fish on a line because the hangman didn't take the imbalance into account. Decapitations caused by too much counterweight. A choke case pissing into a crowd of fine ladies come to see the execution. You could lose your faith."

"What makes you stay with it?"

"Who's to do the job right if not me?" He watched the young man routing the notch. "You got good hands, son. You'd make a fine hangman."

Oscar smiled in spite of his concentration. "I'm a carpenter."

"I was a saloonkeeper. You think anyone sets out to do what I do? I got tired of mopping up after drunks and took an offer nobody else was taking, to pull the lever on a sergeant that spat his bit and raped a sutler's wife. The army paid me forty bucks for it. What are you getting for this job?"

"Not forty."

"I wouldn't take it now. I get a dollar a day to maintain the gallows at Fort Leavenworth and fifty every time I use it. The good people of Shawnee County are paying me a hundred on top of my travel expenses, all because they're too civilized to do it themselves, and on a wife-killer to boot, an axe murderer. You might give that some thought tonight when you're pulling the splinters out of your palms and worrying about next month's rent."

SIX

On the third day of his labors, Oscar acquired an assistant, a slow-thinking but obedient youth of fifteen named Harold, whose father had hired him out to the land office in order to lessen the financial responsibility for his family of twelve. Harold had likely never initiated a thought in his young life, but once an assignment was explained to him it never had to be repeated. And he did good work, untainted by any personal ideas of "improvement" he might have developed over and above his instructions. A surface sanded by Harold would not abrade an infant's delicate skin; a peg he had pounded into place became as much a part of the structure as if it had grown there. Had he time to dwell upon the matter, Oscar might have reconsidered his own pursuit of a skill that was so close to perfectly developed in a boy who could not arrive at a simple sum without counting on his fingers; but the job was only half done, with just two days left to finish, and Harold's gift of concentration without the distraction of thought was the model to emulate.

With his help, the uprights went up wonderfully fast, giving Oscar the time to mortise and tenon the crosspieces. The result, when the platform was erected and the gallows arm—Rudd called it a gibbet, borrowing his terminology from the last century—

swung into place, was a structure that neither swayed nor creaked beneath the weight of those who climbed upon it. Rudd was on hand daily, swigging from his bottle and watching, raising his voice only occasionally to point out a better way. His knowledge of carpentry was extensive, but his coherence suffered as the day wore on, until at dusk he fell into a mumble to which he himself didn't seem to be listening. The whiskey had by this time done its work, although when he took himself away he did not weave or stagger. Both Oscar and Harold brought sandwiches wrapped in waxed paper, but the hangman declined all offers to share in their meals and remained present while they ate, drinking and dominating the conversation with technical details about hanging and grisly anecdotes about bungled executions. Some were too graphic for Oscar's appetite, but as he rewrapped his luncheon, Harold continued eating, chewing with his mouth open, engrossed. Oscar came to believe that the only nutrition Rudd knew came from fermented grain and shop talk.

With an hour of daylight left on Thursday, the gallows was complete, all but the mechanism for the trap. Oscar was using the crude sketch on the back of the plan to refresh his memory when Rudd said, "Tell me again about that linchpin idea."

The young man looked at him. Rudd had been drinking all day, but his eyes were bright beneath their bloated lids. "It's actually a sliding bolt, located in the center of the seam and holding the trap in place like a door. We attach a cable to the knob, run it around a pulley and then up through a hole in the platform, around another pulley, and attach it to a lever on a pivot on the railing, tightening it with the lever in the vertical position. When it's pulled back to the horizontal, it shoots back the bolt and the trap drops open."

Rudd drank and thought. "If there's any play in the cable, Hollingshead and I will both drop through before I can get the noose in place. I'm only getting paid for one broken neck."

"There won't be. I'll wrap the end around a piece of scrap and twist the scrap to hold it taut until I get it tied off. Then I'll cut off the extra. It will be simple enough to test. When you pluck it, it should make a sound like a guitar string."

"You didn't learn that trick from any cabinetmaker in Pennsylvania."

"I spent one summer building rabbit hutches with my father. He decided that if he couldn't keep them away from his crops he'd trap them and fatten them up and eat them at Easter. Between June and August I think I stretched about ten miles of wire making those hutches."

"You're a regular virtuoso, ain't you, lad?"

"I hope not. A jack-of-all-trades is just a blunderer with versatility."

"That sounds like something somebody told you."

"It was the last thing Pickerel said to me the day I got married, just before I left Pennsylvania."

"There's truth in it, but it don't hold out here. There's too much to be done and not enough men to do it. Nor women, neither; coming through Lawrence I got into sore trouble when I shared a ten-cent bed with a bullwhacker who turned out to have teats. Point is you can't expect to get along doing just one thing, no matter how good you are at it."

"Does that go for hangmen too?" Oscar reached out and tugged Harold's floppy hat down over his eyes. The job was almost done, and well, and he had begun to feel a giddy kind of release after days of intense concentration. Grinning, the boy pulled his hat back up and kicked dirt over the front of Oscar's overalls.

"Here, now, watch my boots," Rudd said. "What I said goes for hangmen and saloonkeepers and carpenters and what-have-you. The day's coming when I'll have had my life's portion of stretching necks and up and quit, maybe right in the middle of a hanging; just walk right off the platform and let the sheriff do his own filthy work. Won't that be one for *Harper's Weekly*?" He cackled and drank.

"What will you do then?"

"I don't know. Turn farmer, maybe, only I won't grow potatoes. Old Seamus Rudd didn't die of diphtheria on the boat crossing over so his boy could dig potatoes in America just like his father done in Ireland, and his father, too, all the way back to when that limey Raleigh brought the first foul bushelful back from the Indies. I don't know, though; farming's an iron dollar, especially out here, and I won't go back east and be a damn fireman like my brother Arthur, dead at thirty with his lungs burned through. Rest his goddamn blaspheming soul. No, sir, I'm thinking I'll turn preacher."

Oscar laughed out loud at that. He scooped up his wooden mallet and pounded the head of a peg that wasn't sticking out at all.

"Don't laugh, lad. I've got the silk hat and the vocabulary. There's worse ways to live than pounding a pulpit for an hour on Sunday and eating at a different parishioner's house every night. Nobody asks a hangman to dinner." His mood took a sour turn then. He went on drinking and didn't say another word until darkness came down and he pushed himself away from the upright he'd been leaning against.

"Mind that's a good stout bolt," he said by way of farewell. "I'm only getting paid for one broken neck."

"You said that before."

"It bears repeating when it's my neck."

When Oscar awoke the next morning and squinted at his pocket watch in the early gray, Gretchen touched his arm. In her flannel nightgown with her blonde hair in a braid, she looked even younger than her years. "Promise me you won't go to the hanging," she said.

"I wasn't planning on it. I have to get that bolt as soon as the hardware opens and put it on and then Rudd wants to test the trap."

"That horrible old man."

"When did you see him?"

"Everyone talks about him. He's outside the saloon every morning waiting for it to open, and he's the last customer at night before they close."

"Drink doesn't make a man horrible, necessarily. Though it does make him old. I doubt he's much past fifty."

"He fills the hole where his soul belongs with whiskey. Promise me you won't go."

"Why?"

"You have nightmares enough about South Georgia Crossing."

Her head was on his chest. He bent his neck to look at her. "I've never mentioned them."

"Not when you're awake."

"I didn't know."

" 'Hands like scarecrow's gloves.' That's what you say."

He saw the boy's hands then, swollen and streaked with red. He closed his eyes, opened them, and saw only the figures on the wallpaper opposite the bed, becoming slowly visible in the spreading light. He stroked her hair and kissed her forehead. "Watching another hanging is the last thing I'm about to do."

"That isn't a promise."

"I promise."

The tension went out of her then. She was warm and smelled sweetly of sleep. He could never understand how a man awoke rank and stale, while a woman—or, at least, Gretchen—began the day like a crocus in spring.

"What are you going to work on next?"

"I don't know. I'll go to see Skinner this afternoon and ask if he has anything."

"I wish you were finished with the other thing already."

"I will be, by noon. That's when they're doing it."

He felt her shudder, and tightened his arm about her shoulders. He spoke of all the things he would build, including a house big enough for both of them and many children. He said he'd teach them all to be carpenters, "so they'll have something to do when they're not healing the sick or pleading someone's case before a judge."

"Just so long as they never have to build a gallows," she said.

But he wasn't listening. He was hoping Skinner had something.

Rudd was waiting behind the courthouse when Oscar arrived, with the heavy brass bolt and socket he had bought at the hardware store. The hangman's frock coat was brushed and he had on a clean collar and cuffs. His chin was scraped and pink.

"It's a question of respect," he said, when Oscar commented on his appearance. "Not that the poor devils ever take notice. Where's the half-wit?"

"I told Harold last night I wouldn't need him." Now that the job was almost finished, he felt less tolerance toward Rudd's crudeness. He ducked under a crosspiece and climbed the short stepladder beneath the platform to install the bolt.

Rudd whistled when he saw it. "What's that built to hold, a buffalo?"

"It's for a railroad mail car. Ringgold laid in a supply for the A.T. and S.F. It's designed to withstand a battering ram. I hope it's stout enough for you."

"Just make sure it don't work too stiff. It won't look well if I have to climb down and work it by hand."

"I'll use plenty of oil."

Using a brace-and-bit, he drilled the holes small so the wood would hold the screws tightly, and worked the bolt back and forth many times, applying oil frequently, until it slid as smoothly as a hot knife through lard. "That's it," Rudd said with a cackle. "Pretend you're taking your pleasure from a woman." For the cable, he'd selected another piece of railroad equipment, the pull cord used by conductors to signal the engineers to brake. He tied it securely around the knob at the end of the bolt, adding a dollop of yellow glue to the knot to hold it in place, and ran the cord around the pulleys and through the hole he'd bored in the platform. He used the method he'd described the night before to pull it taut and fixed it to the lever, which at the twelve-o'clock position was nearly invisible against one of the posts that supported the railing. Then he cleared away his tools and invited the hangman to climb up and test it.

"You do 'er, lad. I'll stand down here and watch the trap."

Oscar put out a hand to trip the lever. Someone placed a cold chisel against the flesh between his shoulder blades. He had an image, startlingly clear, of Sergeant Harney striding along the covered bridge, shoving over four dirty vagabonds from behind.

"What's the matter, lad? Don't it work?"

He grasped the rectangle of wood and twisted it to three o'clock. A hinge squeaked and the trap fell open with a thud.

Rudd cackled shrilly. "Lad, you're a genius. You'll want to oil that hinge."

Later, Oscar transferred the stepladder to the platform, helped the hangman carry a hundredweight sack of sand up the steps, and held the ladder while Rudd tied a twelve-foot length of rope to the gibbet.

"There's some as use pulleys and such and anchor the other end to the ground, or get fancy with counterweights, but that's just hoodoo for the rubes. Good hemp's too dear, and after you've lugged it through a couple of train stations you learn to do without the extra length."

"You travel with your own rope?"

"Well, sure. You never know what's available, and then there's the preparation. Give it a feel." He waggled the dangling end.

Oscar closed his hand around it. The fibers were moist and spongy. His hand came away slick. "You oil it?"

"Oil it and stretch it. Whenever you hear about a bungled hanging, nine times out of ten it's because they used dry rope. Fibers catch in the knot and the noose don't close properly. Throws off the torque. I use gun oil, but it's dear. I go through a can a month. Then if you don't stretch it beforehand there's too much bounce and you won't get a clean drop. It's like tying a bucket to an India rubber band and throwing it out the window."

"How did you learn all this?"

"Trying and falling on my arse and trying something different, just like everything else out here. Think those ranchers down in Texas started out roping cattle from horseback? In the beginning they paid little boys a nickel a head to slip a halter over those mean Mexican longhorns and lead them in on foot like Bo-peep's sheep. You don't have to get more'n a dozen boys stomped to death to figure there must be a better way. Same thing with all them chinks laying dead as Confucius under a ton of rock before they worked out how much blasting powder was needed to run a railroad track through a mountain. I'm ashamed to say I strangled my share of deserters and horse thieves on the way to my present system." He leaned the knot tight with a grunt and sat down on top of the ladder. Drawing up the rest of the rope, he began to fashion a hangman's knot, looping a noose and twisting the supple hemp into tight coils, inching his other hand up as he progressed to maintain tension. The hand doing the coiling was a blur. Oscar remembered something from his childhood: watching his mother knitting a scarf for his father, the needles moving too fast to follow.

". . . eleven . . . twelve . . . and thir*teen*, by God!" He set the knot with a jerk and held the noose aloft, a thing of sinister beauty.

"Why thirteen?" Oscar asked. "Is it superstition?"

"Some say that, though I say if it's true they'd have used a rope on Jesus, Old Number Thirteen Himself, instead of four-by-fours. Romans." Resting the noose on his thigh, he uncorked his bottle and drank his contempt for the conquerors of the ancient world. "They built roads all over hell and owned all the forests from England to Africa, but they couldn't none of them use a stick to put up a simple scaffold. Nailers, that's all they was, like your squarehead friend Berensen. No, lad, it ain't superstition, it's patriotism.

One coil for each of the thirteen original colonies, just like the stripes in the flag. American justice. They were all marked for the rope, you know, Hancock and Jefferson and Buchanan and the rest, just for signing their names to the Declaration of bloody Independence. It's our way of thumbing the old Yankee nose at Mother England, the clap-ridden old bitch." He tipped the bottle up. It gurgled twice.

"I don't think Buchanan signed the Declaration of Independence."

"What do I know? I was born in Limerick. Well, lad, should we take her over the fence a time or two?" He rammed the cork back in and climbed down to the platform.

The sandbag was stitched tightly at the top with twine, with an iron ring inserted through a grommet. They passed the noose through the ring, tied it up out of the way, and positioned the bag in the center of the trap, which Oscar had reset. This time Rudd tripped the lever. The trap banged open, the sandbag plummeted through space, and came to the end of the rope with a slam. The hemp creaked where it rubbed against the gibbet.

Oscar said it sounded like an explosion.

"It'll be louder when it's Hollingshead. He's five-foot-eight and a hundred and seventy-two pounds, so I measured a seven-foot drop. The heavier they are, the shorter the rope and the bigger the bang. You want to give the lighter men more traveling time. I heard last year in San Francisco they had to raise the whole scaffold on whiskey barrels to snap the neck of a chink cook that slipped arsenic into his employer's chowder. He came in at ninety-six pounds.

"In Leavenworth they wanted me to stack straw bales under the platform, to absorb the noise," he said, hauling up the bag. "Some of the settlers complained they could hear it in town. I compromised by installing a double trap so it didn't bang so loud at the end of the swing. That thump when the rope catches 'em up short is like a clap on the back for a job done right; also, I can hear the report better when the neck gives out. I can tell the difference between a clean break and a partial by the sound; one's like a pistol shot, the other's more on the order of gravel crunching under a buggy wheel. It helps me adjust for the next one."

"I never realized it was a science."

"It's been developing since the cave. In the beginning they just tied a slipknot around the wretch's throat and dragged him up off the ground. A hundred years ago in England they stretched a timber between two trees and pushed the fellow off a ladder. I could go on for a week, just covering the high spots."

"You've researched it."

Rudd grinned over the neck of his bottle. "Barbers collect razors, actors bone up on the Greeks. If you got the talent, you got the interest, and visa-la-versa. Sweet Mary, I near forgot." He slid a sheet of stiff paper out of an inside pocket and gave it to Oscar.

It was the size and shape of a formal dinner invitation, printed on cheap gray stock bordered in black, and offered the bearer admittance to the execution Friday, July 13, 1866, of Emmett Hollingshead for the murder of his wife Rachel. The sheriff's signature was scribbled in brown ink at the bottom.

"The sheriff don't like public spectacles," Rudd said. "He's deputizing a dozen guards to keep out the wives and shopmen and giving them cards to some local mucketies to make it dignified. I told him it's customary for the hangman to invite an acquaintance. It was a bald lie, but it saves you scratching for roof space across the street."

Oscar held it out. "Thank you. I promised my wife I wouldn't watch."

"I promised mine I'd give up the scaffold as soon as I found someone to take my place. It took her two years to figure out I never looked. That's when she left me. If you start off telling her everything, there's no saying where it will lead."

"One hanging was enough for my lifetime."

He didn't take back the invitation. "That wasn't no proper

hanging. You owe it to God to see how it's done when it's done right."

Oscar smiled. "How did you arrive at that?"

"You've got a gift, lad. Call it good hands or Job's own patience, but God gave it to you and you'd be worse than a sinner if you let it go to waste. I'll not leave what I've learned to a degenerate or an idiot. Some men were born to hang, but nobody deserves to twist and choke like a goose at the hands of a green man. See the thing the way it's intended, and see me later if you want to know more. I'll pay you board and half my day's wages to come to Leavenworth and learn at old Rudd's knee."

"I don't want to be a hangman."

"You can decide that later. Meanwhile you'll make more than you're drawing down as a carpenter. I know you ain't getting rich or we'd never have met. I seen three churches going up on my way into town and only one gallows. If you had your choice of jobs you'd be building a steeple."

Oscar looked at the invitation again, this time without seeing the words. Then he looked up at Rudd.

"I'll come. But you'll be going back to Leavenworth alone."

"Lad, I'd be alone in a riot. I'm used to it."

At a minute before noon, Oscar stood sweating among a small crowd of local businessmen and city and county officials in suits watching Emmett Hollingshead climb the steps Oscar had built. The farmer was led by the Reverend Thomas Millman of the First Lutheran Church droning over a Bible and flanked by two regular deputies carrying shotguns. Hollingshead was slighter of build than Oscar had imagined; it was difficult to picture this frightened-looking man, with a bald spot on the back of his head and his working sunburn reduced by his months of incarceration to a gray pallor, swinging an axe with the force necessary to commit mayhem. He had sweat through his new flannel shirt and his hands were bound behind his back in studded leather cuffs affixed to a wide belt that encircled his waist, itself stained white, as from the dried perspiration of others who had worn it before him. He stumbled halfway up, but was prevented from falling by the deputy on his left, who caught him under one arm and continued without missing a step.

The sheriff, a thick-waisted man in his early thirties, whose stiff-visored cap and heavy drooping moustaches made him resemble a railroad conductor, stood beside Rudd on the platform. He stepped forward and said something to Hollingshead, whereupon the condemned man approached the railing at the front of the scaffold and looked at the crowd with a slow swiveling movement of his head. His voice cracked when he began to speak, but as he continued, it leveled out into a middle-register monotone. He didn't project well. Oscar strained to catch the first pious phrases, then stopped listening when he realized he and the other spectators were being exhorted to obey the Ten Commandments and mind the Golden Rule.

The speech was brief. As the reverend continued reading from Revelations, Rudd fitted the noose around Hollingshead's neck, snugging the knot up under his left ear ("Subaural placement, lad; the hangman's choice. I don't hold with the submental, and the occipital's a notorious decapitator"), then produced a black cloth hood the size of a five-pound flour sack from a pocket and tugged it down over the man's head. He looked at the sheriff, who hesitated, then took off his cap and placed it over his heart, as if watching a hearse pass. Rudd grasped the lever—Oscar saw him flex his fingers twice, improving his grip—and pulled it down. Hollingshead vanished.

It was as simple as that. He dropped entirely out of sight beneath the platform, allowing those who hadn't the presence of mind to follow the movement through the crosspieces only a glimpse of the taut rope above as a signal that the act was complete; that, the bang of the trap, the thud of the body coming to a dead stop at the end of the drop, and—Oscar thought later he might have imagined it, but heard it clearly just the same—a sharp report, as of a maul cleanly splitting seasoned oak or a pistol discharging. The rope creaked and the body turned halfway around to the left, a pendulum drifting to a halt between the uprights Oscar had built.

It was the noise, however, he remembered most vividly; the incontestable sound of the farmer's neck breaking, ending his sad passage in a fraction of a second. Oscar had been prepared for horror, nausea, and the iron taste of self-loathing on his tongue merely for witnessing the act, as he had known at South Georgia Crossing. He experienced none of these things now. What he felt, he saw when he had the chance to isolate it, was excitement, and a sense of satisfaction that went deeper than any he had ever known; and when he raised his eyes to the platform and met Rudd's gaze, he knew that he saw it too.

PART THREE

LEARNING THE ROPES

Experience keeps a dear school, but fools will learn in no other.

—BEN FRANKLIN

SEVEN

Why must you go? There is so much building taking place here."

He looked into Gretchen's eyes, gray now, as if the dye from her dress had bled into them. "That's part of the problem. Every week brings more carpenters into town, single men who will work for less than I need. This is a sound offer. It's only thirty miles."

"It might as well be three hundred. How will you travel?"

"A stage ticket is part of the offer."

"What need has Fort Leavenworth for a civilian carpenter? Doesn't the army have its own?"

"It's a large settlement. Many people live there who have nothing to do with the army. The soldiers protect them from Indians."

"Indians?"

He'd regretted the words the instant they'd left him. "They aren't bothering settlers now. They're too busy trying to stop the railroad from going through. The army is assembling an expedition to drive them off."

She was sitting on the edge of their bed, kneading her hands in her lap. She took her lower lip between her teeth and looked at the wall to the right, where hung a Currier & Ives print in a cheap frame of a snow-covered landscape in Massachusetts. It had come with the room and looking at it seemed to help her avoid crying. "This is my fault. If you didn't have to look after me you wouldn't be forced to leave. This time you may not be so lucky as to meet German-speaking Indians."

"I'll only be gone a month. I'll send my wages to you by the Overland. I won't need them in Leavenworth. My room and board are provided for."

"If I went with you, you wouldn't have to send money here."

"I'd have to find a place for you to live. The offer did not include quarters for a wife. We wouldn't get to see much of each other. I'll be working all day every day, even Sunday."

"But what will you be building? What structure is so important it won't let you keep the sabbath?"

"It's not just one structure. The boom is only starting there. More people are coming in than anticipated; many families are living in tents or out in the open. They need hotels and houses. The merchants who serve them need proper shop buildings. As an experienced carpenter, I'll be working on several projects as a contractor. It's possible I won't touch a hammer the entire time I'm there." Which was as close to the truth as he'd come since the conversation had started.

"I have a bad feeling about it. It's dark." She touched his cheek. "I don't know what I should do if death separated us."

"I survived two years of war. I think I will survive Fort Leavenworth."

"Is survival all you want? We could have survived in York."

He took her hand and kissed the fingers. "In York I might have made a comfortable living building bureaus for rich old women who smelled like pressed flowers. Out here I'm building civilization."

"What shall I do while you're away?"

"Find us a place to live where we won't breathe sawdust and turpentine from morning to night. Make curtains, hang pictures, buy furniture. Good furniture, mind. I'll not sleep in a bed I wouldn't be proud to have built myself."

She smiled. "Will we be so rich, then?"

"As long as there is need for my skill, people will pay what I ask."

They kissed, and he unfastened the first of the many buttons of her dress.

The stagecoach drawn up before the express office was a mud wagon, lighter and less ornate than the famous Concord and built closer to the ground. Canvas flaps were rolled like window shades above the open sides and secured with leather straps, to be lowered to keep out rain and dust, or as much of it as could not find its way in around the edges; local wisdom said the conveyance had earned its name not for its ability to navigate mud as for the amount of it that collected on the passengers. The square box in which Oscar would travel thirty miles, built of unpainted planks reinforced with splints, reminded him of the rabbit hutches he had helped his father build.

He placed his valise and his toolbox—the latter with a board nailed across the top to keep the contents from spilling out during the journey—next to the other passengers' luggage on the boardwalk, watched carefully to see that the man kneeling on the driver's seat stowed the items properly after they were passed up to him by the expressman, then boarded the coach. He'd asked Gretchen to say good-bye at home to avoid contact with the ruffians who loitered near the office whenever a stage came through. In reality he didn't want her to see the man who was sitting in the seat facing his.

"I hope you ain't planning on doing carpentry work in your spare time," Rudd said. "Time's one commodity you won't find at the sutler's in Leavenworth."

"Gretchen would have asked questions if I left my tools at home."

The hangman grinned. He wore a linen duster like Oscar's over his clothes, only Rudd's was older, discolored and tattered where the hem brushed the insteps of his old-fashioned shoes. He'd fixed a chin strap to his battered silk hat. Fresh white stubble had sprouted on his cheeks and chin. "If I'd had your smarts starting out, I might still be married today. I had some damnfool notions about not lying to my wife."

"When will we reach Leavenworth?" Oscar was eager to put the subject behind him.

"Tonight, if we ain't scalped first. These gents don't waste much time once they hitch up to a fresh team."

"What is the Indian situation?"

"Scared as squirrels. I was just greenhorning you about getting scalped. That business on Sand Creek in 'sixty-four dropped the trap right out from under them. They'll raise them some more hell, like as not, but only on the run. I remember when telling a Sioux he might die of old age would get your hair cut off for you and your ballocks with it, but that was before they seen what a load of lead could do to a buck in his prime. They don't seek it. I never thought I'd see the day when I'd pity them wild sons of bitches. I'd admire to make the acquaintance of Colonel Chivington on my scaffold one day."

Oscar had read about the Battle of Sand Creek in a month-old newspaper during the war. That eastern journal had presented the fight in Colorado Territory as a victory. The farther Oscar had moved west, the more frequently he had heard it referred to as a massacre of peaceable Cheyenne, and John Chivington, the militia commander, as a murderer of women and children. There were, it seemed, two truths when it came to the frontier, each equally believable depending upon where one happened to be when he first heard it.

They were joined shortly by a middle-aged woman and a young man who were strangers to each other. The woman, solidly built with a round pleasant face beneath the broad brim of her traveling hat, bound with a scarf beneath her chin, said she had been engaged from a position as cook to a wealthy family in Lawrence to become a chef in a Leavenworth restaurant; to which Rudd responded that he hoped she could do more with buffalo than the mess sergeant at the fort. The young man, a corporal in unfaded blue with gaiters to protect his boots, an oilcloth cape, and all the shine still on the visor of his kepi, announced that he was on his way to an assignment at the fort and that he hoped to see Indians on the way, having enlisted only two weeks before the surrender of the Confederacy and thus missed all the excitement.

"I'm afraid you missed out all around, lad. I was just telling my friend here the injuns are on the run."

"You're mistaken, sir. General Hancock has accepted a commission to patrol the Smoky Hill River and engage any Indians standing in the way of the railroad. I expect he'll be recruiting at Fort Leavenworth."

"I heard the same thing. I also heard he's bringing along that pup who lost control of his horse at Bull Run and come out the other side a general."

"Yes, sir. That would be Custer. He'll be second in command."

Rudd nudged Oscar in the ribs. "That's what war's come to, lad—boy generals and green troops chasing scared injuns from Kansas to California." He mined his bottle out from under his duster and pulled the cork with an apologetic look at the woman. "For my nervous stomach, madam. Travel upsets it."

She shrugged and directed her attention to the last of the bags being loaded aboard. Her interest in her fellow passengers had flagged.

"May I ask you gentlemen what your business is in Fort Leavenworth?" The corporal touched the hollow of his chin, where a downy imperial had begun to grow.

"Fabian Rudd." The hangman swallowed his mouthful and shook the young man's hand. "Oscar Stone, my assistant. We balance the books for the army." He grinned.

"I didn't know that was a civilian job."

"You soldier lads have enough in your kit protecting our like from rebels and heathens. The worst we have to worry about is leaving a figure hanging."

The corporal nodded politely and joined the woman in watching the luggage. Oscar stared at Rudd, who moved a shoulder and leaned forward, lowering his voice to a hoarse whisper.

"You'll learn to stir up dust, too, when you've answered questions for miles. Nobody hounds a bookkeeper asking how he does it."

The stagecoach left on time. What followed was relentlessly exhausting, more so than the same distance covered over three days by oxen. The mud wagon hadn't the elaborate suspension system employed by the Concord, and the travelers felt every rock and hole in their spines and teeth. The woman, apparently experienced, hung on to the seat and the frame and kept her place, but twice the corporal lurched forward and had to grasp Oscar's knees in order to avoid spilling into his lap, apologizing and touching his visor once he'd regained his seat. Dust curled in under the side flaps and settled like flour over everything inside. They lunched in Oskaloosa while the horses were changed, but the thirty-minute respite only made the rest of their journey seem even less endurable by comparison. To Oscar's relief and the corporal's disappointment they saw no Indians, chastened or otherwise. When after dark they topped a low rise and swept down toward the dim lights of the settlement, three miles this side of the fort for which it was named, Oscar ached all over, as if he'd fallen down a long flight of stairs.

"There it is, lad," Rudd told the corporal, "and not a hostile in sight the whole way. Not that a ride in a Bozeman bonebreaker is any improvement over a Cheyenne arrow in your seat. Beg pardon, ma'am." He touched his brim.

The soldier said, "You may be right. I've ridden more comfortably in ambulances."

"Welcome to the West. It's ugly as a washtub and harder'n hard times, but there sure is a hell of a lot of it. Beg pardon again, ma'am."

"Oh, hush up." The woman sounded drained.

They alighted in front of a two-story hotel. Oscar's feet had gone to sleep and he stumbled when he stepped down to the boardwalk, but Rudd was behind him and caught him under one arm. Oscar was reminded unpleasantly that one of Emmett Hollingshead's guards had provided the same service for him on his way up to the scaffold. He was tired, he missed Gretchen, and regretted his decision to leave her and apprentice a trade he had no intention of taking up, all because the hangman had offered him more than he was getting practicing carpentry in Topeka.

"My shack's up the street," Rudd said. "We'll look in on the fort tomorrow." He gave a silver dollar to the hotel orderly who came out to help the guests with their bags, and asked him to deliver his trunk to his address in the morning. The pair then claimed their bags and started walking. Oscar couldn't help noticing that the contents of the hangman's scuffed and dented satchel clinked with each step.

EIGHT

Rudd was given to neither exaggeration nor understatement: A shack was what it was, built of clapboard on a government-owned lot by someone who had never laid eyes on plane nor plumb. The hangman explained that it had been used by the army to store tack and saddles during field exercises outside the fort and that the city had grown up around it. Once it had been presented to him free of rent, he had lain a plank floor over the bare earth, tacked buffalo hides and trade blankets on the walls to keep out drafts, and installed a barrel stove with a crooked pipe that vented out under the slanted roof. There was just room enough for a bed on a painted iron frame, a plain pine table and two wobbly mismatched chairs, and an immense armchair with black horsehair bulging out through splits in the old leather. This was as much of the place as Oscar could see when Rudd lit the lamp on the table; the chimney was blackened and the oil burned with a smutty orange glow.

He asked where he would sleep.

"Bed's built for two." Rudd blew out the match. "You might want to tie your nightshirt up between your legs, just in case I start in to dreaming about Lola Montez."

Oscar, who was often unsure when his companion was making

a joke—particularly when it was accompanied by that evil grin—decided he would sleep in the armchair.

The walls had one decoration only, if one did not count the bright woven blankets, whose purpose was utilitarian. This was a long sheet of what appeared to be butcher wrap, torn at both ends and fixed with tacks to one of the buffalo hides. A series of straight horizontal lines had been drawn its length with a rule and pencil in ranks of five, with blank spaces between each rank. They looked like musical staffs, and Oscar thought at first he was looking at a sheet of music. But instead of notes someone had superimposed rows of stick figures, each with its feet planted on the bottom line. The ones at the top varied in height from the shortest at the far left to the tallest at the right. The figures in the next rank down varied in height as well, but also in breadth, from the conventional vertical line that formed the trunk of the first figure in the sequence to an absolute circle for the last, suggesting extreme corpulence; this one wasn't properly a stick figure at all. The drawings in the remaining ranks were amalgamations of the top two: short and fat, tall and thin, medium and average, tall and fat, short and thin. They looked like cave pictures drawn by a uniquely precise primitive.

They had been executed carefully and with confidence, but without evidence of formal training; Oscar guessed that the same hand had drawn the trap mechanism on the back of the plans for the gallows in Topeka. There was a mark at the right end of each line, and a mark beneath each of the figures. He thought they were numbers but could not make them out in the poor light.

Rudd saw him trying. "You're looking at the sum total of six years and seventeen hangings. You'll not find a chart like it anywhere else in the world, and it's the Lord's own shame you won't."

"What is it?"

"Just scribbles if you don't know what it is you're looking at. For the wretch on the scaffold it's the difference between oblivion, quick and sweet, and choking hell for three long minutes. Or between a whole corpse and a headless one. The numbers there at the end represent heights, from four-foot-ten to six-foot-six. The ones underneath each of them little men tell you their weight and the drop needed."

"The drop?"

"Purely speaking, it's seven feet for a big man of two hundred, with two inches added for each ten pounds lighter in weight, up to eight feet, eight inches for a hundred pounds—that'd be for the chinks in San Francisco, not the robust Micks and Polacks I draw more often than not, but I'm a thorough man and I like to see things through to the end, so to speak. Too short a drop and you've strangled a chink. Too long and you'll need a man ready with an open sack to catch the flying noggin of a son of Old Erin. There's variables, mind, beyond height and weight—weak neck muscles and strong yield equally unsatisfactory results at both extremes—but you can make your adjustments based on your examination. I don't mind telling you if I had this table when I started out there'd have been less suffering in the world."

"You examine the condemned?"

"Just a quick gape and a feel around the collar. I'd be making a nice living now guessing folks' weight on street corners if I'd stayed in New York." He took out his bottle, shook it, frowned, and opened his satchel on the bed to fetch out a full one.

"It seems to me it would be easier just to shoot them."

"Who, the folks in New York? I'm just fooling. Firing squads ain't as efficient as they're made out to be. Shooting an enemy in battle and taking aim at one of your own with his hands tied behind him ain't the same. I've heard of five men, tried in the flames and mean as wolves, all firing live rounds at a trussed-up deserter standing ten feet off and not one of 'em hitting so much as a baby toe. Worse yet, a ball pierces his gut and he gets to sit down and hold himself in until the officer in command makes up his mind to walk up and put a charge through his head. That's the beauty of the rope: It don't think."

"This chart had to be thought up."

"That's just it. All the thinking's done beforehand, and it's more along the lines of an exercise in patience and precision. You get lost in the details of footage and good tight coils and stretching and testing and don't have the opportunity to hesitate like you might when some leather-lunged top kick screams ready-aim-fire in your ear."

"I just never realized there was so much involved." Oscar yawned the last part of the sentence. Suddenly he couldn't keep his eyes open. His sore limbs were as heavy as if he had bags of sand tied to them.

"You ain't heard but less than a tenth of it. You'd best roll in while I lay a fire for breakfast. The school door opens when the sun goes up."

Oscar found a sheet and an extra blanket in a wooden foot locker with Rudd's initials burned into the lid. There was only one pillow in the shack, and so he rested his head on his valise while stretching out in the armchair with one of the wooden chairs drawn up to support his feet. The blanket was coarse and scratchy, the sheet none too clean; the whole place, in fact, smelled like unwashed socks, the stale musk of male neglect, familiar from his months with the 150th Pennsylvania and Collingwood's Raiders. It kept him awake not one moment longer than would the smell of clean linen and his wife's warm fresh skin in their bedroom in Topeka. If he dreamed, he did not remember when he awoke, and when the clink of a stove lid as Rudd prepared breakfast brought him around in dawn's bronze light, he thought he'd been asleep only minutes.

"Outhouse is in back." Rudd, his little paunch poking his faded red flannels out over his belt, used a spatula with a rag wrapped around its handle to turn over a flat piece of meat in a skillet as big as a kitchen table. "You can't miss it. It's as big as the shack."

It wasn't much of an exaggeration. Oscar, who'd been fastidious about his bodily functions all through the war, seeking out bushes for cover when his fellow veterans were content to squat over a slit trench, contemplated the two-hole arrangement and wondered at the sort of person who would share that moment with a partner and what the pair might talk about while they were doing it. When he returned, the aroma of hot grease that filled the shack gnawed at his insides. He was as hungry as he was sore, and he ached in so many places he suspected he'd borrowed some from someone else while in a somnolent state.

Rudd ate his fried salt pork and drank strong hot coffee without conversation, giving Oscar a chance to glance around the shack in the light of day. Coils and coils of rope, some new and stiff and as yellow as corn, some frayed and black with age and tar, still others darkened with oil to a golden saffron, hung from pegs in the walls near the roof where harnesses and halters had likely hung in years past; the ends of the older ropes were corkscrewed where they'd been twisted to form the hangman's knot. Flat cans of the gun oil Rudd used to soften the fibers stood on the two-by-four crosspieces that framed the building, and in the corner where an upright and a crosspiece were joined a concertina leaned, its wooden end pieces polished to a soft sheen from handling. He found it difficult to picture the hangman entertaining himself or anyone else with music, and supposed the instrument had been left behind by someone else, perhaps an earlier apprentice. There were the inevitable rows of empty bottles interspersed among the oil cans, as if placed on display to help Rudd keep track of the amount of whiskey he consumed. None had stood there long enough to gather dust or cobwebs, as had the worn ropes; Oscar assumed his host gathered the empties from time to time and sold them for pennies to a local saloonkeeper or the sutler at the fort to use for refills.

In the corner near the door another surprise, a pair of crude book presses fashioned from furry wooden crates, stood at right angles to each other, their unplaned shelves packed with volumes, many of which had been jammed into horizontal stacks on top of their vertical mates. The arrangement was so precarious that it was difficult to imagine extracting one item without creating an avalanche. Most of the books were old, much older than the shack and Leavenworth itself, and bound in cracked leather. Some, less old but used just as hard, were covered in grimy cloth and burst at the hinges. One of the former, whose leather had withstood the test of endurance better than the others, was nearly as fat as a tree trunk, bigger than the family Bible Oscar had sold along with his father's farm. Were it not crowded on both sides by less substantial companions it would have remained erect on its own quite solidly without support, like a well-fed burgermeister standing in the middle of a busy tavern holding his tankard of ale. Unlike the others, it was shelved spine in and secured with clasps about the fore edge of its uneven pages and stuck out several inches beyond its neighbors, a formidable tome. There were books piled on the floor as well, as if the disaster Oscar had foretold had taken place at some earlier time and left uncorrected. Amid this mound were bundles of printed pamphlets, many discolored with age and flaking away at the edges; one, whose stained and faded title page bore the legend *Newgate Calendar* in English Gothic print, was gnawed at one corner, probably by a mouse or a rat.

The smell of must that arose from this corner, like old clothes discarded and forgotten, was stronger than anything else in the shack. This was the unwashed-socks odor that Oscar had noticed the night before. Everything else in the place was tidy—the cooking utensils Rudd had not used that morning hung on nails near the stove, the bed made and the floor swept clean. The young man decided that the books and pamphlets were consulted too often to bother putting back in order.

"I suppose there is not much to do out here between hangings but read," he said.

"There's enough, depend on it. Months can go by without a gallows bird to make you worth your scrip, then it's hurry up and get it done. Once a verdict's in they don't let the grass grow. If your trap hinge is rusted and your ropes are dried out or a piece of the gibbet's rotted because you let it go too long without dope, your living's done. There's a rumor running about that hanging is filthy work and no one wants it, but it ain't true. There's always some mean sergeant thinks he can do the job better for less pay, and the army's always got its ears out for a low bid. You got to keep your equipment in brass-button order, just like a lighthouse when the sea's calm, and there's no help for it if you'd rather sit around on your arse reading *King Lear*." Rudd scooped another piece of meat off the platter and refilled his cup from the chipped enamel pot.

"You have a substantial library for someone who hasn't time to enjoy it."

"It ain't for pleasure, it's study."

"There's a course for hangmen?"

"There ain't, though there ought to be. It's a heap more practical than poetry or dead languages. Show you tonight if we don't get back too late."

Before Oscar could ask where they were going, the hotel man arrived with Rudd's enormous trunk on a handcart. It was shorter than a coffin but fatter, and had filled the mud wagon's rear boot. Rudd helped him bring it inside, inspected the contents, which seemed to consist entirely of more rope, and sent the man away with an extra fifty cents for prompt delivery. He sat down and gestured with his fork.

"You'd best take that last piece of pork and another cup of bellywash and don't say no sermons over it. It's three miles out to the fort."

"What's at the fort?" Oscar helped himself. The salt pork was superior in quality to the kind he'd bought in St. Louis for the trek west; he assumed it was army meat, which traditionally was splendid until the mess cooks got hold of it. The coffee, however, was burnt and bitter.

"Nothing you won't find at any other, except for one. It's time I introduced you to the Old Woman."

"I thought your wife left you."

A morsel of fat quivered between Rudd's front teeth when he skinned his lips back. "Oh, but we're faithful yet. She don't spread her skinny wooden legs for no one but old Rudd."

NINE

The livery operator was an Irishman like Rudd, but of a more common frontier type, thick-built and burned deep red from the visor of his filthy military kepi to his sweat-stained collar, and from his rolled-up shirtsleeves to his black and shredded nails. His eyes were glittering blue shards and he had a short charred bulldog pipe screwed like a permanent fixture into the corner of his mouth. When he looked up from the stall he was fixing and saw Rudd, he crossed himself and stood, his claw hammer swinging at his side. Evidently neither the hangman nor his occupation were unknown to him.

"I thought you was stretching some lost child's neck in Topeka," he said by way of greeting.

"Stretched and buried. What happened here? The nags you take in don't have the strength to drop dung standing, let alone kick in no stalls."

The liveryman waggled his hammer at the pile of shattered boards. "I went against my better judgment and let a tinhorn talk me into boarding his stallion for five dollars gold. From now on I won't let a beast through the door unless I see its balls pickled in a jar first."

Oscar said, "You ought to put in another upright and use

shorter boards. Then if it happens again there won't be as much damage done."

"If it happens again I'll sell the shebang and run buffalo." The liveryman stared at him as if noticing him for the first time. "You in the lumber business?"

"Mr. Stone's a master carpenter, and you'll find none better this side of Chicago," Rudd said. "I'm taking his opinion on the gallows at the fort. I'm needing the dogcart and an animal that won't blow out in the first mile."

"Dogcart's out. You'll have to take the gig."

"The gig's all right if you've done something about the axle. I near broke it on a pebble the last time."

"It was a rock, and if you wasn't blind drunk you'd of seen it and not hit it. I put on a new elmwood axle. If you break this one, you bought the gig."

"Hitch her up, Finn. I ain't got all day to haggle."

The liveryman tossed his hammer onto the pile of boards and went back into the gloomy back of the stable, to return a moment later pulling a two-wheeled trap. It was a light vehicle, little more than a seat wide enough for two balanced between a pair of high wheels, and Finn pulled it without effort. He laid down the tongue, then led a gray gelding with shaggy hooves out of a nearby stall and harnessed it while Rudd stroked its pale muzzle. "Well, Methusaleh, top of the morning. But then I'll warrant any morning you don't feed the buzzards is a good one for you."

"His name's Jake, and he'll live to shit on your grave." Finn took a bridle off a peg. "That's if you don't get drunk again and run him into a cottonwood."

"He don't need me for that. He's blind in one eye and can't see with the other. But he's got wind, I'll give him that. It's more'n I can say for his sainted mother. You gave me her last time."

"Eleanor's only a year older than Jake, and you know it. I bought her off the Overland."

"She must of rid up top with the driver. When you going to buy younger stock?"

"When it's old. I can't afford nothing better as long as you keep busting up my inventory." The liveryman adjusted the bit in Jake's mouth, then stepped back and mopped his red sweating face with a blue bandanna he took from a pocket. Rudd handed him his bottle. It gurgled twice before Finn tipped it down and gave it back.

"Is he your friend?" Oscar asked as they rode away. The gelding lifted and planted its hooves with the thoughtful deliberation of an old man.

"He didn't throw the hammer at me, did he?"

"He didn't ask for money either."

"Wouldn't take it if I offered it. He considers it bad luck. There's advantages to the work."

"He drank from your bottle."

"Luck's got nothing to do with whiskey."

They passed the last building and started out on the Kansas plain. There was a spring beneath the seat and the tall wheels seemed to glide over ruts. The sun felt pleasant on Oscar's shoulders. It was a far cry from the teeth-chattering ride in the loaded mud wagon.

"Why is there a gallows at the fort? I thought all the military prisons were back East."

"It ain't a prison yet, but it will be. All it needs is the name. The stockade holds a hundred, and it's a central location. When they catch deserters from Riley and Dodge they bring them here. Can't spare the men to take them all the way back East. Desertion in battle is death. It just makes sense to carry it out right here."

"But the war's over."

"Tell that to the quartermasters. They got warehouses in West Virginia and Maryland full of uniforms and rifles and saddles and harnesses just getting dusty and ready to rot. The army's like a sporting woman with a brand-new five-dollar gold piece on her dresser; she's got to spend it on something or bust. If it ain't injuns and renegade whites, it'll be something else, maybe Mexico or Canada. I'm talking about the army now, not the sporting woman. She'd settle for a spring hat."

Oscar, who had no experience of western forts, was prepared for a monolithic structure walled around with a high stockade, patrolled on catwalks by armed sentries. Fort Leavenworth offered only an orderly arrangement of long barracks buildings and stables surrounding a parade ground pounded into hard bare earth by thousands of booted feet and shod hooves, with the Stars and Stripes snapping atop a pole in a stiff wind. The sentry on duty at the entrance to the compound recognized Rudd and waved him on through without asking the identity of his companion. Oscar commented on this.

"That will change come the injun campaign. They learned to be lazy out here while all them brass-buttons was busy winning medals down in Dixie. Come this time next year you won't be able to squeeze a copper through the gate. I may have to buy some new collars for myself and a fresh coat of paint for the Old Woman just to pass muster."

They rolled past the actual stockade around the prisoners' quarters, a disappointing picketlike enclosure less than ten feet high, and came to a stop before a tall narrow building that Oscar mistook at first for a granary. It was clapboard, with a single-paned window placed high on each wall near the roof, and connected to the stockade by a brick walkway. The door was painted an ugly dark green and had a tarnished brass knob above a keyhole into which a normal-size man could have inserted a forefinger.

"Leave it to the army to lock up the one place nobody wants to go in." Rudd stepped down from the gig and produced a ring with a huge brass skeleton key attached.

The hinges croaked when the door opened, and Oscar was certain no one had passed through it in the hangman's absence. Inside, a number of straight wooden benches stood parallel to the walls on an earthen floor, lit only by the sun coming through the high windows. The visitor was reminded of the arrangement in a small barn in York where he and his brother and father had attended a stock auction, except that in the center where the animals should have been led out for the buyers to bid on stood the structure Rudd called the Old Woman.

It was built lower to the ground than the gallows Oscar had erected in Topeka, with a simple crosspiece across the top instead of an L-shaped arm, but wonderfully stout. The twelve-by-twelve timbers that formed the legs were sunk deep into the earth—three feet at least would be his guess—and painted the same depressing shade of green as the door.

Rudd rapped his bony knuckles against one of the uprights. It rang like iron. "Solid hickory. You can't beat them army bridge builders for materials and workmanship. It was here when I came, not that it was appreciated; the wood was dried out and shrunk around the joints. I had some pegs replaced and painted it for the first time. The only other color they had was black, and I wasn't going to do that. My preference was barn red. I thought it might bring some comfort. But any patch in a high sea, as we say." He mounted the steps, motioning for Oscar to follow.

"It's a Thurtell drop," Rudd said when they were on the platform. "First used in 'twenty-eight on a wretch of that name for a murder in England. That means it's a double flap. The earth just drops out from under you, so your feet don't slide and complicate the fall. I considered using the same principle in Topeka, but it takes longer to make and is treacherous if the carpenter don't know what he's about. I hadn't yet made your acquaintance then, understand. See, there's the seam."

There was a straight line through the center of the trap where the flaps met. "How does it operate?" Oscar asked.

To demonstrate, Rudd grasped a three-foot lever set in a slot in the platform and pulled it toward him. The trap banged open, exposing the dirt floor seven feet below. "It's attached to a gear that draws the bolt," he said. "What I showed you in Topeka was a simpler variation, but I can't say the one you came up with didn't answer just as well. I'm told the engineer who designed this one requisitioned the works from a civilian contractor building a drawbridge across the Missouri. Requisitioning, that's what they call it in the army." Cackling, he uncorked his bottle.

"I'd like to see the mechanism."

They descended and stepped between the uprights, where a perfect square of light shone on the ground through the open trap. A hole had been bored through the base of the painted wooden lever so that it could be fitted over the hub of the gear, which was a medieval-looking wheel the size of a dinner platter, toothed around the edges. The teeth engaged the teeth of a smaller gear mounted horizontally beneath the platform, whose teeth in turn engaged a groove filed near the end of a thick iron bolt that passed between staples attached to the bottom of the double flap. Oscar stooped to examine the latter.

"One of the staples is loosening. The wood's mealy."

"I have to keep pounding them back in. I've replaced the flaps twice already. This latest set is white pine. Hickory's scarce."

"They ought to be made of iron, with the staples welded on."

"That's a strange suggestion coming from a carpenter."

"I know wood's limitations. If one of those staples works loose while you're standing on the trap—"

"I see it. Don't throw that back at me. Iron, you say. There's a first-class blacksmith here at the fort. It'll make a hell of a racket, though. They won't like it in town."

"You might reconsider your position on straw bales."

Rudd took a drink and banged the cork back in. "Why not wait a day or two before you start making changes, lad. You're here to learn."

Oscar decided against responding. He wondered if in his nineteenth year he was outgrowing the age of unquestioning apprenticeship.

He spent another hour appreciating the gallows and the ceremony of military execution; setting and resetting the trap, working the lever, learning the order of events and where to stand when the prisoner's sentence was read by Colonel Janning, the commanding officer, and while the chaplain read aloud from the Old Testament. ("Ecclesiastes when he's slept well and filled his belly with breakfast; Revelations when he's hung over.") It was like blocking out the actions of actors onstage. Rudd said the benches were reserved for the officers of the court-martial, guests of the colonel, and in cases of murder, the wives and families of the victims, when they requested permission to see the sentence carried out. When they were finished, the sun had moved, casting the scaffold's gaunt shadow onto the east wall. It looked uncannily like the silhouette of someone's grandmother, bent over her chores.

Rudd saw Oscar looking. "You ought to see her by moonlight. I come here some nights when I've had my portion of breathing company; sit on the front bench sharing a jug with the Old Woman and talking over the day passed. You'll come to it, when she's the only one won't ask you for anything more than a dab of paint now and then and a nail or two when she's ailing."

Again the young man said nothing. He promised himself silently he would never come to that.

From there they went to the commander's office, where Colonel Janning's adjutant, a captain named Burry, informed them the colonel was in Leavenworth for the day and told Rudd that no capital prisoners were in residence or expected. Oscar disliked Burry, a walrus-faced clerkly type approaching middle age who appeared to resent his menial duties and did not offer his hand to either of them; clearly, hangmen did not belong to his social circle.

"Burry'll die a captain," Rudd said when they left the office. "Hasn't got the brains to promote nor the inwards to get himself busted to lieutenant. That's what's running the army until the boy generals get here."

"I doubt he approves of us."

"That's the work, lad. They don't want us until they need us."

Part of their journey back to town took them along the bank of the Missouri, where Rudd pointed out a stern-wheeler heading toward the dock, smoke lisping from its twin stacks.

"Packet boat. No telling how many letters they're carrying from troopers' wives and sweethearts saying they're leaving them. Brawls in the barracks tonight. Nothing to us if all that gets busted is a nose or a hand. If a gun or bayonet comes out, or somebody falls and splits open his melon on the corner of a foot locker, the Old Woman will host a party in a couple of weeks. Same thing, maybe, if there's a woman aboard. There's more boats coming every day—side-wheelers, I'll be bound, with gamblers and actresses—more wagons, and trouble on board each. A lot of folks are running to something, gold or land or work or air that ain't been breathed before. Just as many are running away from something: wives and husbands, failures and the law. You can't fling open a door and not draw some vermin. What you learn here will be in demand a long time."

Oscar watched the boat drift in as its paddles slowed. A deckhand threw a coil of rope to a man on the dock, who gathered in the slack as the hull drew near. "Do you ever think about the men you hang?"

"I think about how much they weigh and how tall they stand and what kind of muscles they've got about their necks. I don't need to know their names, if that's what you mean. That's for the chaplain."

"I don't mean that. Are you never bothered by the concept of killing a man to punish him for killing?"

"Now you sound like one of them teetotaling newspaper editors back East. It ain't about punishment."

"What is it about?"

Rudd drew rein and wrapped the lines around the brake handle. His long face with its knob of a nose was flushed, but not from drink. The slack flesh was pulling away from his cheekbones, creating red pockets beneath the watery whites of his eyes.

"It ain't up to me who I pull the lever on," he said. "I don't come in until that choice is made. That don't mean I ain't give it some thought. I give it plenty. It ain't about punishment. It ain't revenge, nor even justice. It's balance. Take a life, give up your own. Keeps things even."

"But it isn't only killers you hang. Some are just deserters."

"If one man dies fighting because you wasn't there to help, you might as well have shot him yourself. It's the same thing in my mind. You fit in the war. How do you see it?"

"My strongest memory of the war is seeing three men and a boy hang for stealing food because they were starving."

"That wasn't a hanging. It was a strangling. If you don't see the difference you can go on back to Topeka and build hardware stores."

"I don't think I could hang a man who didn't actually commit murder."

Rudd unwrapped the lines. "You'd be surprised what you can do and can't. A bare week ago you didn't have any interest in hanging anyone." He whistled Jake into a trot.

TEN

The *Calendar*'s useless," Rudd said. "I bought a stack off a book-wagon for a penny. The peddler was using them to start fires, said he got 'em from a shop in Boston and couldn't give them away. I thought I'd learn a thing or two I didn't know about how things was done a hundred years ago in Old Blighty, but it's just a shopping list of atrocities committed by the condemned. Not a word about drops or trap mechanics or type of rope. You can have them if you want, scare your grandkids out of stealing candy."

Oscar sat on the floor in the shack, shuffling through the loose crumbling pages of the *Newgate Calendar* in the greasy light of the lamp Rudd had set on the floor between them. A drop of sweat rolled off the end of the hangman's nose and plopped onto the curled pebbled-leather cover of a book bearing the title *Transportation, Incarceration, and Execution: A History of the British Penal System, 1600–1750, vol. I*, stamped in smudged gold. Rudd was on his knees before one of the makeshift bookcases, struggling to remove a volume without dislodging the contents of an entire shelf. He was in his shirtsleeves, and perspiring what smelled like pure grain alcohol through the cotton.

Other books on the shelves and in the shambles on the floor carried such titles as *Paris Under the Terror, Engines of Immolation,*

The Penalties of Heresy, From the Stake to the Guillotine, Drawing and Quartering in Medieval Europe, The Mazzatello of the Papacy, and *A Review of the Bloody Tribunal; or, The Horrid Cruelties of the Inquisition as Practised in Spain, Portugal, Italy, and the East and West Indies.* This last, printed in elaborate hard-to-read italics, covered most of the mottled title page of a tome that lay open atop the pile. There were general medical texts as well, measuring several inches across their spines, with bits of torn paper sticking out of the page ends, as markers, and a number of titles in languages Oscar could not understand, including *La Pregunta* and *Peine Forte et Dure,* and one he could, in German: *Tod bei Brandwunde,* Death by Burning.

With a grunt of triumph, Rudd pried loose the book he wanted, creating a vacuum that was quickly filled when the volumes on either side and stacked on top spilled into it. The book, which he lowered to the floor with both hands—the veins on both sides of his neck standing out with the effort—was the enormous one Oscar had noticed that morning over breakfast, bound in a wonderfully soft-looking leather golden with age and secured with clasps in lieu of a spine stout enough to prevent the pages from bloating.

The hangman unfastened the clasps carefully—his long fingers, abnormally strong from his years of kneading hemp, were surprisingly dextrous—and grasped the cover to turn it back, but paused to stroke the binding. "Go ahead, have a feel." He withdrew his hand.

Oscar touched the material, gliding his fingertips over the blank surface. It felt like velvet. "Pigskin?"

"Human, or so I was told by the same peddler who sold me the *Calendar.* He said the lord magistrate who commissioned the book had a murderer skinned to bind it. Whether the wretch was alive or dead at the time, he couldn't say. Steady, lad, he won't bite. He's been buried three hundred years."

Oscar had snatched his hand back. His squeamishness embarrassed him. "Is it genuine?"

"I'm inclined to think it's vellum; that's unborn calf, to you. A merchant will say anything to separate a man from his poke. Whatever it is, it's held up. The book's dated 1510."

"It must have cost a fortune."

"I traded the rope I used on a trooper who joined the army to escape a charge of strangling his wife in St. Louis. I told the peddler he could get fifty dollars for it back there, more if he cut it up and sold it piece by piece. I didn't lie, but the Jesuits there would give him twice as much for this book. I doubt the fellow could even read. He bought it in a box of atlases and dictionaries from a professor's widow."

Oscar was only half listening. Rudd was turning the ancient cream-colored pages, through which a bookworm that might have been observed by Magellan had burrowed a hole smaller than the head of a pin, at an angle that exposed the oblique edges clear to the back of the book. The text, made up of archaic characters printed in brown ink, was Latin. Oscar asked him if he read the language.

"I never saw the need to learn. I doubt what's written here is more enlightening than the pictures."

As he spoke, the hangman turned back a leaf, exposing an illustration reproduced from a woodcut that filled most of a page. In it, a crude representation of a corpse in a jerkin and breeches hung from a beam laid across the limbs of a pair of skeletal trees. A ladder leaned against the beam and a group of men and women in antique dress stood in a half circle observing the event.

"I gather it was a legal affair, blessed by judge and church," Rudd said. "See, there's the priest with his book, and this fat fellow in the broad hat and ruffles has the bench written all over him. That aside, there wasn't a bit of difference between it and a lynching. As near as I can figure they made the poor bastard climb the ladder, slipped the noose over his head, and shoved him off. He couldn't have dropped more'n six inches. Choked like a chicken. He must of been an Irishman."

"Perhaps he committed a heinous crime."

"Maybe so, but it's been less'n a hundred years since someone decided death was punishment enough without the slow pain. Take a look at this here."

He took a brick of pages in his hand and flipped them to a place he had marked with a scrap of paper; Oscar saw that it was a piece of the manufacturer's label peeled from a whiskey bottle. This illustration, also from a woodcut, showed what appeared to be a naked man spreadeagled on a stone floor with his wrists and ankles bound to stakes, with a square board laid upon his torso and half a dozen cylindrical objects with rings attached to their tops arranged in two rows upon it; weights. A brutish-looking fellow in shirtsleeves and breeches crouched over him, preparing to add another pair of weights to the board.

"Pressing to death," Rudd said. "I read about this before. If the wretch refused to plead guilty and keep his property from being confiscated by the king, this is what he had to look forward to. If he pleaded guilty and left his heirs without a penny, he got to be hanged. Is it any wonder my old da' took ship from the bloody empire?"

"Why do you have this book?" Oscar's chest felt constricted.

"It's a measurement of progress, lad. I admire to rummage through it when some benighted soul calls me a butcher and I ain't in a mood to shut him out." He riffled pages. "See, here's the first proper scaffold, what was designed to collapse out from under the condemned instead of obliging him to take the drop himself. There's the Halifax Gibbet, a beheading machine, and that's a woman burned at the stake; probably failed to get her husband's supper on time. Here's a pretty one of a fellow being broken on the wheel. I wonder if the book's purpose wasn't for the edification of prisoners waiting for their time, or if they was expected to browse through and make their choice, like a wishbook." He cackled. Then he slammed shut the book with a reverberating boom. "It's a noble calling, lad, and in here's the proof. The miserable murderers who designed these engines were no better than the ones they designed them for; hell's bells, you could fill another book with them that came to their end on their own machines, from Cratwell to Robespierre. Meanwhile some of them they executed was guilty of nothing worse than selling gold filings off the king's coins or smiling at their landlord's mistress. We kick the trap out from under killers and deserters and rapists, and we do it quick and painless, sparing the world and themselves their nuisance. Doctors no longer bleed their patients to death to spare them disease, and we've learned right along with 'em. It wasn't so long ago a surgeon couldn't go in a hotel through the front door. The time's coming—I may not see it, but you will—when a hangman is fit to dine with the president."

The young man, embarrassed by Rudd's passion, ran a finger along a row of compressed books and stopped at one entitled *Traumas of the Esophagus and Upper Spine*. He asked about it, as much to change the subject as to quench his curiosity.

"I don't recommend it. There's a chapter about the mechanical effect on the central nervous system of the subaural knot as opposed to the occipital. Claims you can avoid the prisoner disgracing himself in his pants if you slide the knot to the base of the skull. Below the ear's quicker and more sure. I ain't interested in sparing my delicate nose."

Oscar tugged loose the volume, slowing the slide of the others with his hand and avoiding anarchy. He found the chapter Rudd had marked and studied the colored transparencies. It had been an expensive book to produce. "Have you ever tried it?"

"Once you got a dish perfect, you don't spoil it by changing from cinnamon to pepper."

"It looks as if you spend most of your wages on books."

"Ain't much else to spend them on in Leavenworth, after food and underclothes. You see that hand?" The hangman thrust out his right, palm up.

Oscar had noticed before how muscular Rudd's hands were. The sinews stood out like piano wire and his palm rippled visibly when he flexed his fingers. The young man could not have encircled one of his wrists with both hands. His own father, whose forearms had thickened prodigiously over years of milking cattle, had boasted none bigger.

"That's from working with rope," Rudd said. "I can roll a spoon into a ball with one hand, and break a whiskey glass from inside just by spreading two fingers. There ain't a woman between here and Dublin will let a hand like that touch her face. That's why I got the money to spend on books." He raised the hand in front of his eyes and leered at it. "Too bad they don't know what they're missing. A man with a hand like that can pleasure a woman all night and tie flies with the other."

Oscar felt himself blushing. The hangman's cackle sounded like sticks breaking. Suddenly Rudd rose on his knees and groped behind the books on the top shelf. He cursed, leaned in closer to extend his reach, made a hoarse noise of satisfaction, and withdrew his hand in a tight fist. He opened it beneath Oscar's nose. A black sphere the size of a stunted orange rested on his palm.

"A rubber ball?"

"*Hard* rubber, lad. Policemen back East carry clubs made from it." He flipped it above the young man's head.

Oscar cupped his hands involuntarily and caught it. He turned it over in one hand. It was very hard, and gave only a little when he tightened his grip.

"That's the ticket, lad. Squeeze it like you expect juice to come out. You're to live with it day and night and work it even when you're asleep. Eat and drink with one hand, squeeze it with the other. Every time I catch you not squeezing it I'll dock you a nickel."

"Why?"

"Because this dry spell can't last, that's why. Next time the Old Woman throws a party, she'll be using a rope you worked. If you haven't the hands for it, the guest of honor won't fare much better than that lost child with the board on his chest."

He could not tell if Rudd was having him on, but he knew shortly. Thirty minutes later, with a platter of bacon and cornmeal mush waiting on the table, he put the ball down next to his plate to draw out his chair. Rudd snorted loudly, produced a tiny memorandum book with a grubby leather cover and a gnawed stump of yellow pencil and made a mark on one of the dog-eared pages. "That's a forty-five-cent day, Mr. Stone." He laid the book and pencil within easy reach on the table and sat down.

Oscar could not cut his bacon with only one hand, so ate the strips with his fingers while squeezing and rotating the ball with the other. Having to lay down his fork in order to drink from his cup of water slowed him down, and the hangman was through eating before he was. Rudd then announced it was Oscar's turn to wash the dishes. He had to brace the plates against the side of the shallow basin to scrub them with the rag, and had to swish the utensils around in the water one-handed rapidly until they surrendered their clots of grease. A plate slipped while he was trying to wipe it dry, and he dropped the ball in order to catch it before it broke; there was a snort behind him, pages turning, the scratch of a pencil. "Down to forty cents, Mr. Stone."

Sometime in the night, light came pink through Oscar's eyelids. He opened them to see Rudd standing over him in his nightshirt, the lamp in one hand and the notebook and pencil in the other. He found where the ball had rolled out of his hand when he fell asleep and resumed squeezing.

"Thirty-five cents," Rudd said. "One more tonight and even the chink cooks won't let you in their company."

Later—it could have been minutes or hours—he awoke with a start and groped in a panic between his body and the arm of the horsehair chair until his hand closed about the ball. He began squeezing it frantically, as if to make up for lost time. Presently he realized that Rudd was snoring and that his lapse had gone unnoticed. For a long time after that, Oscar lay awake in the dark, squeezing, squeezing.

ELEVEN

On the last day of May 1866, a trooper named Ervine, walking punishment detail at Fort Riley with a log over one shoulder for reporting to duty drunk, threw his log at a guard, crushing the man's skull, stole a horse, and rode forty miles to a stagecoach stop in Washington County, where he raped a backward serving girl and stole a fresh mount. A citizen's committee led by a former colonel of the Kansas militia caught up with him near Marysville and prepared to lynch him, but a patrol that had been tracking Ervine all the way from Fort Riley intervened. Returned to the fort in irons, the trooper was awaiting court-martial when an answer arrived to a communication sent to Columbus, Ohio, where he had been recruited, informing the commander that Ervine was wanted there under the name Creasey for cutting the throat of a clerk named Oliphant in the course of robbing a dry goods store. Oliphant had lived long enough to identify his assailant, but it had taken the Columbus police months to establish that Creasey had joined the army under an alias and been assigned to a post out West. From June to August the case remained in the newspapers while the state of Ohio and the Department of the Army argued the priorities of their particular grievances against the prisoner. At length it was agreed that Ervine/Creasey would stand trial for desertion, rape, two counts of horse theft, one count of armed robbery, and two counts of murder before a military court, with a civilian prosecutor employed by Oliphant's family assisting the army. Conviction was swift, after which the prisoner was ordered to be removed to Fort Leavenworth, where he would be hanged by the neck until death released him from his worldly obligations.

Trooper Ervine arrived in an ambulance, escorted by eight cavalrymen under the command of a lieutenant. Although the route bypassed the town of Leavenworth and no schedule was released to the public, a crowd of more than a hundred people lined the road approaching the fort from the west, eager for a glimpse of the hunted felon who had managed to finesse the Grand Army of the Republic into abetting his escape from justice. If the mild-looking fellow who stared out at them with frightened eyes disappointed his audience, no such indication was given. Any sudden color in the drab flatness of the American plain was sufficient entertainment.

Rudd prepared for the occasion by giving the Old Woman a fresh coat of green paint, replacing one of the hinges on the Thurtell flap, and selecting a rope from among his favorites, a remarkably pliant one of Indian hemp, into which the amber drops of gun oil vanished almost upon contact, like liniment into thirsty flesh. He spat after them for luck, rubbing the spittle into the fibers with the ball of a broad thumb, and stuck out his right hand, commanding Oscar to grasp it. Prepared for the test, the young man obeyed, squeezing the calloused hand with fingers long accustomed to the pressure of the hard rubber ball. The hangman grinned, and after giving those fingers a final twist that only a few weeks before would have left them numb, let go and tossed him the rope.

"Work it good, lad. Not too much oil, mind; you don't want it making a mess of your cuffs up there on the platform in front of everybody."

"*My* cuffs?" He felt a protest rising in his throat.

"I'm talking general. Ervine's the most famous gallows bird the Old Woman has seen since she's been in my charge. She'll never forgive me if I put him in a carpenter's hands. You'll know it's ready when you can run your fingers against the grain with your eyes shut and don't hear a thing. We'll be kinder to Ervine's neck than he was to that store clerk's."

"He sounds a fit fellow for hanging."

"Oh, he's hempstring, all right, but that part ain't our concern. What *is* is how he feels about it all."

"I imagine he's against it." Oscar smiled.

"You'd be surprised how many ain't. Murder's just a step to suicide for some. We had this corporal for a while that shot his lieutenant over a misunderstanding. The lieutenant pulled through, so the judges of the court gave the corporal life. He filed a protest from his cell, demanding execution. Well, you don't acknowledge communication from a madman. The next thing he done was smuggle a letter out to the *Weekly Herald* in Leavenworth, stating his case, and they ran it. It got picked up by the eastern papers. Before you could say Jack Ketch, every old maid and pettifogging editor in the country wrote the army demanding that it do as he asked or turn the lunatic over to an asylum where he belonged; some said let 'em go, he was suffering enough on his own. I got a rope ready just in case and prepared the Old Woman, washed and set her hair, as we say, for the big day. I was curious to see how a man swung who wanted it and if it differed from the common. Would he give a little hop just as the trap opened, make a head start? And how would it affect the drop if he did? I had a whole list of questions to ask him for when it came time to take his measure. I don't think I ever looked forward to a thing with more curiosity and trepidation."

"What happened?"

"What usually happens when you got your tongue all set for a thing? Nothing."

"Nothing?"

"The army put a guard outside his cell day and night, in case he tried to do the job himself. He didn't, and after six weeks when the letters stopped coming they shipped him to New York to serve out his sentence. I ain't heard a thing since, so I assume he gave up his demands. That, or he made good on his suicide, which was probably what the army was waiting and hoping for as soon as no one was looking. I can't say I wasn't relieved when he passed out of my hands—there was just too many variables, and whatever went wrong would of went wrong in front of the whole country—but part of me is still wondering what it would of been like to hang a man that wanted it."

"Maybe Ervine will answer your question."

"I doubt it. I seen him when they brought him in. He's got rabbit eyes. I hope he ain't the kind to blubber and beg for his life up on the scaffold. It's messy and unsatisfying."

"How can you find out?"

"The measuring will tell me all I need to know. That's when the brass chips off and you see whether it's iron underneath or just cheap foil. A man's true character emerges when he's got a hangman's fingers around his throat."

Oscar thought of the strength in Rudd's hands and swallowed as quietly as possible. "What if he's the kind who blubbers and begs?"

The hangman grinned and held up his bottle. "Six or eight slugs of Dr. Barleycorn's the cure, half an hour before the chaplain comes. Five won't do it for a big man. Nine makes a small one stumble on the way up the steps. I ought to draw up a chart for that as well." He drank.

"Aren't there regulations against it?"

"There's regulations against everything, that's the army. You can't follow 'em all without breaking some others. The commander who was in charge when I first got here was temperance through and through. I had to smuggle the stuff in under my hat on the pretext of taking some measurements I'd forgot. But Janning likes a good port with dinner and brandy after, and he'd rather hang a man smooth with a glow on than honor the Pledge with a coward. I use the term loosely, mind; no man knows what he's got in him until he climbs them steps. I've seen men with a brow and a chin you'd put on a statue break down and whimper like a schoolgirl just at the sight of me in my working clothes, and little birdy-necked jaspers with wet lips and eyes white all around that step up onto the trap and stand there like they're waiting for a train. There's no chart for that. Draw one up and I'll put you in my book."

"What book is that?"

"I told you before I don't propose to finish out my days kneading ropes and working levers. The books I've been showing you are all right as far as they go, but they take too long to read and there's nary a one written by a man who's done the thing written about. I mean to set down everything I know about the profession, all the things I've told you and a deal more I ain't, have it printed up and set between boards, and make it available to every penal institution in the land. Call it a *McGuffey's First Reader* for hangmen. Care to hear the title?"

Oscar nodded. No other response seemed appropriate.

Rudd corked his bottle, set it aside, and hooked his thumbs inside the armholes of his vest, like a minister announcing the subject of his sermon. "*Gravitational Execution*, by Fabian Timothy Rudd, D. S." He unhooked his thumbs, unstopped the bottle, and swigged, as if in reply to a toast.

"Department of Sanitation?"

"Doctor of Suspension, damn your eyes. It's honorary, but I expect it to be made official once the book becomes the standard text in college courses. Don't look at me that way, lad. We can't keep recruiting our master executioners from the street. What's to prevent a common strangler from usurping the imprimature of a public service, if not a diploma and the sanction of a great familiar body? *I* may not, but you'll live to see the day when the science of practical dispatch is taught in every American university, with a copy of *Gravitational Execution* on every desk, right next to the inkwell and slate."

"I have no reason to disbelieve you. Nothing has surprised me since the war." Oscar went on kneading the rope.

Rudd drank, and his mood turned sour. "That is if the old maids and pettifogging eastern editors don't talk Washington into outlawing the death penalty. They done it in Michigan twenty years ago, all because they brought a brass band and baskets of chicken to a good public hanging and got ashamed of themselves for it. All they had to do was send the band home. They think they're against execution, but they ain't. They just don't want to see it. I never cared a fig more for the frogs than I do the damn English, but you got to hand it to them Frenchies. The guillotine was the quickest and least painful invention ever got up for separating a man from his sins, but it was bloody and hard to look at, so they done away with it. The man who can make the rope do what the guillotine done, as swift and clean as that but without the unpleasant display—that man will save the profession."

He continued to drink and talk, but with less optimism, until he sank into indecipherable muttering and finally put his chin on his chest and began to snore. Oscar put aside his rope, turned up the lamp on the table, and reached across to take the bottle from Rudd's hand before it spilled. As he did so, he caught sight of his fingers next to the hangman's. In the low dirty light he could not tell where his left off and the other's began.

If looks were any indication, Colonel Emlen Janning would have served out his life in the Prussian military had he or his parents not emigrated to America. His head, when he uncovered to scratch his scalp, was bullet-shaped, falling off sharply behind the close-cropped crown to his collar, and his eagle nose and sharp cheekbones threatened at any moment to gnaw through the thin layer of shining skin that covered them. He trimmed his fair beard so close to his jaw that he appeared clean-shaven until he moved his head and a ray of sunlight canting through the high windows overlooking the gallows glittered off the golden hairs. Oscar, a descendant of Bavarian peasants long accustomed to losing their sons and their chattel to press gangs raising armies to fight Napoleon, felt a deep-seated aversion to the man on sight.

They had not spoken. The colonel, in parade dress with coils of gold braid on one shoulder, mounted the steps to the scaffold some twenty minutes after Rudd and Oscar had taken their places near the lever that operated the trap, and stood on the opposite side with his white-gloved hands folded before him while the drummer with the company band rattled a rhythmic tattoo on the snare suspended from a strap across one shoulder. Hangman and apprentice wore crisp collars and cuffs, Oscar in his wedding suit and shining bowler, Rudd in his frock coat and striped trousers, brushed and pressed for the occasion, and his silk hat, its dented side a workman's badge with its own kind of shabby dignity, like a farmer's clean overalls worn for a trip into town. His grim face showed animation but once, to tip a wink at Oscar the first time he looked Rudd's way. His mouth remained turned down at the corners like a pallbearer's.

The benches were all occupied by officers from Fort Leavenworth and Fort Riley, including Major Alfred Gibbs, Riley's ranking officer. Gibbs, bearded and sun-browned, wore the scowl customary of an old campaigner who was preparing to turn over his command to a younger man, a lieutenant colonel then on his way from Washington to head up the Seventh Cavalry. There was a delay before the prisoner's appearance, during which the drummer stopped his sticks. The mood of edgy anticipation that filled the silence combined that of a crowd attending a funeral and of an audience awaiting the delayed performance of a play. Isolated dry coughs broke the stillness like sticks popping in a fireplace.

Finally Trooper Ervine entered, led by the chaplain in his captain's uniform and clerical collar, reading from Revelations, and flanked by two members of the military guard, with six more following in column-of-twos with bayoneted rifles on their shoulders. Ervine's shuffling footsteps in ankle chains did not keep time with the drum. His face was pulpy gray and Oscar could see the whites of his eyes all around the irises. He had seen them before at close range, when Rudd had handed his apprentice a roll of measuring tape like a dressmaker's and instructed him to gauge the prisoner's height. The man had actually flinched when one of Oscar's knuckles grazed his temple during the procedure, as if he had touched him with the rope that would be used to hang him, and had breathed swiftly and heavily throughout. When Rudd encircled the base of the man's neck with his hands in order to determine the strength of the muscles, Ervine's knees had buckled; a guard standing nearby had come forward to steady him physically. That night Oscar had asked Rudd if he was planning to administer alcohol before the execution.

"Not in this case, lad. He'll perform come the day, or I'm no judge. It's the braggarts you need to watch. They don't give themselves the chance to be afraid, and so it all comes out on the way to the scaffold."

Oscar was dubious, but with the assistance of the guards the condemned man climbed the steps without missing any, the links of the chain connecting his anklets clinking against the edges, and when the chaplain stopped reading and Colonel Janning asked Ervine if he had anything to say, the trooper astonished Oscar by tipping back his head and singing, in a clear but slightly uneven tenor, a hymn Oscar remembered from his childhood. When the last ringing note ceased, Rudd slipped the noose over Ervine's head and then the black hood and stepped back from the trap, looking at Janning. Once again the colonel bared his bullet head and lowered his chin in a courtly nod.

Rudd, however, made no move to operate the lever that stood between Oscar and him.

Silence stretched, broken in half when Jannings cleared his throat. Oscar looked at the hangman, who continued to stand with his head lowered and his mouth downturned, staring at the boards at his feet. Then his eyes moved toward his apprentice. One lid moved downward, then up.

Oscar stared. He tried to shake his head, but was conscious that it would not move according to his will. The officers seated on the benches coughed and cleared their throats. Ervine stood unmoving except for the dark hood billowing out and in with his breath.

Rudd directed his gaze across the building, where it became lost in the middle ground. His hands remained crossed in front of him, where they might have been carved from the same hickory as the Old Woman for all they moved or showed that blood was coursing through them. A rill of perspiration started under Oscar's collar and crawled down between his shoulder blades. It felt like a fire ant looking for a place to sink its mandibles.

The movement when it came was sudden. Without consciously thinking, Oscar reached out, grasped the polished roundness of the lever, and jerked it toward him. The black hood with Trooper Ervine's head inside dropped out of his line of vision. He heard the squeak of the hinge, the thump of the trap, the bang when the rope jerked taut, and underneath it the splitting crackle of the spinal column parting. The platform twitched twice beneath his feet, the physical extension of Ervine's nerves and muscles making his legs kick. Then it swayed in accompaniment with the creaking of the rope as the body completed its semirevolution to the left.

Oscar felt a wave of nausea that reminded him immediately of South Georgia Crossing; but he didn't vomit. He felt hot, fevered, disconnected from his body and from that platform and the tall narrow building filled with men in uniform. He did not recall descending the steps from the gallows or making his way through the standing officers to the fresh air outside, or whether he did it under his own power or with support from Rudd, who walked beside him. He did not feel part of the earth until, standing near a crowd of civilians from Fort Leavenworth who had been allowed to gather on the edge of the parade ground while the hanging was taking place, he found himself grasping the hand offered him by Colonel Janning.

"Thank you," said the commander. "I had no idea Mr. Rudd had such a capable assistant. You'd be advised to look to your health, Rudd. You're no longer indispensable to this garrison."

"I ain't concerned, Colonel. There's always more men to be hanged than there are to hang 'em."

Oscar said something in response to Janning's compliment, and then Captain Burry approached the colonel with fort business and the young man was forgotten. Oscar turned away, more to avoid the hand Rudd was raising to clap on his shoulder than anything else, and found himself looking into the blue of Gretchen's eyes.

She wore the bonnet and cape she'd worn aboard the wagon from St. Louis, powdered with dust from the stagecoach ride from Topeka and from her journey aboard whatever conveyance she'd taken from the town of Leavenworth. Her face was dead white. Then she turned and fled, the crowd closing in behind her like water running out of a sluice.

Part Four

LOOSE KNOT

Traveling is a fool's paradise. . . . My giant goes with me wherever I go.

—RALPH WALDO EMERSON

A fugitive and a vagabond shalt thou be in the earth.

—GENESIS 4:12

TWELVE

It ain't work for a married man, lad. The women don't understand, and God bless them for that, because I don't know as I could sleep next to one that could. The bald fact is there's jobs to be done in this world that most don't want, and don't want them that does it, but they want the jobs done no less. I ain't saying I don't miss my Cynthia; there's nights still when I think I might of got her to stay if I went at it hard enough. But I wouldn't of had Cynthia even if I had. She'd of hated us both, me for what I am and her for staying. Brighten up, lad. There's women of a certain stamp'll crease the sheets with a hangman just for the privilege of saying they did, and not take money for it, neither. It ain't like being a priest. And there's this to consider: You don't have to lose no sleep over your reputation. You're still a hangman whether you give to the poor or steal canes out from under widows. It's freedom I'm selling you, lad; liberty and security. The army don't offer that and neither does the Homestead Act. Now put back that gear and join old Rudd. Just because he drinks alone most of the time don't mean he wouldn't welcome company." He blew the dust out of a glass and filled it from the bottle.

Oscar ignored him, packing his valise. He'd pursued Gretchen through the crowd, only to arrive at the spot where she'd alighted from the ambulance that had brought her along with the others just as it gained speed, carrying her back toward the town of Leavenworth. By the time he and Rudd had driven back in their hired gig, he learned she'd boarded the stagecoach for Topeka. She'd made the bone-shaking journey to surprise him, only to subject herself to it all over again to escape him. He knew without question that she'd overheard Colonel Janning's congratulations and drawn the only conclusion possible.

"She'll not listen to you, lad; and even if she did, what would you tell her? 'It's the first neck I ever stretched, I feel bad I done it and I won't never do it again'? It ain't like you forgot to stop at the baker's on your way home, or let her birthday pass, or said her mother's face reminded you of the south end of a mule you seen in St. Louis. Even if she does take you back, you'll never know peace. One day you'll be reading her hell for putting too much cornstarch in your long-handles and she'll remind you about the time you turned hangman after you promised her you wouldn't. Then it starts all over again."

"I don't care. She'll have the right. If it means begging on my knees for the rest of my life, it's no more than I have coming. I might as well get used to it now."

"It'll be a lie."

It wasn't just the words that made Oscar stop throwing shirts into the valise and look at the man sitting at the table, still in his hanging clothes, with the bottle in his hand. Rudd's tone lacked utterly the edge of irony that rimmed most of his pronouncements, and the horse-toothed grin the young man had expected to see was nowhere in evidence. The hangman's long comical face had the dignity of Smollett the druggist when he was discussing his daughter's future in the wilds west of Pennsylvania; of Pickerel the carpenter when he was rubbing his sandy palm along the smooth wooden surface of a mahogany cabinet searching for flaws.

"What would be a lie?"

"My Cynthia was a God-fearing woman, Christian to the bone.

She said Jesus had no forgiveness for a sinner who wasn't sorry. Without it, all you'll get for your begging is splinters in your knees."

"But I am sorry."

"You're sorry you gave her hurt, that's plain enough. What's just as plain is you've got no regret for springing the trap on Ervine. I'm drunk, lad; I ain't blind. I seen it on your face when he came to a bang at the end of that rope, just like I seen it in Topeka when Hollingshead shot through the hole in the gallows you built. You're a born hangman. You can give it up and go back to your planes and chisels and never again see a rope put to any use other than hauling a bale of straw into a loft, but there's one thing you'll know that you'll share with every twentieth man you see, and none other: the smell of the air you're breathing when a man you sent to glory finishes his swing. It's like fresh grass and good whiskey and verbena on the throat of a warm woman. You can get away from the smell easy, but you'll not outrun what you felt the first time you smelled it. *She* knows that right enough, and it's why she taken off rather than stay and hear what you had to say."

Oscar shook his head and resumed packing. "I don't believe men are poured in a mold. If I thought that I'd never have left York."

"Might could be it's the mold that made you leave. They don't hang so many back east. If God wanted you to build hope chests and houses He'd of found some way to make you stay. But let that rest. There's another reason you ought not to chase after her and leave what you started here, and it's better'n any one you can think up to throw against it. It's duty."

Oscar looked around, but he had run out of items to place in the valise. There was nothing left to look at but Rudd. "There is no shortage of hangmen," he said.

"There is of good ones. Rope's cheap. Any cowhand that ever threw a loop over a calf thinks he can hang a man for stealing his horse. Talk to him about subaural knots and trap mechanics and drop ratios and he'll look at you with all the intelligence of a jackrabbit. Every time some wretch dances under some tree limb, sticking out his tongue and shitting his pants, it's because there was one less professional hangman handy to do the thing proper." He thumped the cork back into the bottle, deep enough to require a knife to dig it back out, and thrust a finger at Oscar. "If you're prepared to shoulder the responsibility of every lost soul who dies like an animal, go on ahead and get your wife and saw your boards. If you can pound nails and not count one strangulation for every nail you pound, you made the right choice. You've got a gift, lad. It's yours to throw away if you like. Just ask yourself before you do if you're ready to let others pay the price."

Oscar was silent for a moment. Then he closed his valise and buckled the straps. "I have to go after her."

"If you have to, I can't argue you out of it. You know where I'll be when you come to your senses. I ain't got quite enough material for my book yet."

"Good-bye."

"God save you, lad."

He caught the evening stage to Topeka. It might have been the same mud wagon he had ridden out on; certainly it was no more comfortable. The jostling kept his thoughts from settling into a useful pattern. He tried to plan out what he would say to Gretchen, but whenever he began to string the phrases together, one of the wheels would strike a rock or a hole and they would fly apart while he grasped for a purchase on the wagon's frame. When he became too exhausted to repeat the attempt, he wedged himself between the door and his valise and slept. He dreamed in fragments, not of Gretchen or of their life in Topeka, but of his hand on the polished handle of a lever and the feel of the slight resistance of the trap mechanism just before it let go, and of the vibration beneath his feet when the flap dropped open. He saw a man in a black hood with a rope around his neck fall from his vision, as suddenly as a magician's velvet cloth dropping from a thing he had made vanish.

Topeka was awakening when the stagecoach rolled to a stop. New buildings had gone up since he'd left, and the frames of newer ones still were poking up from fresh foundations. The clerk behind the desk at the Baron Hotel, a young man with fair hair thinning along both sides of the center part, handed Oscar his key, but informed him that Mrs. Stone had left the night before with a bag.

"Where did she go?"

"Lawrence."

"Lawrence? You're mistaken. That's twenty miles."

"I'm sorry, Mr. Stone. That's what she said. She left you a message." The clerk retrieved an envelope from the pigeonhole that had contained the key and gave it to him.

The note was brief, written in Gretchen's round, clear hand. It informed him that she had engaged a trap and a driver to take her to Lawrence, where the Overland operated a stagecoach route to Independence, Missouri. Her intention was to book passage on a steamboat to St. Louis, and ride the train from there back to York. She asked him not to follow her. If he did, he might succeed in persuading her to come back with him, which was something they would both come to regret. She could not respect a husband who failed to keep a promise. She apologized for having to draw all their money out of the bank to make the journey, and said that if he would write her father he would be reimbursed. She signed it, without a closing endearment, "Gretchen Smollett."

He slept that night in his clothes on top of the counterpane in their turpentine-smelling room, intending to rest before following her. He woke with the sun in his face and went to the livery to hire a vehicle. He didn't get that far. The freight office was on the way, and he stopped outside it for full five minutes before going in and buying a ticket on the next stagecoach to Leavenworth. Putting the ticket in his pocket on his way out, he encountered Gretchen's note. He took it out, crumpled it without looking at it, and tossed it into the muddy street.

"Welcome home, lad. Don't waste your time thinking. Work's the cure. Them iron flaps we ordered are all finished and waiting for us at the blacksmith's. Platform's going to need shoring up to take the weight. You wouldn't know where we could find a good carpenter, would you? What's that? I was laughing too hard to hear. The bottle? Well, sure, you can have a pull. A cup? You know where they are. Say when."

He remained in his clothes for a week, ate nothing, drank much, let his beard grow. When he sobered up enough to see himself in the mirror where he shaved, he liked its look and trimmed the edges, cutting himself in several places. He put on sticking plaster, went out to the bathhouse, and came back to eat an enormous breakfast of salt pork, eggs, pancakes, and two pots of coffee. Afterward he found his hard rubber ball and sat in the armchair squeezing it, switching hands every five minutes or so. He could feel the tendons in his fingers drawing up. He asked Rudd if any condemned prisoners were in or expected.

"Nary a one, though I expect a busy time next year when they send out that expedition from Fort Riley. They're clearing injuns from the railroad right-of-way. Desertions always go up when there's fighting. All deserters ain't for hanging, but some are desperate enough to do anything to keep from going back."

"What do you do while you're waiting?"

"Well, there's the books, and the saloons, and Hester's there on the east end of town. Mind, she won't charge you the going rate. Girls that wouldn't think twice about snuggling up next to a gutty old buffalo runner turn out to have principles when it comes to hangmen."

"Is that all there is?"

For answer, Rudd grinned and refilled Oscar's glass.

Autumn came, and then winter, with its razoring winds and snow that swept across the plain with nothing to pile up against. Oscar and Rudd installed the iron flaps, reinforced the platform with four-by-four timbers, and stacked bales of straw between the

Old Woman's legs to muffle the noise when the flaps dumped open; the iron added a ringing echo to the bang. The work didn't take up enough time. Oscar used a scraper to remove four coats of paint from the hickory, returning to the shack each night to cough up lungfuls of chips and dust and scrub the itchy residue from his skin. He took one of Rudd's old ropes and traded it to the sutler at Fort Leavenworth for a gallon of red barn paint the man had been hoarding, telling him it was the rope he and Rudd had used to hang Trooper Ervine, and got a slap on the shoulder from the old hangman for the cheery look the new color gave to the gallows. "She's blushing, I'll be bound," Rudd said. "The Old Woman ain't looked this good since she came out."

But time still crawled. Oscar went to Hester's, a three-story brick house on the very edge of the prairie and one of the town's rare permanent structures, and paid an exorbitant sum for an hour's company with a horse-toothed redhead in a bed whose linens preserved hair oil stains from customers who had preceded him. The woman hadn't half Gretchen's imagination. Walking home sour and unsatisfied, he bought a flat pint in the Smoky Hill Saloon and put it in his pocket.

"Texas, now, *there's* a man's work," Rudd said. "A place the size of Europe, packed full of Comancheros, old guerrillas, and deserters from both armies, and I ain't even counting Mexicans. I hear they're hanging 'em every hour down in El Paso, regular as trolleys. A good suspensionist could make his fortune there if he could find a way to hold on to his scalp during the journey."

"I'd risk it," Oscar said.

"Possess your soul in patience, lad. Rate you're going, you won't know one end of a rope from the other come the time you're needed."

"I'm not drinking any more than you."

"You ain't drinking any less, neither. It takes years to develop a resistance to tanglefoot. It's like arsenic: You take a little bit and then a little bit more over the years, then you marry a woman who don't like darning your socks and throws a fistful of rat poison in with your eggs, and all you do is you belch and tell her she's getting to be a fine cook. But if you eat that same fistful all in the beginning, you won't live to court her. Drinking's a science, no less than hanging. It ain't for amateurs."

"I guess you're the expert."

Rudd grinned. "That ought to sting, but it don't. I been where you are. A man needs a wife, and if he don't have that, he needs work. God invented liquor for men that didn't have either." He fished inside a vest pocket. "I been saving this. I didn't know how to answer it. I'm young enough not to say no right off the bat, but just old enough not to say yes. I considered telling you about it, but I was afraid you'd take the offer and leave me here without no company. But you ain't company when you're like this." He flipped a square fold of flimsy yellow paper onto the table.

Oscar struggled up out of the armchair, grasping one of the arms for support when the whiskey rushed to his head, and picked up the paper. It was a telegraph blank, filled out in the operator's square hand:

> F T RUDD
> FORT LEAVENWORTH KANSAS
> FOUR MEN AWAITING EXECUTION FEDERAL JAIL TWO
> MORE STANDING TRIAL CAPITAL MURDER STOP
> HANGMAN QUIT STOP WILL PAY TRAVEL HOTEL MEALS
> TWENTY FIVE DOLLARS PER HANGING
>
> TOWNSEND PHELPS
> US MARSHAL
> DENVER C T

THIRTEEN

Townsend Phelps was a clerkly looking man in his early thirties, fine-boned and clean-shaven, with weak eyes he sought to dissemble by carrying his spectacles in an inside pocket and taking them out to peer through quickly when he thought no one was looking. He favored brown, in his suit and necktie and soft narrow-brimmed hat and glossy handmade boots, and carried a cane with a gold ferrule and a matching band at the base of the crook. Three points of a nickel-plated star poked out the top of the watch pocket of his vest. All this Oscar observed through the window of the Concord coach before it rocked to a stop in front of the office of the Leavenworth and Pikes Peak Express Company. He'd expected a reception committee of some kind, and under the indifferent regard of his fellow passenger, a mining supplies salesman who traveled with a white handkerchief tied around the lower half of his face to protect his asthmatic lungs from dust, had spent the last mile brushing his bowler and changing into a fresh collar and cuffs. He'd removed his duster, folding it with the soiled side in, and used the brush to eliminate brown streaks from his suit. "They're expecting a professional, lad," Rudd had said. "Don't go in looking like a common tradesman."

The marshal's weak brown gaze lingered on him briefly when

he alighted, then slid to the salesman, a cadaverous man in a baggy black suit whose face, uncovered now, fell away below his cheekbones like the stalk of a withered melon. Phelps started that way. Oscar inserted himself between them and grasped the marshal's hand as he was raising it to greet the salesman, introducing himself as he did so. Confusion stirred behind Phelps's face, then hardened into a resolve with the sheen of steel. In that moment Oscar adjusted his opinion of the man's character. He had begun to learn that people in the West were sometimes less than what they appeared, but just as often more.

"I wasn't expecting someone so young," Phelps said. "Your wire said you were an associate of Mr. Rudd's."

Oscar had determined that his age would be brought up, and was just as determined not to discuss it. "I understand your regular man resigned."

"They don't stay for long. I'll take you to the hotel. Have you brought anything besides the valise?"

Oscar said he had not, and accompanied the marshal to the American House, a square frame building with a two-story porch. Phelps informed the clerk who registered the guest to send the bill to his office. "As soon as you're settled in I'll take you to the jail. I imagine you'll want to see the facilities."

"I'll see them now." Oscar placed his valise on the desk and asked the clerk to see it was taken to his room.

"The jury returned a verdict against the last two defendants yesterday," said Phelps as they went out. "They robbed the bank and rode down a little girl getting away. You'll be hanging them as well."

"That's an even six. This is a busy town."

"Gold attracts filth. We just got the Copperheads cleared away from before the war when it seems the whole of both armies came out here to make their fortune in the mines, some of them without even bothering to muster out. They jump claims, shoot each other for card cheats, rob stores for a stake, and carve up whores just for the fun of it. And that's just the murderers. I've got a man on the top floor who escaped from jails in Kansas, Minnesota, and Iowa on the same charge of larceny, and fifteen stock rustlers in the basement. I need every inch of space those six men are taking up."

"I'll do what I can."

"I'm not complaining, just stating the situation. When I came out here there was no jail at all. The local law confined prisoners by throwing a buffalo hide over them and staking it to the ground. If the territorial governor and the chief justice hadn't authorized me to find a substitute, I doubt the buffalo would have held out. Here it is. It used to be the post office."

The carpenter in Oscar was impressed with the building. It was two stories, with outer walls built of one-inch boards nailed twelve deep to a thickness of one foot. Phelps explained that he had had the lower floor torn out and replaced by one built entirely of joists nailed together with five-inch spikes, ten inches thick. He'd coated the cell walls with brown mortar and whitewash and installed steel bars an inch in diameter with three inches of space in between. Finally he'd surrounded the building with a twelve-foot fence with a catwalk on top for the guards to patrol. It was easily the sturdiest construction in a city of frame buildings built to endure on the foundations of the log cabins that had preceded them. Oscar said he hoped the gallows was in keeping with the rest of the building.

"That's part of the problem."

Inside, a series of turnkeys unlocked heavy oak doors to grant them passage down a corridor between cells where men rested their forearms on the crossbars, their eyes following the visitors like those of bored animals. A door at the end led into a room with bare whitewashed walls in which slouched a gallows constructed of parched and twisted pine. Light showed through many of the joints. Shaking his head, Oscar walked up to the structure and pushed against it with one hand. It swayed.

Phelps said, "It should be torn down."

"It shouldn't have been built in the first place. Whoever did it used green wood and didn't own a level. Who was responsible?"

"Your predecessor. Washington allocated funds enough for seasoned oak and skilled labor. It's pretty clear he did the work himself, using substandard material, and pocketed the difference. I didn't report it, because we needed a hangman. The kind of man necessary was the kind that refused the work, and the kind that usually volunteered wasn't that much different from the men who were awaiting execution. This one thought he could raise his salary by threatening to quit with four men stacked up and two more in the chute. I accepted his resignation immediately. When he tried to withdraw it, I told him I'd have him up on charges of misallocation and embezzling. The prospect of sharing a cell with one of the men he was going to execute didn't appeal to him. He left on the next stage."

"What sort of hangman was he?"

"What sorts are there? None of his subjects came back to complain."

"That's a foolish statement, Marshal. Are you a fool?"

Bright spots appeared on Phelps's cheeks. His tone remained even. "I'm smart enough to know how little I know about anything but keeping the peace. That's why I wired Rudd. Are you as good as his recommendation?"

"I'm better than my local competition. There isn't a nail worth salvaging from this grotesquery. Are the men who worked on this building still available?"

"They are. Washington will stand the cost. The first man is sentenced to hang in ten days. Can you do it?"

"No. I will need two weeks at least, and a day for testing."

"Impossible. Two weeks from today is the very date set for the second hanging."

Oscar walked around the gallows. He was not reevaluating it; in his mind, it was already gone. His footsteps rang off the walls of the empty room. He was taking a mental measure of its dimensions. He stopped and put his hands in his pockets. Phelps remained where he'd been standing, framed between the warped legs of the scaffold.

"If you give me *three* weeks, I may have the answer to both our problems."

"The first four men are to have been hanged by then."

"They will be. You will be ahead of schedule."

The marshal said nothing, waiting.

"Fifty years ago in England," Oscar said, "Newgate Prison introduced a gallows capable of hanging a dozen men at a time. I shouldn't think it would be difficult to design one that could hang six."

Phelps's eyes opened slightly. "Six at once?"

"Of course. Any gallows could hang six in order. Any, that is, but this." Oscar kicked the base of the leg nearest him. The entire structure shuddered.

"It's never been done."

"I just got through telling you it has."

"Not in this country."

"A great many things have been done in this country that had never been done anywhere. Denver is one."

"They already think we're barbarians back East. A mass execution would confirm it."

"Six men is six men, whether you string them out or dispatch them together." Oscar shrugged. "If it's your reputation you're concerned about, I can't help with that. I'm proposing a solution to your present problem that will prevent a similar one from occurring in the future."

"I have to think about it."

"That is your privilege. In the meantime, please give me the names of the workmen who built this prison and tell me where they can be found, and I will engage their services immediately. Judging by the amount of new construction I observed on the way here, there is no time to lose."

"I think you'll find them free."

Phelps's lips were compressed into a thin smile. It made Oscar curious, but he asked no questions. "If you can let me have your decision by tomorrow morning, I will draw up the plans."

"Are you a draughtsman as well as a hangman?"

"After a fashion. A jack-of-all-trades is just a blunderer with versatility."

"That's an unpopular notion out here."

"I'm not in a popular profession."

"You are at the moment. Build your killing machine, Mr. Stone. If Denver must become a slaughterhouse, it should at least be efficient."

Oscar's curiosity was satisfied when he met the foreman. He was a Negro in his middle twenties, just under six feet tall, and built all of squares and rectangles, with his neck sunk like a post into the horizontal line of his shoulders and his arms extending straight down his sides like ebony timbers. His tightly coiled hair lay close to his flat temples as if a plane had been used to crop them. His name was Gibeon.

"Gibeon what?" Oscar asked.

"I ain't chose yet. Lincoln was took and the man that owned me snuck through the Yankee lines in a bonnet."

"Do you get much work in town?"

"I get work." The man's slightly raised chin placed a blockade across that path of inquiry.

His only remark upon being shown the sketch Oscar had made on a sheet of American House stationery was a long low whistle. Asked if his men could manage such a construction, he folded the paper—into a perfect square, the other noted—and poked it into a pocket of his worn white cotton shirt. He wore it, and his patched and faded dungarees, with an elegance often found lacking in a tailormade suit.

"Not without proper wood," he said. "Beg your pardon, mister, I wouldn't use this here on a outhouse."

They were standing in the whitewashed room containing the old gallows.

"Certainly not. You don't want to have to build an outhouse more than once. You will use seasoned oak, the best that can be had, for the best price you can get, but in any case the quality is more important than the cost. I mean for it to stand."

"It'll stand. Can I use my whole crew? There's five, counting me."

"Are they the crew you used to build this prison?"

"Yes, sir."

"You may. Can you finish in three weeks?"

Gibeon's face looked troubled. Oscar knew a flash of doubt, which evaporated when he realized the foreman was struggling to keep from grinning. "We can do it in two, if you pay us for four."

Oscar grunted. "I can see why you don't work more often."

"That ain't why."

"We'll pretend it is."

They shook hands.

FOURTEEN

Oscar had never known two weeks to pass so quickly and enjoyably.

His room was comfortable and clean. The bill of fare in the hotel restaurant boasted that it was a match for any in New York and San Francisco, with some justification; no less an authority than Major Collingwood would have praised the ham served in champagne sauce with pearl onions on the side. There was dining and dancing at the Windsor Hotel, and residents and visitors could choose between attending the theater or buying chances on roulette and cards at the Denver Hall, where employees carrying buckets of water worked their way among the customers, discreetly sprinkling the earthen floor to settle the dust, but Oscar, after sampling these diversions, found himself spending most of his time in the stark room at the rear of the jail, sharing sandwiches he had had made up at the American House with Gibeon and his crew of carpenters and filling their cups from the bottle he'd brought.

The men were young and black, all former slaves, including two who had run away before the war and worked menial jobs throughout the hostilities to avoid drawing attention to themselves from Copperhead spies gathering information for the Confederacy. Every one was a master-quality carpenter, who once told what was expected of them never had to be told again, and even made improvements upon some details. They were on the job from first light to well past sundown, measuring and mitering by lantern light and pausing only to help themselves to water with a dipper from a wooden bucket and to eat the food Oscar brought. The first time he showed up with a cheap picnic basket he'd bought at a local dry goods store, they regarded him with suspicion, muttering brusque thank-yous and retiring to remote corners to dine in silence, but when Oscar made suggestions and asked questions that demonstrated both a knowledge of carpentry and the assumption that what he said was understood without need for explanation or condescension, they began to warm to him by degrees. Three days went by before a casual reference to something that had happened during the war alerted them to the fact that Oscar had fought for the Union, whereupon Silvanus Johnson, who looked no older than nineteen, volunteered the information that he had served under General Ferrero, and rolled up one sleeve to show a bump on his forearm where a minié ball had been working its way to the surface ever since Petersburg. Oscar learned that he'd been correct not to flaunt his service, as the crew was cautious of white men who sought their loyalty by suggesting they had fought for their freedom. "What side was they fighting on at Harpers Ferry?" muttered the brutish-looking William Penn Cartier, who bored mortises to uniform depths with the precision of a Swiss watchmaker. They told stories of the Underground Railroad, wondered aloud about the fates of family members sold down the river, and laughed, while their victim squirmed good-naturedly, about practical jokes they had played on each other while they were building the jail, sometimes under the very nose of the myopic Marshal Phelps; offering their cups for refilling and frequently adding water from the bucket when there was work yet to be done that they didn't want to have to re-do when they were sober. Oscar found them better company than either Rudd or Pickerel or Smollett, and he marveled at their craftsmanship. The gallows grew at a rate he found wonderful. The superstructure was as level as a billiard table and would have supported a ship of the line.

When it was finished, in fact, it reminded him of a ship, built to withstand the highest seas, and measured to contain the maximum payload. It stood fifteen feet long and twelve feet high, with a flight of steps climbing one end and a massive beam extending its length, strong enough to support a combined weight of sixteen hundred pounds, or eight men averaging two hundred pounds apiece suspended by ropes. (In technical terms this was called, ironically, the live load.) The beam was twelve inches in diameter and treated with creosote to prevent rot and promote flexibility. Oscar was particularly satisfied with the trap mechanism, which was an improvement suggested by Gibeon over the design Oscar had envisioned: Instead of a series of traps, the workers had installed two planks the length of the platform, hinged on the outside edges and secured with a series of draw bolts welded to a single bar attached to a trigger arm, which when manipulated, created a single extended opening through which all six men condemned by the Denver court would plunge simultaneously. The simplified design minimized the chances of a malfunction and eliminated the embarrassment of one of the prisoners outracing his fellows to oblivion. To this arrangement Oscar had added one suggestion, that a lever be installed atop the platform to spare the awkwardness of his having to descend the stairs to operate the mechanism. He believed with Rudd that the executioner should stand on the same level with the condemned and perform his function within full view of those observing.

"You know a heap about carpentry for a hangman," Gibeon had said while studying the sketch Oscar had made to explain the apparatus.

"You know a heap about hanging for a carpenter. How did you guess it would be indecorous if the men were executed out of order?"

"I seen my share of nigger lynchings. And I know what it's like to suck the hind tit your whole life."

"You haven't the monopoly," Oscar pointed out.

"Never said I did. You ain't answered my question. How's a man that knows what you does about working with wood end up hanging folks?"

"Wood is scarce out here."

Gibeon didn't pursue the subject, and neither man asked the other any more questions about his past. If there was an etiquette native to the frontier, that was its basis.

Now Oscar smacked a hand against the staircase railing. It rang dully. "What color should we paint it? The gallows at Fort Leavenworth was green when I made its acquaintance; it's red now. In England they prefer black, but that strikes me as redundant."

Gibeon scowled in thought. "Paint covers cheap wood. I'd varnish it, bring out the grain. It looks good in the courthouse."

"Varnish would look well against the whitewash."

"We could rig it up with doilies and lace curtains," Cartier said. "Maybe plant some flowers in a box there under the platform, if they don't kick it over."

Oscar surrendered the point without comment. "Let's test it. Then we'll decide."

He'd spent an hour inspecting the ropes at Vawter's Dry Goods, finally selecting six made from an inferior grade of Chinese hemp that nonetheless exceeded the quality of anything grown in North America, and had busied himself oiling them while watching the gallows take shape; feeling as he did so like Madame DeFarge knitting before the guillotine. Now he produced them from a gunnysack and held one up, coiled into a supple figure eight, for Gibeon to take.

"If it's all the same to you, Mr. Stone." He kept his hands in his pockets.

Oscar lifted his brows, but asked no questions. He turned to the others. None came forward. Shrugging, he returned the rope to his other hand with its companions and mounted the steps. Using the carpenter's stepladder, he tied each of the ropes to the crossbeam, leaving plenty of slack for trimming later—he had yet to weigh and measure the prisoners—allowing two feet between each pair. He'd had bags filled with a hundred pounds of sand apiece and brought to the jail. These the carpenters shouldered without protest and carried to the platform, but they made no move to assist him as he knotted the ropes around the drooping necks and placed them atop the trap, nor did they linger on the platform as he took his place beside the lever, scrambling down the steps instead as if he might propose substituting men for sandbags.

The lever was beautifully made, turned on a lathe, with a shoulder sloping from the shaft into a rounded handle, hand-rubbed to a satin finish, and seemed to mold itself to Oscar's grip. He grasped it tightly and pulled. The long double flap dumped open with a chunk and the six weighted bags slammed to the end of their ropes, making the unstretched hemp thrum. He felt the buzzing vibration in the soles of his feet, but the great oaken frame neither swayed nor shook. It was as a thing carved from stone.

At the moment of release—he knew not why, did not think it mere curiosity—his eyes sought Gibeon's face where the foreman stood on the floor before the gallows. It was gray from pallor, but there was satisfaction in the eyes, the sum of the factors he had rapidly noted—stress to the joints, the behavior of the crossbeam under the burden of the sudden live load, the clean solid action of the two long planks swinging on their hinges—coming out to what he had expected but had not allowed himself to hope. His crew, craftsmen though they were, shared only the pallor; two had looked away when the bags descended. There was not a true master among them. And when Gibeon's gaze met his, Oscar felt a pang of profound regret that their association was at an end.

Oscar descended the steps and shook each man's hand. When he came to Gibeon's he hung on to it a half second longer. "Hanging pays well," he said. "You'll never run short of work."

This time the foreman let his grin break through. "That's just it, Mr. Stone. How would you know when you was finished?"

Minutes later, alone in the room with the structure that dominated it, Oscar told himself the emptiness he felt came from being alone. He placed the flat of his palm against one of the uprights. It was smooth and warm, as if life still pulsed within. He bent his arm until his forehead touched the oak, filling his lungs with the smell of sawn wood and strong pitch for the last time. He would never again supervise the construction of a gallows, or of anything else built of wood.

FIFTEEN

The six men condemned to die on the Denver gallows were as follows:

Leonard Quill, a Choctaw already marked for hanging in Fort Smith, Arkansas, for the murder of a deputy United States marshal who attempted to arrest him for the crime of selling whiskey in the Indian Nations. After escaping from the Fort Smith jail, he had committed murders in Missouri and Arkansas, then shot a territorial judge in Boulder for the purpose of stealing the judge's buggy horse. A citizens' posse had pulled him out of a saloon tent in a mining camp twelve miles north of that city, having identified him by means of the judge's horse tethered outside the tent. The federal authorities in three states had agreed to allow Quill to stand trial in Denver for the Boulder murder, with the understanding that if acquitted he would be returned to Fort Smith to face execution for the murder of the deputy marshal. The jury had delivered a verdict of guilty after deliberating for thirty minutes.

King Thompson, for murder and cannibalism. Snowed in with his two prospecting partners near Pikes Peak, he had cut the throat of one while he slept and decapitated the other with a spade during an ensuing struggle. When dug out by a rescue party ten days later, Thompson had been unable to offer a plausible explanation for his partners' disappearance. A search of the cabin uncovered butchered body parts and bones, the latter tossed into a pile in one corner like discarded table scraps. The first proceeding had ended in a mistrial when the jury deadlocked over the question of desperation and delusion. A second trial convened two weeks later had convicted him.

Titus Jefferson, a Negro employed at odd jobs, for the murder of a postal clerk during a fight said to have started when Jefferson looked at the clerk's wife while passing the couple on a Denver boardwalk. The clerk's appendix was ruptured, causing death from peritonitis one week later. The defendant's plea of self-defense was rejected.

C. L. Matoon, for the kidnap and repeated rape of the daughter of a Bohemian farmer. Inebriated and distrustful of non–English-speaking foreigners, the unemployed teamster had taken the sixteen-year-old off her father's buckboard while the farmer was inside a Denver feed store and spirited her away to his shack outside the city limits, where he held her for three days—until deputies broke down his door and shot him in the neck when he reached for a revolver. There was some confusion in court over whether the girl had been as unwilling as the prosecution insisted, but in the end he was sentenced to hang as soon as his wound healed.

John Tyler Lawrence and Edgar "Bud" Sutpen, for armed robbery and murder. Former mining partners having gone bust on an empty shaft, they had stolen three thousand dollars from the Colorado National Bank at gunpoint and gotten out without shedding blood, only to trample to death a five-year-old girl who wandered into the street as they were riding out of town. Apprehended by a citizens' posse, Lawrence had broken down in tears during the trial while Sutpen remained stone-faced, unblinking even when the sentence of execution was read.

Newspapers in three states and two territories filled columns with the grisly details of the careers of Quill and Thompson and to a lesser degree Lawrence and Sutpen, whose single foray into crime paled in comparison to what the James-Younger Gang was doing in Kansas and Missouri, and hinted salaciously at what had taken place in Matoon's shack before the deputies came. The Titus Jefferson case, however, was forgotten as soon as the court was through with him.

It was the West, whose towns of clapboard and canvas continued to fill with men who had spent four years practicing the methods of rapine and murder. Into their midst came eastern carpetbaggers and women of putative virtue, and soon other, newer depredations moved in to crowd Denver's "Half Dozen" off the closely printed gray pages. Relaxing in his room evenings, Oscar spread open the *Rocky Mountain News* and read of train robberies in Nebraska and pistol fights in Texas and remembered what he had told Gibeon about hangmen never being idle.

Then the flaring nostrils of the press, lifted always to the wind from the territories, caught the scent of Marshal Phelps's wonderful and terrible new gallows, and of the prospect that the six men waiting out their lives inside the mortared walls of the federal jail would join one another presently upon the same scaffold at the same time, and within a week of its completion there was not a vacant room to be had anywhere in the city. Men in bowler hats and dusters, with the telltale stain of purple ink beneath their nails, climbed off Concords and mud wagons, barking imperious instructions about the handling of trunks packed with bales of writing paper and Western Union blanks and bottles of whiskey. Chewing cigars and tipping pocket flasks, they swarmed like box elder bugs around the entrances to the jail and the marshal's office, demanding to be let inside and bellowing questions so close together that a shotgun barrel would have had to be jammed between them to pry open enough room to insert an answer.

Upon coming down for breakfast on the day he was to take the measure of the condemned men, Oscar found his customary corner table occupied, as were all the others in the hotel restaurant. He divined immediately the nature of the noisy, ravenous diners and knew it was only a matter of time before they learned who he was and turned their fulsome attentions upon him. He decided to eat later, and take advantage of the breakfast hour to report to the jail.

Journalists, however, were not all herd creatures. He found a number of unfamiliar men loitering on the front steps, eating sandwiches and scribbling with pencils upon thick folds of paper propped upon their knees. They were resolved to a long wait and paid no attention to the young, well-dressed man carrying a satchel until he was halfway up the steps. The deputy on the other side of the door, who was waiting for the marshal, recognized him and moved quickly. Oscar was inside with the door shut and locked while the men on the steps were stirring themselves.

"They're like maggots." The deputy, a man close to Oscar's age, had a deep purple bruise below one eye that drew up that side of his face. The clerk at the American House had said a party of officers had been necessary to break up a brawl started by a pair of rival newspapermen in the Criterion Saloon the night before.

"Maggots only feed on diseased flesh. I understand they tried to batter down a door to question Jefferson's wife yesterday."

"I'll be happy when you've hung those men, Mr. Stone."

"No more than I. The gallows may have been an ambitious idea."

A room on the second floor where the turnkeys rested and played cards had been reserved for Oscar's use. There was a table and chairs, and a set of scales borrowed from a local doctor for the weighing. This was a heavy piece of cast iron covered with white enamel, extending upward in a narrow neck from a treadle where the subject stood to a cylindrical canister at eye level, where a stationary needle drew attention to the pounds and ounces marked out on a rotating barrel. It reminded Oscar disturbingly of the counter scales employed by butchers, but was less awkward than the balance type that required a man to sit on one side while plates were added to and subtracted from the other until both sides were suspended at the same level. He was not sure that it was as accurate, however, and had arranged for five- and ten-pound sacks of grain to be brought from a nearby mercantile in order to satisfy himself that it could be trusted within a reasonable margin of error.

He asked the turnkey stationed outside the door to bring in the first of the prisoners, then produced a roll of dressmakers' measuring tape from his satchel. The bag contained nothing else apart from six flat pint bottles of Old Pepper whiskey, individually wrapped in muslin to prevent them from clinking together. He hardly expected he'd need all six, and hoped he would be leaving with as many as he had brought.

Awaiting his first appointment, he had a sudden attack of panic, not unlike stage fright. The reality of what he'd come to Denver to do had not visited as long as he dealt with inanimate things like ropes and wood and bags of sand. It was not so easy, now that he was about to meet the first of his subjects, to divorce himself from the fact that he was preparing to hang someone without help for the first time, and that somewhere in the excitement of proposing a novel solution to a logistical problem he had agreed to multiply those circumstances by six. Upon his first independent outing he had chosen to go beyond the experience of the man who had tutored him. He thought of his brother Jacob, wringing the necks of two woodcocks at once when he, Oscar, could not end the misery of even one. Who was he, of all people, to make a circus of a grim business?

He unwrapped one of the bottles from the satchel, tugged out the cork, and poured the warm balm down his throat. It entered his stomach with the sting of acid and spread like a blanket, bringing a flush to his face and making his extremities tingle. As the tide of heat ebbed, his fear went with it, leaving behind a numbness that stood for courage. He had never felt as close to Rudd as he felt at that moment.

A key rattled in the outside lock. He returned the bottle to the satchel and placed the bag under the table as the turnkey prodded in a prisoner he identified as King Thompson, the cannibal killer of Pike's Peak.

Oscar, who had learned to form no prior assumptions based upon a man's reputation, was surprised nonetheless to find himself facing a fellow smaller than he, with a weak chin and the vague, naked-looking eyes of a man accustomed to wearing spectacles. A number of muddy brown hairs stuck out on one side of his bald scalp. His hands were manacled and secured by a length of cargo chain to a broad brown belt buckled around the waist of a pair of overalls that were evidently his own, if the stained and tattered knees of a hard-rock miner were any indication. Certainly he looked like some kind of burrowing rodent. Thompson was likely still in his twenties, although the lowered head of a defeated man and his shuffling gait made him seem decades older; his ankles weren't shackled, but might as well have been. His gaze remained fixed on the floor.

He weighed one hundred thirty-eight pounds, with the manacles. Oscar had considered asking the guard to remove them, but decided against it for the reason that he would be wearing them when the trap was sprung, with an additional pound or two when his ankles were chained. He rounded off the figure at one hundred forty in his pocket notebook. The man showed no emotion when Oscar measured him for height—he stood five-feet-four, including his thick-soled work boots, when asked to stand erect—but his breathing quickened when the hangman begged his pardon and felt of the muscles at the base of his neck, the air hissing in and out of his nostrils in shallow gusts. The muscles were thick and knotted, as befit a man who had been engaged in hard physical labor for months in the close quarters of a subterranean shaft.

Then came the difficult part. In an even voice, Oscar asked, "Are you a devout man, Mr. Thompson?"

"What?" The whites showed around the shortsighted eyes.

"Are you a man of faith? Have you made peace with your fate?"

"I'm a good Christian. It's a better life I'm headed for."

"Please understand that I am not assigning guilt. Do you feel justice has been done in your case?"

The prisoner was silent a long time.

"I reckon it has," he said then. "I shouldn't of done what I done. I reckon I was out of my head, but I went and broke two Commandments and I'm a man who pays his debts."

"Two?"

Thompson lowered his head—but not before Oscar noted something sly crawling into his murky eyes. "I coveted Philpot's wife just before I slit his gullet. I reckon I would of coveted Sully's too, if he'd had one. I'm enslaved to Jezebel."

Oscar thanked him for his time.

The bald head came up then; the jawline strengthened slightly. "I practiced envy, and I partook of the flesh of my fellow man. I'm ready to be judged."

The prisoner was removed. It had not been necessary to find a way to smuggle a bottle into the man's overalls.

Leonard Quill was a more likely fit for the portrait the press had painted. Manacled like Thompson, with the addition of leg chains in tribute to his successful escape from the jail in Fort Smith, the Choctaw was nearly six feet high and very broad through the chest and shoulders, with an enormous head and features to match. His skin was the color of tarnished copper, his nose thick and flattened at the end so that the nostrils showed, as large as eggs. He had heavy lids, plucked of their lashes, and his mouth resembled an old axe cut that had not quite healed over in the base of a stump. His hair, black and without luster, had been cropped off in jail to the corners of his jaw. In his homespun shirt with its burst seams and tight gray cotton trousers, he stood in the middle of the room like some powerful engine strapped down for the night.

The barrel atop the scales whirled and stopped at two hundred twenty-two. Oscar's hands could not encircle the great neck, which felt like the limb of a tree. Quill's pulse was strong and steady in his throat and his breathing didn't change. Asked if he was a devout man, he skinned his upper lip back from a row of brown and uneven teeth like neglected pickets.

"If that means do I believe in hell, the answer's yes. I sent my portion of men there, including two you don't know about."

"Do you think justice has been served?"

"Yes, in the case of them six I kilt."

"Thank you. You may return to your cell."

The man's dark irises filled the spaces beneath the thick lids, as if the openings themselves were empty. "I'll do justice on you, too, hangman, tomorrow. What they couldn't do in Fort Smith they won't do in Denver."

The turnkey grasped the back of Quill's belt and spun him toward the door.

The Negro, Titus Jefferson, appeared fierce, but Oscar decided this was due more to the fact that his face was still cut and swollen from his fight with the postal clerk than to natural temperament. He was five-eight and his weight came to an even one hundred sixty in two sets of chains. He stepped on and off the scales obediently and although he trembled a little when his neck was probed, Oscar did not feel that whiskey was necessary. He said he had faith in Jesus and that he would be tried fairly in the court of heaven.

"Justice?" he repeated. "It took four years to free me and five minutes to find me guilty. I ain't experienced enough of it to answer one way or the other."

C. L. Matoon, the teamster convicted of kidnap and rape, fought when the turnkey tried to force him onto the scales. A two-foot length of hickory stick struck the back of his neck, he fell into a swoon, and Oscar wrote down an approximate figure while the turnkey held him under the arms atop the treadle. He'd been out of work many weeks at the time of the abduction; the muscles of his neck were slack and spongy. His lower lip shook during this part of the examination and the guard kept a tight grip on him to prevent his knees from buckling. His eyes rotated wildly in their sockets. Oscar asked no questions. He removed the unwrapped bottle of Old Pepper from his satchel and slipped it inside the man's dirty striped shirt. When the turnkey protested, he unwrapped another bottle and gave it to him. It went into his hip pocket and he half carried the prisoner out the door.

Bud Sutpen was next, followed by John Tyler Lawrence, the two busted miners who had ridden down the little girl while leaving the bank they had robbed in Denver. Oscar rather liked Lawrence, who had overcome his fit of remorse in the courtroom to accept his sentence without rancor, even with good humor; he told Oscar a joke involving a prospector and a prairie dog that the hangman promised himself to remember to pass on to Rudd when he returned to Fort Leavenworth. He cared less for Sutpen, a bitter and foulmouthed defeatist who blamed the man who had sold the pair a claim to an empty shaft for everything that had happened afterward. They both fell squarely in the middle of Rudd's chart and whiskey was not required in either case.

Oscar thanked the turnkey for his efforts, closed his satchel, and descended the stairs to the ground floor, feeling as weary as he ever had after a skirmish during the war or a day pitching hay into the loft of his father's barn. He looked forward to stretching out on the counterpane in his room for an hour or two before coming back to adjust the ropes on the scaffold according to the figures he had recorded. When the deputy at the front door opened it to let him out, he found twenty men waiting for him, shouting questions and scribbling on thick folds of paper with stubby yellow pencils.

SIXTEEN

On the morning of the hanging, Marshal Phelps reversed his decision to bar visiting journalists from the event. Previous policy had restricted the audience to federal officials, the families of the condemned and their victims, and the gentleman from the *Rocky Mountain News*; but he was a practical man as well as an efficient administrator, and there were hints in Washington, where the wire services had carried the story of the super gallows, that Congress might intervene with an eye toward the 1868 election. He despised bureaucratic meddling and usually kept it at bay by bending with the wind before it mounted to a gale. Benches were borrowed from the Presbyterian church and set up in the room to accommodate the backsides of the guardians of the free press, and the bare wall behind the scaffold was hung with red-white-and-blue bunting intended for the city's Independence Day celebration. The effect, however, was deemed too festive. To add gravity, portraits of the martyred President Lincoln and his schoolmasterly successor, Andrew Johnson, were removed from the courthouse and mounted at the ends of the bunting, with a bit of black crepe encircling the likeness of the Great Emancipator in a final flare of patriotic inspiration. Oscar thought it looked as if the men who were to hang were stumping for public office.

When he entered, the room smelled distinctly of camphor. Some of the scribes in attendance had come from climates where spring was well advanced, and had retrieved their overcoats and mufflers from storage for the journey into the high thin cold air of Colorado Territory. But the perverse imps of the Divide had chuckled grimly and pulled a "hot southerly" from their sack, drawing a warm wind from New Mexico Territory to raise the mercury into the sixties; the odor of sweat permeating wool had begun to overtake the mothballs. As Oscar walked up the aisle that led between the rows of benches to the gallows, feeling like the bridegroom at a bleak wedding, pencils scratched furiously at coarse paper. A graphite cloud rose and settled over collars, cuffs, and gaiters. He felt himself described and pigeonholed, his physical features exaggerated, his personal history cast aside and a more dramatic one substituted, a living first draft.

Just inside the door, off to the right and cramped behind the crowded last bench, a photographer had folded and leaned his tripod and camera against the wall and now busied himself blowing dust off his glass plates and arranging them on the lid of a brass-bound trunk with his name and purpose stenciled on the side: G. F. MAKEPEACE, LANDSCAPES AND PHOTOGRAPHIC PORTRAITURE. He was not with the press, whose gray fibrous paper would not reproduce photographs. Oscar suspected the execution would be recorded in all its static, deceptive detail for purchase by the morbidly curious from the windows of portrait studios across the country, and perhaps find its way into the pages of a sensational book. And he felt the ground shift beneath his feet as the West entered a new and exhibitionistic phase.

He climbed the steps he had climbed a hundred times before, to test the trap and stretch the ropes, but when he took his place beside the lever and turned to face the spectators, he felt as if the platform were suddenly much higher, allowing him to look down upon dozens of upturned faces, and the owners of those faces to scrutinize him, his dress and grooming and comportment, as if he were the first actor upon the stage of a play whose seats had been sold out for weeks. He experienced again that numbing panic he had known in the room upstairs when he was preparing to examine the first of the condemned men. Had he been careful enough with his measurements, and particularly faithful to Rudd's chart? Had he worked all the bounce out of the ropes, so that the shock was sufficient to break the bones? Had he worked them too much, and would they hold? He had heard of executions in which the ropes broke, and the poor, half-dead wretches had to be lifted from the ground and carried back up the steps and held upright while fresh nooses were prepared and the procedure repeated. To Oscar, that was worse than strangulation or even decapitation. He thought of the mortally wounded woodcocks whose sufferings he had compounded for his failure to wring their necks on the first attempt, of the look in their disturbingly human eyes, agonized and accusing. By what thought process had he, on his first assignment without Rudd's counsel, decided to compound by six the likelihood of failure in the interest of merely saving time?

Marshal Phelps had applied for, and received, funds from Washington to appoint additional deputies from among the local population for the day of the hanging. These were posted at all the entrances to the jail and at the corners of the room where the gallows stood, to maintain order and prevent morbid onlookers from gaining access to the execution. He had had special passes printed and numbered, and had handed them out personally to invited guests who signed for them in his office. Rumors had circulated for weeks that members of what the newspapers called the "Lawrence-Sutpen Gang" were planning to disrupt the execution and break free the robbers of the Colorado First National Bank. Although Phelps knew beyond question that no such gang had ever existed, he had stationed his regular men at both ends of town to stop and question strangers attempting to enter before and during the appointed hour; journalistic fables had a way of making themselves come true once they made their way into the hands of certain adventurous and impressionable readers. The deputies leaned on shotguns in doorways, and the barrel of a rifle poked out over the edge of the false front of the building across the street from the jail.

Now came the marshal himself, walking up the aisle with the jerky stride of a neophyte actor attempting to cross a stage without appearing unnatural. He'd had his hat blocked and his suit brushed and pressed, and his stovepipe boots glistened with fresh blacking. He carried his cane like a swagger stick, with the crook down and the gold ferrule slanted up behind him; Oscar suspected it was more weapon than affectation, and wondered if it was loaded with lead, the better to crack open recalcitrant skulls in lieu of shooting. On first sight, the hangman had put him down as an appointed official who had won his post by way of a political favor, but he had learned through observation that Phelps was a man of decision and foresight, who for reasons of his own preferred to let others think he was the carpetbagger he appeared. All was not as it seemed this side of the Thirty-fifth Parallel.

Oscar nodded to him as he walked past the platform and planted himself on the opposite end. There had been a brief discussion in the marshal's office the day before, during which Oscar's own sketch of the gallows had been used to block out where the principals would stand; not counting the prisoners, for whom the ropes were already in place, their lengths adjusted according to the figures in Oscar's notebook and the men's initials penciled in above *X*'s made by the hangman. He had spent an inordinate amount of time deciding upon this order. The logical first choice, to place King Thompson, the shortest, at one end and the tallest, Leonard Quill, at the other, with the remaining four graduating between, had struck him upon reflection as grotesquely comical, a flesh-and-blood replication of the stick figures in Rudd's chart, and was therefore out of the question. As a craftsman he was moreover dissatisfied with the picture presented by the opposite gradation of the dangling ropes, which when the scaffold was awaiting its subjects would make the structure itself appear out of level. Similarly, he had vetoed placing the taller men in the center and the two shortest on the ends, mimicking an Egyptian pyramid. At length he'd settled upon an up-and-down grouping of alternating heights, and blast anyone who compared it to an arrangement of steam-driven pistons. After that, with Stone's own position dictated by the placement of the lever, it had been comparatively simple to anchor the tableau with Phelps at the far end and leave plenty of room in between for the ministers and the guards to pick their places.

The important business of praying in public for the souls of the condemned had fallen to the Reverend David Tupper, pastor of the Methodist church. The local Catholic bishop had been considered and rejected on the basis of Bud Sutpen, whose hatred of all things papist had made itself known at the top of his lungs when a priest of that faith had come to give comfort to a prisoner awaiting sentence for patricide; peace officer and executioner both were eager to avoid an additional excuse for a scene on the platform. Tupper, narrow-built and luxuriantly bearded, with a curly fringe of hair that stopped precisely where the tall crown of his flat-brimmed black hat began, entered first, impressively reciting the Book of Revelations from memory with the Bible clasped shut and clutched to his breast, with the prisoners shuffling behind, chained ankle to ankle, arms pinned to their sides by coarse leather belts buckled tightly behind their backs, the men arranged in the order in which they were to stand upon the platform. Jail turnkeys in uniform brought up the rear, two to a prisoner, paired shoulder to shoulder and armed with two-foot lengths of hickory stick polished to a high hard gloss. Only the two men at the end carried firearms, a double-barreled shotgun and a lever-action carbine. In the event of a break, the men in between were drilled to go down on one knee in order to give the two at the rear a clear field of fire.

Quill, the big Choctaw, was incommoded further by a cylindrical lead weight contrived by the marshal. Acting upon Oscar's report that the prisoner was not prepared to serve his sentence quietly, Phelps had ordered the molten metal to be poured into an iron paint bucket, with a cast-iron ring inserted in the top and hung by an extra length of chain from the belt around Quill's waist. This forced him to take short steps with his knees bent to avoid banging them. Placed second in formation between bank robbers John Tyler Lawrence and Bud Sutpen, Quill placed his feet carefully on the steps, pausing in between and wheezing heavily. Oscar had shortened his rope an additional inch and a half to allow for the surplus.

Each of the prisoners was offered an opportunity to speak. Sutpen and Quill were silent, the latter out of breath as well as sullen. Jefferson, the Negro, told "Mr. Phelps" he might as lief "get to the gettin'." Lawrence delivered a short, ineloquent speech of tear-choked apology to the parents of the girl he and Sutpen had trampled. His partner punctuated this address by leaning forward and dribbling a gob of spittle onto the planks at his feet. King Thompson—christened "The Cannibal King" by the press—sang a hymn that strained his vocal cords, along with the ears of many present; when C. L. Matoon chimed in with a bawdy, drunken rendition of "Sweet Betsy from Pike," one of the guards lined up along the back rail stepped forward and jabbed him in a kidney with his stick, choking off the lyric.

Now came the nooses. The second shortest rope, after Quill's, was reserved for Matoon, the abductor and rapist, in compensation for his weak neck muscles. Adjusting the knot, Oscar smelled half-digested spirits, confirming that the teamster had taken advantage of the bottle he'd been given to settle his nerves. He swayed when he stood on the trap, but there was no sign on his flushed face of the panic the hangman feared. The bitterness in Sutpen's eyes was interrupted only when the hemp came between them and Oscar's; it came out the top unaltered. Lawrence's expression was resigned despite a greenish pallor, Thompson's pious and sly. Titus Jefferson fixed his gaze at a point on the wall opposite, above the heads of the spectators. Only Oscar was aware of the quivering in his body.

He made double sure the knot was snugged into the hollow below the black man's left ear and moved on to Quill.

As the noose slid over his head, the Choctaw bent his knees suddenly and bumped his pelvis forward. The lead weight intended to subdue him swung forward in a short arc and cracked against Oscar's right leg just below the kneecap. A bolt of pain shot up his thigh, a flash of nausea overtook him, and he stumbled.

Phelps had stationed the guard with the shotgun behind Quill. The man sprang away from the rail and thrust the twin barrels against the broad base of Quill's neck, earing back both hammers in the same movement. The prisoner froze.

The marshal closed the distance between him and the hangman in two strides and caught him under the arms.

Oscar extricated himself, placing a hand on Phelps's shoulder for balance. "I'm all right."

"Are you sure? I heard the crack."

"It was broken once on that spot. It can't be again." He worked his knee twice, took his hand away and walked around in a circle. The pain had retreated into a glow in the center of the bone. He nodded at the marshal, who hesitated, then raised a hand toward the man with the shotgun. Both returned to their places, but the weapon remained raised and cocked.

Oscar stood to one side of the Choctaw as he fixed the noose in place. The ugly gash of mouth was open in its picket fence grin. Oscar jerked the knot tight, a little more emphatically than usual. Quill flinched. The grin went.

Six five-pound sugar sacks had been purchased from a Denver emporium and stained black with a dye made from boiled walnut husks. These Oscar tugged down over the prisoners' heads with brisk efficiency, feeling through the skin of his back the disappointment of the gentlemen of the press as he did so; he suspected most of them had their descriptions of the condemned men's facial contortions already half written in their minds. At the end he circled behind the line and resumed his position beside the lever. He tried not to limp. He grasped the smooth handle and looked at the marshal. At the rear of the room, the photographer held his burning stint above his stack of magnesium powder.

Oscar expected hesitation from Phelps, and he got it. It was as difficult for a decent man to give such an order without pause as it was for a man of any sort to avoid flinching when a snake struck at him from behind a pane of glass. And it was impossible for a man of duty not to follow it up with a slight nod.

Phelps nodded. Oscar pulled. Powder flashed.

SEVENTEEN

HEARTLESS DESTRUCTION OF A HALF DOZEN LIVES
BY LEGAL PROCESS

Six Men Swept to Their Doom in the Space of a Heartbeat

Circus Atmosphere Prevails at Multiple Hanging

Church Group Here Decries "Legal Lynching"

Hangman Cool as a Cucumber

"All a Matter of Natural Law," Says He

The stacked headlines took up most of the third column of the eight-column broadsheet Oscar found tacked to the door of Rudd's shack. Someone—Oscar could guess who—had underscored "Hangman Cool as a Cucumber" in thick pencil. He set down his bag and tore off the page to read it.

The masthead belonged to one of the eastern journals that Colonel Janning, the commander at Fort Leavenworth, received by dispatch rider ten days after they appeared, and shared generously with junior officers and other acquaintances when he was through reading. The gray paragraphs below the bold print provided a more or less accurate account of the hanging in Denver, along with details of the crimes of which the men had been convicted and a report of the interview to which Oscar had submitted the day before the event. The New York editor had lifted the story from the wire after it had appeared in a newspaper in Nebraska.

A brief paragraph described Oscar as a Union veteran and a former citizen of York, Pennsylvania, currently residing in Leavenworth, Kansas, where he served as assistant to Fabian T. Rudd, hangman at the military fort there. In response to a question about the size of the assignment he'd agreed to undertake in Denver and his ability to carry it out, he had said, "It's all a matter of the natural law of gravity, which remains unaltered whether one man is to be hanged or six."

He was amused and a little chagrined to learn that he had struck the reporter as "a solemn fellow for his years of twenty-five or so, in height a little below the average, bespectacled, and attired more in keeping with a clerk in a bank than grim Charon to the underworld." Did he look as old as that? There was, he was relieved to note, no comparison to a cucumber in the text; that had been added by whoever had composed the headlines, along with the business about a "Circus Atmosphere." In fact, the event had taken place with all the sobriety appropriate to its nature, unless one counted C. L. Matoon's brief impromptu concert, alluded to even more briefly by the gentleman from Nebraska.

A related item, separated by the boldface line, "Outrage in the Lord's House," referred to a meeting in the basement of the First Presbyterian Church on Fifth Avenue, where one Mrs. Jerrold Godacre, chairwoman of the Committee to Reclaim the Lost and Wayward, made mention of barbaric practices in certain western venues that would shame even the Church of Rome. "Are these scrubbed savages so fearful of having wronged the innocent," asked she, "that they must slaughter them wholesale before the hand of the righteous can be raised?"

On the day he left for Leavenworth, Oscar had read the account of the hanging in the *Rocky Mountain News*. It had been as close to the truth as the one borrowed from the Nebraska paper, and the editor had seen no reason to add inflammatory headlines or articles about disgruntled church wives. What different places were New York and Denver.

A line scribbled in pencil at the bottom of the coarse newsprint informed him that Rudd had gone to the fort and would be back that evening. Oscar used his key, plopped down his bag inside the door, felt behind the books in the crowded press until he found Rudd's spare bottle, and made himself comfortable in the armchair.

While waiting for the liquor to take effect, he thought about the job he had done in Denver. Considering the amount of sleep he had lost and the anxiety that had dogged him throughout the final twenty-four hours before the affair, the hanging itself had been anticlimactic. The trap had fallen open smoothly and all six men had shot through the space like so many plummets. The ropes had caught with a reverberating boom that Oscar had felt through the soles of his feet, and six necks had snapped in a single report. Leonard Quill alone had violated the subsequent peace, twitching his legs for perhaps a second and a half and jingling the chain between his ankles, a chillingly merry sound. Then he joined the others in that graceful half turn to the left. Oscar had made note of that slight ripple in the smoothness of the event and calculated that a drop of an additional half inch would have prevented it. Rudd's chart needed adjustment.

In the main, he was satisfied. Negro and white man and Indian had been served equally, and the machinery of justice in Denver was back on its tracks. He had shaken Marshal Phelps's hand and boarded the stage two weeks later after having passed on most of what he knew to an eager young turnkey named Muldrow. This fellow had been among the guards who had escorted the condemned men to the gallows, and had approached the marshal asking to be appointed to the permanent post of executioner in Denver. Oscar had found him a good listener and a quick learner, and was satisfied that the young man was motivated more by personal advancement than morbidity. He'd hoped to be able to stay long enough to guide Muldrow through his first hanging, but an attempt at suicide by the prisoner accused of murdering his father had delayed that trial indefinitely and no other capital cases were imminent; Phelps's budget would not stretch to pay Oscar's expenses another day. He'd spent most of his last night in town transcribing his notes from his pocket book to a sheaf of pages and had left them with his young successor the next day, along with his best wishes.

Lack of sleep, the exhausting ride in the mud wagon, and the effects of whiskey quickly combined to send Oscar into a deep doze. When he awoke, the room was dark but for the lamp glowing on the table and Rudd was clunking pieces of firewood into the stove.

"About time you stirred. I was afraid you'd froze to death. You got to feed a fire to keep it burning, or don't they teach that in Pennsylvania?" The old hangman swung shut the stove hatch and turned Oscar's way. His long face and bulb of blue-veined nose were flushed from the heat and some assistance from the bottle, which had migrated to the table from the floor beside Oscar's chair. He had on his battered high hat; but then he only removed it to sleep and to show respect on the scaffold when death was pronounced.

Oscar asked him what was happening at the fort.

"Nothing no muckety six-rigger like yourself'd take an interest in. Just your garden-variety hanging, one customer only. One of Custer's boys got a hot spark up his ass on account of Fetterman and took himself a Sioux child's scalp. They sent him here to make an example of. He goes Friday."

"I know about Fetterman. Who's Custer?" The December previous, Captain William J. Fetterman and a relief force sent out from Fort Phil Kearny to aid a woodcutting detail under attack had been ambushed and wiped out by a party of Sioux and Cheyenne in Wyoming Territory.

"He's that boy general that took over the Seventh at Fort Riley. He's already got himself in Dutch for shooting deserters without authority, on account of he's such a hard-ass he makes deserting look like fun. I figure I won't be idle until Washington recalls him."

"You mean *we*."

"Oh, this circuit's too tame for your like. Didn't you read your notices?" He waved a hand toward the newspaper page Oscar had let fall to the floor.

"Yes. Apparently I swept six men to their doom in the space of a heartbeat."

"I wish it was that fast. Sometimes their pumps are still working when the sawbones gets to them; not that they're aware of it."

"I'm some kind of ogre. 'Cool as a cucumber.' "

"That's eastern thinking. They got an officer on every corner and a courthouse every other block and jail space for a thousand. They can afford to hang 'em one at a time and take a week in between, and still manage to snap more necks in a year than we will in ten. Hangings are easy to ignore when they go on all the time. I've went eight months at a stretch watching the Old Woman gather dust, but let you clear half a dozen cells in an afternoon and they think we're all stringing them up like Christmas balls. Well, they got to sell papers, and folks back East like to think they're better than someone. The point is, thanks to this stunt in Denver you're just about the most famous hangman since Jack Ketch."

"That isn't the reason I did it."

"I know that. Don't you think I didn't consider something just like it two years ago, when I had four men awaiting execution and three more capital court-martials going on betwixt here and Fort Snelling? I'll warrant there isn't a rope man anywhere that didn't entertain the notion at one time or another. The difference with you is you went ahead and done it. Now's the time to turn it into serious jingle."

"Jingle?"

"Money, you bullet-headed Bavarian. Gelt. Gold. Banknotes and double eagles. You don't even need to advertise for business; the scribblers have seen to that. Well, here." He slung the dilapidated leather pouch he called his "kit" up onto the table from the floor where he had dropped it and unbuckled the flap. It was a dispatch case of the type carried by army couriers, with U.S. embossed on it in worn letters; he often used it to carry ropes and an extra bottle. From it he drew a fistful of yellow Western Union flimsies and held it aloft, the way the old-time headsmen pictured in his grisly books hoisted their trophies for the inspection of spectators.

"Telegrams?"

"Offers. Work. The kit's full of 'em, and there's a bushel more back at the fort. They been boiling in ever since the papers came out. Here's one from Omaha, and Fort Dodge, and Jefferson City, and clear down in Santa Fe—I didn't think they read anything but Mexican there." He pulled pages from the crumple and glanced at them. "They're all addressed to you. I took the liberty of opening them, seeing as how you're my apprentice. 'The Honorable Oscar Stone,' that's how they know you in Virginia City, wherever that might be, I'm guessing not Virginia. Lola Montez don't get this kind of mail. They all have someone they want you to hang for a fee, and they'll pay the freight besides."

Oscar picked up a wire that had fallen to the floor in front of his chair. It was from a captain of the Texas Rangers in Fort Worth, offering him a hundred dollars and expenses to hang a Comanche raider named Knee.

"I just got off a stagecoach. I'm sick of them."

"In five years you won't be able to find a coach betwixt San Francisco and Cincinnati. The railroad's in Kansas now; by Christmas it'll be in Denver. There's a fellow named Pullman's designed a car with beds that swing down for sleeping and a restaurant on wheels and even-by-God a rolling saloon. You can get drunk in Michigan and not sober up until you reach the Pacific. The whole country's on the move. It ain't fitting for a lad like yourself to sit on the pot and just watch it fly on past."

"I don't believe that about a rolling saloon. How would you keep the drinks from spilling?"

"I don't know, but if there's a way they'll find it. I got faith in this country." Rudd drank.

"What's wrong with Leavenworth? The pay's good and it's steady work."

"It ain't no such a thing. This lad Custer just up and shoots deserters like they was sage hens, and there's talk in Washington of not even doing that, just give 'em stockade time. That means you and me'll only be hanging rapists and worse. I don't guess we'll never run out of *them*, but like I said there's dead spots for weeks when you draw your pay just stretching rope and pumping your pistol. Any day now some leather-lunged senator from Ohio's going to call for the army to cut expenses. It won't be the brass-balled officers they show the door, you can depend on that. Meanwhile the territories are crawling with carpetbaggers, claim-jumpers, horse thieves, highwaymen, white slavers, tinhorns, bad injuns, bushwhackers, rustlers, bunko-steerers, jayhawkers, goldbrickers, gunmen, Jezebels, and Mormons, all just waiting their turn on the scaffold. If I was your age, I'd *walk* down to Topeka and catch the first coalburner west before the rush."

Oscar reread the telegram. "Knee" didn't sound like much of a name for a renegade. He leaned forward and slid it up over the edge of the table.

"Well, do you mind if I eat first?"

"It would be my great pleasure if a famous hemp man such as yourself would consent to break bread with an old neck cracker from County Limerick. The main course tonight is liver and onions. Appetizer's onions and liver and it's liver and onions for dessert."

"No wine?"

"Just tanglefoot. Aged in a boot." Rudd took his skillet off its nail and blew dust out of it.

The liver was tough and stale, and Oscar wondered if the old hangman had taken to cooking with the gun oil he used to lubricate his ropes; but the smell of onions frying reminded him he hadn't eaten since breakfast. He took three helpings. Afterward he put their plates in the tub to soak and sat back down at the table. The dispatch case had been removed, but the pile of telegrams had merely been shoved aside to clear room for the settings. He rustled his fingers through the paper.

"Everything I know about hanging I learned from you. You should be the one answering these offers."

Rudd cut himself a plug and chewed it.

"Travel's a young man's game. This old gut of mine can't take the variety in diet." He poured a slug of Old Pepper over the tobacco.

"What happens when the army shows you the door?"

"I use it. I never stay past my welcome. I ain't Andrew Johnson."

"What then?"

Rudd grinned, showing bits of gristle and Brown Mule between his horse teeth.

"I said the week we met I didn't intend to finish out my time dropping traps out from under cowards and killers. Five years from now I expect to doze away my afternoons all week in some country parish, delivering the Word on Sunday and eating fried chicken with the famblies of the congregation. The Lord knows I got the bona fides. I know the Book of Revelations backwards and forwards, thanks to the good chaplain. That's more than the man knew that married me the first time."

"The first time?"

"I didn't say I was figuring to be no priest. A man of the Protestant cloth needs a respectable woman to wash out his collars. A hangman ain't got that choice."

"You may have to give up drinking."

"That I may." He picked up the bottle. "But I ain't a preacher just yet, now, am I?"

EIGHTEEN

In Jefferson City, Missouri, in October 1867, Oscar Stone hanged a former guerrilla named Frank Strang for slaughtering a family of five and stealing thirty-eight dollars and change from a tobacco can in the family's home. Strang delivered a speech of profane defiance and dropped to his death without a wriggle. On his way there from Topeka, Oscar sat in a day coach and watched scenery roll past at forty miles per hour that had taken him three weeks to cover by wagon only eighteen months earlier. He could not identify the spot where he negotiated with German-speaking Indians for the party's safe passage but he thought of Gretchen.

January 1868 found him in Lincoln in the new state of Nebraska, where some storekeepers had not yet altered their signs to reflect the name change from Lancaster. Lumber was borrowed from the capitol building project to erect a gallows, upon which Oscar stood holding down his hat with one hand in a blizzard and working the lever with the other. The condemned, an unemployed surveyor, had strangled his wife during an argument over a bad investment in land with nonexistent salt deposits.

He spent the last six months of that year in Cheyenne, Wyoming Territory, on retainer to the Laramie County Sheriff's Office, carrying out sentences connected with shootings, knifings, bludgeonings, and one case of murder by bass viol in the orchestra pit of the Cricket Theater. He was considering an offer of a permanent post with a handsome salary by the citizens' vigilance committee when a bullet pierced the floor of his room from the saloon below; he checked out and left the end-of-track town the day after Christmas.

In Sublette, Kansas, he celebrated his twenty-first birthday alone in his boardinghouse room, drinking Hermitage from the bottle and smoking cigars while awaiting the governor's answer to a request for a stay of execution in the case of Mary Elizabeth Spellacy, convicted of poisoning her lover's wife with a peach cobbler laced with arsenic. The wife of the local minister of the First Baptist Church had organized a letter-writing campaign to spare Sublette the infamy of becoming the first city in Kansas to hang a woman. When the governor, who was facing reelection, commuted the sentence to life imprisonment in the new state facility at Topeka, Oscar greeted the news with mixed emotions. About slipping the noose over a female head he had not been much concerned—the decision to do so had been made by others before he arrived on the scene—but he'd had misgivings about weighing and measuring a woman and examining the musculature of her neck; this seemed to him an impropriety, like searching her person, and he would rather have left the task to a woman, if one could be found who would do it and whom he could trust not to commit some error that would prove disastrous. On the other hand, it was his private theory that women faced death more resignedly than men and he was disappointed not to be given the chance to put this conviction to the test. Offered his full fee to compensate him for his inconvenience, he accepted half and boarded a stagecoach for Fort Dodge, where a shotgun killer awaited his attention.

Throughout 1870 and '71 he recrossed his own path several times. Murderers during this period ran to a narrow assortment of types—cowboys who had fallen out among themselves, cardsharps who hid palm guns up the same sleeves with the ace of spades, buffalo hunters sick of each other's association—and their faces, handlebarred and brown, pinched and pale, bearded and dull, all ran together in the memory of the man who hanged them. He learned to identify the city where he was staying by the excellence of the poached eggs at the Drovers' Cottage in Abilene, the heated towels provided daily by the Comanche Hotel in Dallas, and his inability to secure a bed in Boulder not already occupied by thousands of ticks. The frontier was a place of extremes, with nothing in between: Fresh oysters and heavy cream were to be had at the King's Rest in Denver, while the scarcity of water in Tucson forced a Navajo hotel steward to bring a basin of gray murk to guests in order of seniority. Oscar forbore shaving during his tenure there. By the time he returned to civilization he'd grown accustomed to the beard, and from then on trimmed it only, after the fashion of President Grant. The money was good wherever he went—a proper hanging by a man trained in the science was one luxury even the barest-boned of mining settlements decided it could afford in the interest of a more genteel future—and he ate well where the food was decent. He filled out during these years. While a tailor in Omaha was measuring his waist for a new suit, it occurred to Oscar that if it weren't for the occasional hardship of a stagecoach ride over a washed-out road, he was in danger of becoming absolutely stout.

In the autumn of 1872, he decided he'd earned a holiday. In the lobby of his hotel in Kansas City, he stopped to mail his regrets to the mayor of a place with the unpromising name of Gila Head, then walked to the station and bought a ticket on a train to St. Louis.

He scarcely recognized the city. A roiling metropolis when he had first come to it, with preposterous mansions standing stiffly among grogshops and houses of ill fame, it had spread out in both directions along the Mississippi and west across the green flats, replacing the tipis of friendly trade Indians with brick colonials, newspaper plants, and bookstores. Paddle-wheelers lined the levee as of old, with foreign dockworkers abusing one another in their patois of French, German, and English; but Oscar, sensitive to the subtlest shifts, could feel that the balance of energy had tilted in the direction of the great echoing vaulted depot where oily black locomotives discharged and took on fresh loads of passengers and freight, exhaling steam about the legs of men in bowlers and women in sail-brim hats and capes hurrying to and fro with their bags and umbrellas. He gave a black porter twenty-five cents for recommending the Southern Hotel and hired a four-wheeler to take him and his luggage there. In a pawnshop in Denver he'd purchased a large trunk to carry his ropes and a full set of balance plates he'd ordered from a failed meatpacking plant in Chicago, for the purpose of testing frontier scales; the name of the defunct theatrical touring company from which the trunk had been acquired could still be read in outline where the painted letters had been scraped off. He concluded it was the nature of his profession that made him feel like a feeder off carrion whenever he profited from the calamities of others. This vacation was long overdue.

Among the usual collection of loafers and hotel guests loitering about the overstuffed chairs in the lobby, reading newspapers and smoking, he spotted the familiar furtive figure of a reporter in front of the tobacco stand. Many past encounters had taught Oscar to recognize the breed by their soiled collars, bowlers in need of brushing, and pockets stuffed with stubby pencils and folds of newsprint. The man had seen the bellman wheeling in the oversize trunk on his cart, and as he pretended to inspect the wrapper of the cigar he had just bought, his gaze searched the lobby for its likely owner, coming to rest at last upon the thickset, bearded stranger in spectacles signing his name in the register. Too late, Oscar thought that he should have used a pseudonym. A dollar to the clerk, charged against the newspaper's expense sheet, and by the time the afternoon edition came out all of St. Louis would know that Oscar Stone, the famous western hangman, was visiting the city. Even as he accepted the key to his room he saw his hopes for an undisturbed rest fly out the front door.

Upstairs, he found the bed made, the carpet freshly swept, and the sash raised to clear out whatever odors had been left behind by the previous occupant. When his bags and trunk arrived, he tipped the bellman and gave him money to buy a bottle of Hermitage—or Clark's, if his preferred brand was unavailable—and drew a hot bath to wash off the grit of travel.

When someone knocked on his door, he half expected the reporter from the lobby, come to request an interview. But it was the bellman, with a bottle of Old Gideon and an apology; Clark's was unknown in the city, and the bartender had sold the last bottle of Hermitage only that morning. Oscar tipped him anyway, filled a hotel tumbler, and a few minutes later stretched out naked in the steaming tub with the back of his head resting on the lip and the glass on the floor within easy reach. Almost immediately a cloud of cinders detached themselves from his neck and floated to the surface. Pullman had yet to design a car that could repel them completely.

Belatedly, he groped for his cigars in the pocket of his coat where he'd hung it on the back of the chair. Unexpectedly, paper crackled. He drew it out.

The desk clerk in Kansas City had handed him the telegram as he was checking out. Preoccupied with getting his luggage to the station on time, Oscar had stuck it in his pocket without opening it. He opened it now. It was from a federal judge in Helena, Montana Territory, inviting him to be the first man to operate the city's new "hydraulic gallows," the first of its kind west of Chicago. The prisoner who would be the first to die on it, one Barnet Menteith, had been convicted of murder and arson after an altercation in a saloon. Oscar had no idea what a hydraulic gallows was, but the term intrigued him enough to make him consider undergoing the rigors of traveling to such a remote location, deep as it was in undeveloped country.

When the water began to grow tepid, he scrubbed himself with the first cake of white soap he had seen in weeks, rinsed and toweled off, and dressed for dinner. It was early in the evening, and he hoped to find a vacant table at the Planter's House.

He was fumbling with the studs in his shirt when another knock came on his door. It was the journalist from the lobby, looking particularly shabby against Oscar's starched linen and black broadcloth. His derby was in his hands and his dark hair stuck out in tufts as if he had cut it himself. There were streaks of gray; apart from that and the maturing effect of rimless spectacles, he appeared no older than Oscar. His manner was shy and somewhat callow, but the hangman had learned to be wary of dissembling reporters.

"Mr. Stone, I think?" The man's smile was tentative.

"You have the advantage."

"Mark Kellogg, sir. I'm a newspaper correspondent."

"I'm on holiday, Mr. Kellogg. I'm not giving interviews."

"Oh. I hope you'll pardon the interruption." Kellogg turned.

Surprised by this surrender, Oscar said, "What journal do you work for, Mr. Kellogg?"

The man hesitated. His face actually colored. "Strictly speaking, sir, I'm not actually with one at present. I'm making my living as a telegrapher."

"I'm not sending any wires, either."

"No, sir, I'm sure you're not. Not that you wouldn't have anyone to send one to; that is, I'm sure you have many, a busy man like yourself—" His flush deepened.

"What do you want, Mr. Kellogg?"

Kellogg filled his lungs as if he were about to plunge into the deep end of a lake. His words came out in a rush. "The thing is, sir, I *want* to be a correspondent, but none of the newspapers in St. Louis will give me the chance unless I'm willing to write obituaries and advertisements for harness shops and gentlemen's emporia. My great wish is to go out West and write about the frontier, where history is being made. I've sent wires everywhere, and so far the only answer I've received is from the *Bismarck Tribune*, offering me an interview if I will pay my own travel expenses. I thought—"

"Where is Bismarck?"

"Dakota Territory, sir; it's brand-new, and as yet unincorporated. I thought that if I could arrange an interview with you and sell it to the *Missouri Democrat*, I could make enough to finance my trip."

Oscar kept him waiting while he finished with his studs. If it was a gambit, Kellogg played it well. Finally he shook his head. "I wish I could help you, but I'm hungry. If the Planter's is still as popular as I remember it, it will be filling up by now."

A sudden smile illuminated Kellogg's rather sad face. "The headwaiter is my cousin. I'm sure something can be arranged."

The Planter's House was one of the larger hotels located among the narrow twisting streets of the old French quarter, and resembled a hospital. A long, undecorated corridor led to the restaurant, lit as by day with crystal chandeliers and polished brass Chesterfield lamps. As Oscar had feared, most of the tables were occupied by gaily chattering diners in evening dress. Liveried waiters bustled among them bearing covered platters on shoulders with epaulets like Napoleon's marshals. As Oscar admired a large oil portrait of Charles Dickens, a celebrated early guest, Kellogg spoke to a white-haired waiter with a long Gallic face, whose abundance of gold braid identified him as the maître d'hôtel. Very shortly the visitors found themselves seated at a linen-dressed table in a private room paneled in gleaming black walnut.

"I know a French headwaiter when I see one," Oscar told the would-be reporter. "I assume you're related by marriage."

Kellogg appeared sheepish. "I gave him five dollars when you weren't looking. I'm afraid I lied to you, Mr. Stone. I have no relatives in St. Louis."

"That's rather a large sum for a fellow who can't afford passage to Dakota."

"It'll mean a week without luncheon, but I've made greater sacrifices." He picked up a silver fork, looked at it, and set it down. "You're not angry that I misled you?"

Oscar let the fellow wait while a young man in epaulets filled their crystal glasses with water from a pitcher.

"I should be furious," he said when they were alone again. "I would be under most circumstances, but I'm here to rest. How do you intend to pay for your meal tonight?"

"The mushroom soup is the least expensive thing on the bill of fare, and it sticks to your ribs."

"How old are you, Mr. Kellogg?"

"I'm thirty-six."

"You look younger. How old do you think I am?"

"I thought we were contemporaries."

"You're twelve years my senior."

Kellogg hesitated. "The beard—"

"I wasn't asking for reassurance. A year on the frontier is worth seven in the states."

"Like a dog." The telegrapher's smile died when Oscar didn't respond.

"The point I was making is I am not impressed by people who impose hardship upon themselves to no good purpose. The West will do that without your help."

"Your pardon, sir. I felt—and I still feel—the purpose *was* good. I intend to work in Bismarck."

The waiter returned while Oscar was contemplating his companion's grave face. "That being the case, you'll need to keep up your strength. I will order for us both." He held out a hand for the menu.

"I can't accept your charity, sir."

"We'll call it a deposit against a favorable article in the *Missouri Democrat*."

"I can't promise that. It wouldn't be ethical."

Oscar smiled for the first time, but the other was serious. "I should tell you that with those principles you may find success elusive. Journalism is not an ethical profession."

"Someday I hope it will be. It certainly will not unless someone makes the first move."

"Which will never happen if I allow you to starve to death in St. Louis. Since I don't intend to do that, what alternative would you suggest?"

"Come to Bismarck and I'll buy you dinner."

"What, buffalo hump steak and prairie oysters?" Oscar was quite enjoying himself.

"I'm told the hump steak in Dakota is the finest to be had between Minneapolis and the Great Salt Lake. I can't answer for the prairie oysters."

The bargain sealed, Oscar conferred with the young waiter, who was candid about the quality of the items on the evening's bill of fare, and ordered an array of dishes that covered every square inch of the tablecloth. When they couldn't force down another bite, the table was cleared and the waiter brought a bottle of port.

Oscar breathed in the strong, tar-sweet bouquet and told again his autobiography, sparing the grislier details of the hanging at South Georgia Crossing and leaving out his marriage entirely. So many grotesque tales had been printed about his early life that he answered such questions slowly and carefully to make sure he was understood and to avoid spreading misinformation for failing to listen to himself repeating the same tired phrases. No, he assured Kellogg, he had not practiced his profession as a child, hanging toads and rabbits he'd captured alive on his father's farm. Yes, he was a veteran who had fought for the Union. No, he was not a war hero who refused to hang a fellow Yankee, nor did he hold the exclusive patent in Washington on a trap mechanism he had designed. He had, it was true, made a number of improvements on existing mechanisms, but he did not delude himself that he had come up with anything that others had not. For that, he supposed, one would have to go back to Archimedes.

"The hangman?" Kellogg attempted to appear knowledgeable.

"No, the engineer."

Paper rustled. Notes were read. "Isn't hanging a bit of a far cry from carpentry?"

"Not really. Many of the same rules of craftsmanship apply."

"Would you care to provide an example?"

Oscar drank, held the port in a pool in his mouth, then swallowed. He leaned forward and tapped a finger on the table in time with his words. "If you take your time with a thing, you can't help but do well. Do well every time and you're a craftsman. Do it with *respect*, and you may one day become a master. Without it you're just a man with tools."

"That sounds like a lesson learned by rote."

"The words of a very wise man."

"Do you consider yourself a master?"

"Not yet. So far I'm only a craftsman. But I have the respect."

"Do you still practice carpentry?"

He shook his head. "The same wise man told me a jack-of-all-trades is just a blunderer with versatility."

Kellogg spent a few minutes questioning him about the six-man hanging in Denver, which Oscar dismissed as "a routine matter, actually. If they'd been dispatched one at a time, we wouldn't be having this conversation."

"But it's the hanging that made you famous."

"Ironic, is it not? In York, I helped my employer build seventeen school desks in less than three weeks, which I believe is still some kind of record. Nobody published a line."

The reporter folded his sheet to a fresh square. "Have you ever hanged a man you thought was innocent?"

He saw Titus Jefferson's face on the platform in Denver.

"That isn't my decision. They were all tried and judged before my services were engaged."

"Isn't that avoiding the question?"

"I'm an instrument of justice, Mr. Kellogg. I have no more influence upon how it works than the gallows itself. As a matter of—"

A young woman with her hair tied back came through the curtains carrying a broom and dustpan. When she saw that the room was occupied, she started to excuse herself, then saw Oscar staring at her and ducked out quickly.

"Mr. Stone?" Kellogg looked up from his sheet.

Oscar rose. "Your pardon, Mr. Kellogg. I just saw someone I used to know."

"The girl?"

"My wife." He went out through the curtains.

Part Five

MRS. KETCH

Hanging and wiving go by destiny.
—*THE SCHOLE-HOUS FOR WOMEN* (1541)

NINETEEN

Gretchen was wearing a crinoline, years out of style but in keeping with the Planter's insistence upon behaving as if America were still a colony of Europe. When Oscar emerged from the private dining room and looked about, he glimpsed the skirt's bell shape gliding around a corner. Hurrying his pace, he nearly collided with a waiter carrying a tray full of stemware and a folding stand. By the time he disengaged himself and turned the corner, there was no sign of his wife.

The nearest door led into the kitchen, a room nearly as large as the restaurant itself, and a calamity of white-hatted chefs bent over stoves as long as Conestoga wagons and waiters calling in new orders and demanding old ones, both groups crying in a mulch of languages and making threatening gestures with spoons and empty trays. Dollops of cream and melted butter flew about like shrapnel. Gretchen was not there either.

Outside the street entrance to the restaurant, a confused doorman in crushed red velvet informed the flushed gentleman who emerged without hat or coat that he knew nothing about a *Madame* Stone. A *Mademoiselle* Smollett who answered the gentleman's description was employed to clear tables and clean the private rooms; she and the doorman often exchanged pleasantries, but no personal information. She had come out moments ago without waiting for the door to be opened for her, and gone away in the first in a line of four-wheelers for hire in front of the hotel. *"Non, monsieur,"* he said when asked if he'd overheard where the driver was to take her, nor did he know where the *mademoiselle* lived; perhaps *Monsieur* Capet, the manager of the Planter's House, could provide that information. Distractedly, Oscar handed the doorman a coin without looking at its denomination and went back inside. The *"Merci, monsieur, merci"* that followed him indicated he'd been rather more generous than intended.

He found the hotel lobby, all green marble and deep red mahogany, and asked for *Monsieur* Capet. The clerk knocked on a door behind the registration desk, conferred in murmurs with whoever opened it, and presently a small man in velvet lapels and Napoleon III imperials came out and approached the desk. Capet listened to Oscar's request without interruption, then shook his head. It would be quite impossible for the management to provide the home address of hotel employees to outsiders. When Oscar asked him if he might reconsider his position, discreetly producing a folded banknote from his wallet, the little man thrust out his pointed beard and replied coldly that if the Planter's House did not change its menu to include Yankee pot roast and corn-on-the-cob when *Monsieur* Thomas Jefferson bought St. Louis from Emperor Napoleon I, it certainly would not alter its rules for a bribe. He turned away.

"Pardon, monsieur."

The new voice startled Oscar, who had been so intent upon his business with Capet that he had not noticed Mark Kellogg, his dinner companion, coming up beside him. He must have seen Oscar coming back in from the street and followed him.

The greeting, in what sounded to the hangman to be perfectly accented French, caused Capet to turn and face the reporter, who smiled and entered into a long and involved string of phrases in that language, in which Oscar recognized only Gretchen's name and the word *amoreaux*, which he supposed had something to do with love. Kellogg must have overheard what he'd told the hotel manager, but since he had said nothing about his relationship to the woman he was asking about, he concluded that Kellogg had the instincts of a true journalist.

Whatever he was saying, it didn't appear to be working. The little man began to shake his head early during the speech and continued to do so in a metronomic rhythm. Then he stopped, listening intently, with his gaze on the desk blotter and a thoughtful scowl pulling the points of his moustaches toward each other. When Kellogg finished, Capet drew himself up to his full minuscule height, touched the waxed tips, and spoke a few words to the desk clerk, who nodded and went through the door at the back.

A tense silence followed, during which the manager stood staring straight ahead as if no visitors were present. Kellogg caught Oscar's eye in a sidelong glance and winked. Oscar did not respond; the moment seemed to be balanced more delicately than a gallows trap, and he was afraid it would open beneath his own feet if he celebrated prematurely.

At last the clerk returned bearing a half sheet of stiff paper, which he gave to Capet. The manager glanced at it and handed it back. He spoke directly to Oscar. The *mademoiselle* was living in an apartment at 44 Market Street.

Oscar was too relieved, and too busy memorizing the address, to thank him. "*Merci, monsieur,*" Kellogg said, "*merci boucoup,*" and steered his companion away from the desk.

"It's within walking distance," said the reporter when they were out of earshot of Capet and his clerk. "The doorman can direct you. Pay attention to all the numbers, mind; there's little rhyme or reason to how they're laid out in this town."

44 Market Street. The information committed to memory, Oscar opened his eyes. "For someone who claims he isn't French, you speak the language like a native."

"A native of Quebec, perhaps. I spent two years there looking for work. Oddly enough, the only job I managed to land was as a hotel clerk." He laughed.

"What did you say to him?"

"I told him the mademoiselle was your mistress, that you had fallen out, and that you wished to tell her in person that you've decided to leave your wife."

"She *is* my wife."

"I know, but if I'd told him that he never would have given up her address. If, for instance, I'd said you were leaving your mistress to return to married life, he probably would have had us thrown out. The French are romantics."

"I can't thank you enough."

Kellogg's sheepish smile returned. "Paying for your half of dinner would be more than sufficient. I had to give the waiter all I had."

Oscar produced his wallet and held out a fistful of banknotes.

"That's more than enough for both our meals," Kellogg protested. "You gave me a good interview. If I weren't saving for Bismarck, I'd have paid your half and not said a word about it."

"If you like, you can call it payment for my first French lesson." Oscar held out the money until the other accepted it. He put away the wallet. "About my wife."

"We'll just say the interview was over when the young lady came in." Kellogg extended his hand. "Good luck, sir."

Oscar shook the hand with the grip he usually reserved for the lever.

Turning the last corner indicated by the doorman, Oscar wondered if the directions were accurate. He found himself in a cramped block of high-gabled buildings left over from another era, many of which showed no sign that their parched and curling boards had ever seen a coat of paint, and all of which seemed to be sagging into their foundations, their porches missing pillars, with holes in their roofs through which stars showed. Where there were street lamps, the coal-oil flames glowered behind filthy glass panes, illuminating little beyond themselves. It was not in any way the sort of neighborhood where the daughter of a prosperous York pharmacist would choose to live.

He walked past 44 and had to retrace his steps when the numbers appeared to be going in the wrong direction. The fanlight above the door was dark. Mounting the shifting steps of a porch in an advanced state of collapse, he struck a match and confirmed the number in flaking gold paint on the glass. A rusty bellpull rang asthmatically when he manipulated it.

The woman who answered it, after a long time, represented a type of person Oscar knew too well: the German landlady. Short, stout, impeccably dressed for that neighborhood in Victorian black crepe with an ivory brooch at the throat, she wore her white hair pulled back into a bun so tight the skin of her forehead shone like polished granite. She had greedy black eyes and her mouth was a hairline crack. She would be waiting at the bottom of the stairs with her cash box the morning the rent was due and snoop around the tenants' rooms when they were out. He smiled, removed his hat, and asked her in German if *Fraulein* Smollett was at home.

The crack thinned out further. His use of the language had not endeared him. Her reply was in a formal German so precise that he was certain she had been born to a class that seldom employed it: She had rented a room to a *Frau* Smollett, but she had left twenty minutes ago.

"She is out for the evening?" He was so anxious that this was the correct interpretation of her response that he forgot and spoke in English. When she started to shake her head, he began to repeat the question in German, but she interrupted him in heavily accented English.

"No, *mein Herr*, the young lady packed her things and moved out."

"Are you certain?"

"Yes, *mein Herr*. I could not have been mistaken about so

unusual a thing as a tenant moving out in the middle of the night. She was in such a haste I double-checked my books to make sure she was not sneaking out. It is a terrible responsibility being a landlady, *mein Herr*. People are forever taking unkind advantage."

"Did she say where she was going?"

"No. I would suggest you try the train station, or one of the missions, as there is no other place for a young woman to go at this time in the evening. Well, there is *one*; but even they would not take her with her little boy." Her mouth was pressed so tight now the crack appeared to be spreading.

He came out of his slump as if struck from behind. "Boy?"

"Boy, *ja*." She held out a hand wrinkled like crumpled paper at a height just above her waist. "*Fier, funf.* Four or five." She was as proud of her careful English as she was of her High *Deutsch*.

He turned away without thanking her, and almost fell when a loose board on one of the steps slid out from under his foot.

He walked three blocks before he saw a two-wheeler and hailed it. During the ride to the depot he concentrated on not thinking. He'd asked the driver to hurry; the shaggy gray's shoes rang on the pavement like someone banging a bell with a hammer, the flimsy vehicle shuddered and swayed, he leaned forward in his seat as if he were the one doing the pulling. In front of the building he leapt out before the wheels stopped rolling, dug in his wallet, and gave the man the last of his cash, not waiting to see if it was enough or to hear "*Merci, monsieur, merci*" yet again as he pushed through the heavy door into the hall of shrieking wheels and huffing steam.

He didn't see Gretchen among the people waiting on the platform or sitting on the wooden benches. A line of cars was moving on the track, and he watched the windows closely, looking for her profile, until he realized they were slowing down; the train was coming in, not departing. He waited, twitching, behind an old man counting out coins from a deep pouch onto the ledge in front of the ticket clerk, then nearly knocked him down as he lunged at the window. He asked what trains had left within the past thirty minutes. The clerk, young and arrogant-looking, with a full set of muttonchop whiskers, kept him waiting while he consulted a long schedule tacked to the wall of the booth, then told him that the 8:58 to Denver had pulled out on time and that the 9:17 to Chicago was five minutes gone.

"Did a young woman buy a ticket on either one of them? I believe she's traveling with a small boy."

"I've sold many tickets today, sir. I seldom look at faces, only money." The young man's gaze was fixed pointedly beyond Oscar's shoulder. He knew there was a line behind him.

She would not flee west, he decided. (*Was* she fleeing? Yes, she was fleeing; he'd seen the expression on her face when she'd recognized him.) He asked when the next train was leaving for Chicago.

Again the schedule was consulted. The clerk produced a turnip watch from a vest pocket and appeared to check it against the time on the big clock on the wall opposite the booth. Behind Oscar, someone let out his breath in a whispered oath. "Twenty-five minutes." The watch face snapped shut.

Oscar said, "I'll take a compartment."

Now the clerk opened a book that resembled a narrow ledger and ran his finger down a column. "The compartments are taken. Plenty of room in the coaches."

"A coach, then. How much?"

A grimy list of fees was stuck to the wall across from the schedule; there seemed to be no end to the amount of information at the young man's disposal. "Sixty-two fifty."

As Oscar reached for his wallet, he suddenly realized what he would find. He took it out anyway and spread it open to stare at empty leather. He cursed himself for not drawing from his cash in the Southern Hotel's safe. It would take him forty minutes at least to go there and return to the depot. "When is the next train to Chicago after this one?"

Schedule again. "Eight-fifteen A.M. There are some compartments available on that one." The clerk's tone now was clearly sneering; he'd seen inside the wallet.

Oscar thanked him and turned away. A big man in buckskins and a black beard, who smelled of stale buffalo hides and fresh whiskey, snarled something at him, but stopped in mid-sentence when he met the hangman's gaze.

He was halfway to the exit when he realized he was still holding his empty wallet. He slid it into his inside coat pocket, missing it the first time, and kept on walking. He would not be on the morning train to Chicago. The city was too big; there were too many stops along the way, more than enough to swallow a young woman and a small boy. His own footsteps echoed back at him, joining the hoarse reverberating blasts of steam whistles among the groined arches overhead, distorting into words spoken in an old woman's voice with a heavy German accent: "Boy, *ja. Fier, funf.* Four or five."

TWENTY

John Audubon Pilot appeared too young to be the director of the St. Louis office of the Pinkerton National Detective Agency, and apart from having grown a chestnut-colored beard that he curled with an iron after the fashion of an ancient Greek philosopher, he did nothing to inspire confidence in his maturity. His cravat, red with a pattern of yellow diamonds, was too gay for the dour oak-and-leather furnishings of his office, he did not pull his coat on over his vest and shirtsleeves when he got up from behind his desk to shake Oscar's hand, and even the flamboyant way he smoked his pipe—normally a stolid prop—put his visitor in mind of a college student recently freed from the disciplines of the parental home. He kept on waving the match after it was clear the flame was out, and the novelty of being able to blow smoke rings at the ceiling had not yet worn off. Oscar did approve of his conscientious note-taking in the leather-bound memorandum pad spread open on his blotter, but did not care for the bantering nature of his questions.

"Gretchen Smollett; so she's returned to her maiden name, though I see she's taken the social precaution of amending it to Missus, because of the boy, if we can go by that *Frau* Smollett business. You're quite sure the boy is yours? Well, how certain are any of us, when you come down to brass tacks? If she's gone into hiding, I don't think we can count on her continuing to use Smollett, but we'll put it under 'aliases' beginning with Stone, and start a list. You said her landlady told you she'd been renting from her only three months?"

"Yes, I went back. I gave the woman enough money to rent the room for a week, for the privilege of looking through it. It's an attic room, clean and furnished, but a sloping wall takes up most of the space. I can't imagine why she didn't ask her father for help, if she couldn't afford anything better. Or just go home to York." He didn't add details: how long he'd spent touching curtains Gretchen had drawn open and shut, sitting on the bed where she'd slept for three months, walking around the room breathing in the air and analyzing it for her particular scent. This fellow would probably have made some coarse jest about retaining his services as a bloodhound.

"Dead, possibly," Pilot went on, "or perhaps Daddy and daughter fell out over her deserting you. I'll wire the Philadelphia office and have them send someone around to the house. You say she didn't have any friends at the Planter's?"

"No, all the employees I spoke to said she was pleasant, but very private. They didn't even know she had a son. I've written to her father, by the way, but I don't know if he'll respond. She didn't really desert me. I deserted her when I violated her trust."

"Another woman?" The Pinkerton had the eager face of a reporter, not Mark Kellogg's kind of reporter.

"Not a woman. Work. I'm a professional hangman."

"I know. Read about you in the *Democrat*. Heard of you before, of course, from that six-rig job you did in Denver. I was up at Amherst at the time. You were the big demon around campus all that year. I didn't agree; I thought, There's pluck for you. When they offered to promote me to director I asked for a frontier assignment, but this is as close as I got. So Gretchen didn't endorse your choice."

Oscar ignored the implied question. "What are the chances of finding her?"

"Worlds better than they were before you walked into this office. We've found assassins and poisoners and copperhead spies the federal marshals had given up on. Unless she's grown a foot or moved to South America—or possibly even then—we'll find your wife. Your son, too." He rose and tugged down his cuffs. They were linked with tiny gold manacles. "How long will you be in St. Louis?"

"I'm not sure. A week or ten days. After that I may be in Montana."

"I doubt we'll have her before you leave. Is there a place we can write you where the letter won't have to follow you about the wilderness for a year?"

He hadn't thought about that. His movements since the hanging in Denver had been publicized with such regularity that he was accustomed to receiving offers for work at the hotels and rooming houses where he stayed; he was not interested in any that arrived after he'd moved on. After a moment he said, "Send it in care of Fabian T. Rudd in Leavenworth, Kansas. I'll keep him informed of my whereabouts."

Pilot entered the information in his notebook. "Please feel free to check in with us any time. If there's no news on Mrs. Smollett—Mrs. *Stone*," he corrected himself—"in six weeks, there will be no point in wasting any more of your money. But we'll have something. We never sleep, you know." Smiling, he jerked a thumb over his shoulder at the all-seeing eye in the framed lithograph on the wall behind his desk.

"Please caution your people not to approach her. If *I* frightened her, there is no telling how she'll react to a detective."

"No need to worry about that. Agency policy in noncriminal cases is to surveil, not apprehend, unless the client orders otherwise." He held out his hand. When Oscar took it, the Pinkerton hung on. "Try not to let the fact that she ran when she saw you spoil your appetite. Sometimes, love is very close to fear. Closer than hatred."

The sudden flash of sensitivity caught Oscar without words to respond. He tightened his grip and then they broke contact.

"Oh, Mr. Stone."

He'd started for the door. He paused and turned. Pilot was still standing behind his desk, supporting himself on his hands with the memorandum book between them, like Napoleon at his maps. It was difficult to spend much time in St. Louis without being reminded of the Little Corporal at every turn.

"Back East, they don't understand what you're doing, but Mr. Pinkerton does. He just signed a contract to provide security for the railroads against renegades and bandits. I imagine we'll be sending business your way."

Oscar nodded. He was still without language. Closing the door behind him in the reception room with its framed sepia photographs of fugitives tracked down and brought to justice by the Agency, he said aloud, "I've never wanted for business, Mr. Pilot. Not since I gave up carpentry."

The male secretary seated at the desk looked up from his writing and unpinched the glasses from his nose. "I'm sorry, sir, were you addressing me?"

He shook his head with a polite smile that cost him the rest of his energy and left.

There were other offices lined up on both sides of the corridor, behind frosted-glass doors with numbers painted on them in shiny black enamel, some with names, depending upon the stations of the men who occupied them. It was a warm day; most of the transoms were tipped open, and as he walked he heard different-pitched murmurs drifting out through the openings, with a word separating itself from the drone here and there like a leaf floating down from a crowded branch: *divorce . . . pilfering . . . past . . . mistress . . . larceny.* Words used by *clients,* husbands and wives and employers and worried parents, the sort of people who had lost control of their lives to the extent that they had to pay a stranger to help straighten things out. He was one of them now. Oscar Stone: son of Ernst Stein, brother of Jacob, veteran of the Southern Rebellion, husband—was he still? yes, he had received no papers to the contrary—husband of Gretchen, then, master carpenter, hangman. Client.

Why had she run?

On the way back to the hotel he stopped in a saloon. The trademark batwing doors separating the entryway from the main room identified it, even though it bore scant resemblance to the loud, profane, tobacco-splattered hells of Abilene and Tucson and a dozen other places—tent towns, end-of-tracks, hide-processing centers stinking of rot and swarming with flies—whose names he could not have been expected to remember even when he was living in them. The dimly lighted, cedar-paneled interior belonged more to an English gentleman's club than an emporium where liquor was sold to the public. Men in bowlers and stiff collars sat at the tables drinking, smoking, playing cards, and conversing quietly. Here, the guns were small and well concealed; if someone were to fire one at the ceiling to make a point, he would be arrested on the spot and the details of the affair would be discussed in the newspapers for a week. Just across the river, the guns began to vanish completely. There was scarce work for hangmen in such a place as St. Louis, and what there was went on inside an enclosure closed to the public, conducted by a faceless former turnkey whose name never appeared in print.

It was no place for a notorious character like Oscar Stone. He bought a bottle of Hermitage from the barman and took it back to his room.

He'd planned to stay as long as three weeks, but his enthusiasm for a holiday away from ropes and scaffolding had gone on the 9:17 to Chicago. However, he needed the rest. He attempted to lose himself in the theater, only to find that the ticket the hotel concierge had bought at his request admitted him to a play with "real-life" backwoodsmen in the cast, popping stage pistols at patently false Indians and spinning yarns about past adventures while squatting around a simulated campfire. He left during the second act, while the hero was romancing a savage princess; the preposterous lines about love undying made him think of Gretchen by contrast.

The concert he attended the following evening was even more grotesque. The program of Mendelssohn was pleasant and the orchestra accomplished, but during intermission he was accosted in the lobby by a woman swathed in emeralds and rods of green silk, who recognized him from the pen-and-ink likeness that had appeared in the *Missouri Democrat* with Kellogg's article. (Was the description the reporter had given the illustrator that accurate? It made him look like a sad rabbi.) She told him she thought hanging was "ghastly, but utterly *ghastly*," and plied him with questions about the ghastly details until her escort steered her away. He returned to his seat and remained for the rest of the concert, but could not have been said to have heard a note.

A few days later, bored and out of reading material, he visited a bookshop, where a well-dressed man with silver hair struck up a conversation with him over a book he was considering, imported from England, entitled *Literary Character*. The gentleman, who had made his fortune investing in the fur trade, mentioned that he was acquainted with the author. The discussion continued along literary lines for several minutes, at the end of which Oscar was asked if he wasn't the professional executioner the man had read about in the paper. Oscar confessed that he was, thinking that that would end their acquaintance, but the gentleman then surprised him by inviting him to a dinner party he was giving the following evening.

"Mr. Kellogg will be there," he added, just as Oscar opened his mouth to decline. "He's a friend of my daughter's."

In that moment, Oscar realized he missed Kellogg. Rudd was

the only friend he had on the frontier, and the reporter was the only man who had shown him affection in St. Louis. He accepted.

It was a pleasant enough affair, held in the cavernous dining room of one of the large mansions that had been built near the river during the 1840s. The guests, beautifully attired in bright-colored gowns and blue-white shirtboards, sat at a long table and feasted on venison, a confusing array of soups, vegetables deep-fried in butter, gumbo, and creamy nougat for dessert, with a different wine served before each course. A string quartet made up of Creole musicians sawed on their instruments throughout. He had not the chance to speak with Kellogg, who was seated at the opposite end of the table, although they managed to share a glance and a smile while some blowhard was going on about the sport of shooting buffalo from a train in Nebraska. The conversation was positive, incessant, and indescribably boring. As the night ground on, with dishes appearing and disappearing amid tinkling feminine chitchat and chortling masculine non sequiturs, Oscar found himself belching discreetly behind his linen napkin to make room for yet another helping of steaming Something and actually wishing someone would ask him about his work, just to change the subject from President Grant, the Indians, Monsignor Whoever's audience with the Pope, and the soaring price of buffalo robes as opposed to the dwindling supply of buffalo.

At last the dinner broke up. The women retreated to the drawing room while the men migrated to the host's study, where cigars and cognac were served and the topic became the strategic placement of the rips in Lotta Crabtree's tights. Oscar took out his watch and wondered if ten minutes was sufficient before seeking his leave.

"No need to stand on breeding when you're bored," murmured someone at his elbow. "It's expected at these things."

Startled, he stared at the fellow in the ill-fitting dinner suit, then smiled when he recognized Kellogg. "Are you bored?" he asked.

"Certainly not. I'm drunk." The journalist swirled the honey-colored liquid in his balloon glass as if to illustrate the fact.

"You don't behave as if you were."

"That's how you tell. When a man staggers and slurs his words, it's a sure sign he's faking. I'm roaring. If I weren't, I'd be as miserable as you."

"I'd hoped it wasn't so obvious."

"Only to me. I'm practicing for the frontier. You haven't told me if you liked my story."

"It was entirely accurate."

"A diplomatic answer." Kellogg touched his spectacles. "I suppose I'll learn to exaggerate when I'm quit of civilization. Did our host tell you why he felt compelled to invite me?"

"He said you're a friend of his daughter's. Which is she?"

"She's away at school. I hardly know her name, and I'm sure she's forgotten mine if she ever knew it. She was arrested last month for taking part in a riot for women's suffrage. I managed to keep her name from appearing in the *Democrat.* I thought her father might be grateful enough to influence the editors into hiring me full-time. So far all I've gotten is an invitation to this party."

"Perhaps he'll make you an editor."

"I hope not. I'm bound for the wilderness. Everything worth reporting in St. Louis happened twenty years ago. I want the sting of sulfur in my nostrils."

"You'd be surprised how soon you get your fill of that," Oscar said.

"I'm no tyro, Mr. Stone. I was a telegrapher with the Army of the Potomac."

"That must have been interesting."

"Not really. I sat around a lot. General Grant had a habit of cutting the lines before a major battle, to avoid receiving conflicting orders from Washington."

"Sound policy."

"Indeed. It's a shame he isn't a better president." Kellogg emptied his glass and set it on a nearby pedestal table, almost missing it the first time; it was the first indication he was truly inebriated.

"Thank you, Mr. Stone. The money the *Democrat* paid me for the interview will get me as far as Lincoln, where a job is waiting for me in the telegraph office. My first two weeks' wages will buy a ticket to Bismarck."

"Thank you. For the lesson in French."

"May I ask if you found your wife? I'm not asking as a journalist."

"Not yet. I have hopes." Oscar looked again at his watch. He wasn't concerned about the time; he wanted this conversation to end.

Kellogg drew the correct conclusion. "Good luck, Mr. Stone. I hope you find *your* Bismarck."

They parted. Oscar shook hands with his host, accepted the plump pink palm offered him by the stout hostess with black-dyed hair, and took his leave, vowing never again to cross the threshold of the wealthy. He walked back to his hotel to relieve the uncomfortable pressure in his stomach.

In his room he poured himself a glass of Hermitage, poured another, and retired to what he had decided would be his last night in that bed. The next morning, after checking out and arranging to have his bags and trunk taken to the depot, he dropped by the Pinkerton office to ask if there was any news of Gretchen. There wasn't. He told John Audubon Pilot that for the next three weeks he could be reached at Helena, Montana Territory.

"What's there?" Pilot asked.

He felt in his pocket for the wire from the federal judge. "A hydraulic gallows."

TWENTY-ONE

A bone-jarring, tongue-lacerating stagecoach ride over rutted roads frozen as hard as bedrock deposited Oscar at last in Helena, a clapboard city whose most prominent feature was a wooden fire tower perched atop a bald hill in its center, an ominous sign. His route had in fact taken him past vast patches of new growth where flames had leveled whole forests, and he had been in residence in the International Hotel for only a few hours when he learned that the establishment was nicknamed "the Phoenix" for the number of times it had been rebuilt after burning to the ground. There was a fire bucket on every corner and a local ordinance required smokers to extinguish all stubs on pain of jail. He resolved to cut down his consumption of cigars for the duration of his visit.

His journey through wild, unsettled territory, and the temporary nature of most of the city's structures, had not prepared him for the comfort of his room on the second floor or the cosmopolitan cuisine downstairs. He had a private bath—a luxury even among the more populous regions to the immediate east and south—and found the poached salmon served in the dining room to be the equal of anything he had sampled in St. Louis and Denver. He was braced and invigorated by the clear cold air and the view through the window of snow—in September!—on the foothills of the Rockies, but there was a stench of char everywhere from the most recent fire. He kept the longest and most reliable of his ropes coiled on the floor beneath the window, with one end tied to a leg of the cast iron heating stove, for swift egress in the event of an alarum during the night.

The sooty smell carried with it an odor of desperation that mocked the pretentions toward civilization. The assay office was closed. Placer gold mining was coming to an end in the area, and Oscar was told that investors were being sought to finance operations in quartz and other hard minerals, so far without much success. The judge who had hired him confided that Helena was locked in a tense struggle with Virginia City to become the territorial capital: "Without that designation, the next fire may obliterate it for good."

The judge, a diminutive dandy with false teeth, Satanic whiskers, and an extravagant taste in tailoring, was nevertheless sober on the subject of the challenges faced by his city and his court. His chambers were temporary and consisted of a book press stuffed with thumb-blurred legal volumes, a heavy carved mahogany desk, and a tattered Mexican flag captured at Monterrey—the only items he had managed to rescue from a fire that had gutted the courthouse in August—but they conveyed something of the gravity of the man, transforming a storage room of the Central Brewery into a hall of justice in spite of the kegs stacked along one wall. He spoke with his large head sunk between his shoulders and his small hands folded on the desk's leather top.

"If we're to have any chance at all of becoming the capital, we cannot afford to create even the slightest impression of lawlessness. When we hang Barnet Menteith, we must do it in such a way that no Virginia City demagogue can say that lynch law presides in Helena. That's why we developed the hydraulically operated gallows, and it's why we selected you as its operator. You are well regarded everywhere."

"Not everywhere. In the East they think I'm a butcher."

The judge clacked his teeth in irritation. "In the East they think we should still belong to France. They're content in Washington to let the frontier go its own way to hell, short of civil war. No elected official even in Virginia City would dare suggest you are anything less than what you are."

Oscar had no intention of entering into a dispute between cities. "Menteith is the murderer?"

"There's no controversy over his case. He shot a bartender for refusing to sell him liquor while he was in an advanced and violent state of drunkenness and hurled a lighted lamp at a wall in an attempt to cover his escape. Bartenders come and go, but arson is serious business in Montana."

"What, precisely, *is* a hydraulically operated gallows?"

The judge raised his black brows. They reminded the hangman of Pickerel, the cabinetmaker of York. "You're not familiar with the mechanism? We sent to Murfreesboro for the plans. They've been using it to hang ex-guerrillas in Tennessee for two or three years."

"I haven't traveled east of the Mississippi since 1866."

"I'll arrange a demonstration."

The gallows was built stoutly of ponderosa pine, whitewashed for purposes of preservation rather than appearance, and looked like the skeleton of some prehistoric beast. A twelve-foot board fence had been erected around it to mask it from curious eyes and could be entered only through the back door of the courthouse, where carpenters and plasterers were noisily at work restoring the gutted interior. The charcoal smell was especially strong while Oscar and the judge were passing through it, and the hangman kept a handkerchief pressed to his nose and mouth to avoid coughing; he wondered if he was developing an allergy. The hammering and sawing diverted him not at all. Woodwork no longer held any attraction.

The hydraulic mechanism was simple—disappointingly so, given the anticipation and the hard miles he had covered in order to examine it: A wooden bucket filled with water stood on a small platform beneath the scaffold, above another platform supporting an empty bucket, attached by means of ropes and pulleys to the trap. When a jail turnkey the judge had pressed into service set the standard hundredweight sandbag onto the trap, the weight released a pin connected to a hinge on the single wooden leg that held up the top platform, causing it to tilt and spill the contents of the upper bucket into the lower. When the lower bucket was filled, the platform it was standing on descended beneath its weight, working the pulleys that freed the trap. The sandbag sped through the opening and slammed to the end of the rope tied to it.

Watching along with Oscar from the ground, the judge removed his soft hat. Oscar kept his on. A bag was not a man.

"In a way, I'm asking you to take part in your own obsolescence." The jurist put on his hat. "Since the prisoner himself sets the mechanism into operation, the presence of an actual hangman is redundant. Once this catches on, the executioner will be nothing more than a common technician."

"That is all I am now. You've merely added a fresh spectacle for the entertainment of the public."

"The public is not invited."

"Then your contraption serves no purpose whatsoever."

"It removes the onus from the human conscience. No man is responsible for taking the condemned man's life, not even the condemned man. The sentence is carried out by the laws of physics. I believe you said something to that effect in Denver."

"It's a deception. In Mexico, where they execute by firing squad, the men with rifles are informed that only one of the weapons is armed with live ammunition. They are not told which one. That way every member of the squad may believe that it was not he who fired the fatal bullet."

"I heard the same thing when I was down there in 'forty-seven. I thought it humane and practical."

Oscar faced him. "It's a myth. *All* the rifles are armed with live rounds. The odds of one man missing the prisoner are too great. Mexico is a Catholic nation; guilt and expiation are its principal commodities. I'm distressed to learn that the standard has spread this far north in Protestant America."

"I'm sorry you disapprove. Would you rather not preside?"

"I've come too far to make that decision, and spent too much of Washington's money. I'm a taxpayer too." Oscar took out his watch, but he didn't look at it. "I'd like another demonstration."

The turnkey pulled the sandbag back up onto the scaffold, then descended the steps and reset the mechanism; a delicate task that reminded Oscar of baiting and setting a mousetrap. Finally the man filled a spare bucket from a water barrel nearby and refilled the bucket on the upper platform. This time, when the bag was set on the trap, Oscar looked at his watch and followed the sweep hand throughout the mechanical activity that transpired. When at last the lower bucket was full and its descent sprang open the trap, he looked at the judge.

"Twenty-one seconds. Is there a way to make it work faster?"

"A second or two, perhaps. We experimented rather a lot to get it where it is. If the water is poured too fast, most of it splashes out and the pulleys won't move. We had quite a deep layer of mud out here before we had it right. Is the time so important?"

"Not to you or me. To the man standing on the trap it's forever. When he can follow the operation, he can tell how close he's coming to the end and prepare himself. I make it a point not to delay once the hood is in place. You're asking this fellow Menteith to wait with his hands shackled and a rope around his neck for as long as it would require you or me to take three long puffs on a good cigar. Have you ever had a rope around your neck?"

"I'm happy to say I have not."

"It itches fiercely. In such a situation even a strong man can work himself up to a fine apoplectic fit in twenty-one seconds. What will your Virginia City demagogue make of that?"

The judge scowled satanically. "I'll see about speeding it up."

"Unless you can cut the time in half, don't bother. Does Helena have an orchestra?"

"Orchestra?"

"Music." When the judge didn't react, Oscar pantomimed playing a violin. "It's a poor city that cannot boast one talented musician."

"The firefighters have a brass band, but they don't get much chance to practice. I look to the day when we have fewer fires and better concerts. If you're suggesting we accompany the execution with a musical program—"

"I am, although not for the amusement of spectators. Would it be possible to arrange a private concert tonight? They needn't comb their hair nor put on uniforms."

"I'll talk to Chief Bullock." The judge smoothed his beard. "You're an interesting study, Mr. Stone. I can't decide whether you're an authentic eccentric or affecting the role *pro bono publica.*"

"We're all eccentrics, Your Honor. Out here, it's what passes for normal." He turned back toward the courthouse, with its smells of sweet wood and sour ashes.

The temporary firehouse was a dank livery barn, ammonia-reeking, heated to an unbearable temperature on one end by a barrel stove and freezing on the other. The five-man band occupied the middle ground seated on folding chairs. Captain Bullock, the conductor—lean, gristly, and moustachioed in a white helmet, brass-buttoned blazer, and blue woolen trousers with a black satin stripe—had, in spite of Oscar's request not to go to any trouble, turned out his men in full uniform. Cornet, tuba, and trombone gleamed. The drummer fiddled tirelessly with the shoulder harness supporting the bass between his knees and the cymbalist sat with his great shimmering disks propped like trays on his thighs.

Bullock never spoke directly to Oscar. Baton in hand, he raised his eyebrows to the judge, who asked the hangman if there was any tune he particularly wished to hear. Oscar replied that he'd be content to listen to the entire program. After a cacophonous few moments during which instruments were tuned and spit valves cleared, Bullock tapped his wooden music stand with his baton. Oscar produced his watch.

The musicians were better than he'd feared. The trombonist came in a little behind on some of the livelier tunes, and once the cymbals clashed a split second early, throwing off everyone's tempo, but such mistakes were more to be blamed upon lack of rehearsal than a deficiency in talent. The drummer kept a steady beat and the cornetist could have held his own on any open-air bandstand in the States. The program itself was the standard mix of marches and popular melodies, mournful and sprightly, with the occasional surprise of a tune that Oscar had heard for the first time in St. Louis, only two weeks before; he would never cease to marvel at how swiftly music traveled across country whose residents often did not know who their new president was until three months after the election.

He timed each selection without comment. When the band finished the last piece, he asked them to play again four whose titles he had scribbled on a shirt cuff with a pencil borrowed from the judge. This time they dragged a second behind on two of them and came in nearly two seconds ahead on another, but he supposed that could be corrected in rehearsal. Before making his decision, he asked them to play two of the tunes once again. Then he snapped shut his watch and returned it to his vest pocket.

"Thank you, gentlemen. The last tune is the one I will ask you to play at the hanging."

"The last?" The judge lifted his expressive brows. "Do you think it appropriate?"

"My first choice was 'Tenting Tonight on the Old Camp-Ground,' but it's too slow. The opening chorus came in at thirty-nine seconds, nearly twice as long as what I require. Twenty-one is the ideal. I would ask Chief Bullock to keep a record during rehearsals and try to duplicate that time on each playing."

"I would in my turn ask why." These were the first words the fire chief had addressed to Oscar.

"Humanitarian reasons, and practical. I will inform Mr. Menteith that the trap will open beneath his feet on the last note of the first chorus. It will give him something to concentrate upon while he waits out his last seconds. For reasons I have already discussed with the judge, the alternative might be untidy."

Bullock smoothed his handlebars, regarding him with eyes of stone. "Well, we certainly can't have an untidy hanging."

It was the first truly private execution Oscar had attended. Present upon the platform were the judge, a federal marshal named Gordon, and Barnet Menteith, the convicted murderer of a Helena bartender and the arsonist responsible for a serious blaze in a hurdy-gurdy house on Bridge Street. Spectators on the ground were restricted to the band, a pair of deputy marshals who had escorted the prisoner from the jail, and the turnkey in charge of the hydraulic machinery, the last on hand to ensure that the pins and pulleys operated properly. Bullock's musicians—pressed, brushed, moustache-waxed and bootblacked—stood in parade formation with music sheets attached to their instruments, facing their conductor.

Menteith was a big, redheaded Scot whose defiant scowl was white at the corners from the muscular effort involved in maintaining it; his breathing was quick and shallow, a warning sign that had not been present when Oscar weighed and measured him and examined the muscles in his neck. On that occasion he'd been cold-eyed and arrogant. There was nothing on Fabian Rudd's chart to indicate just when a man's nerves might snap. Some men's never did, even when faced with the ultimate test of climbing the steps to the scaffold. Some broke when sentence was pronounced, others during Oscar's examination. A Missouri bushwhacker in Lawrence, Kansas, had joked about looking forward to getting his hands on John Brown in hell, then when the barber arrived to shave him for the last time flew into a tear-filled rage and had to be dragged back to his cell. He had gone to the gallows stubbled but icily calm.

Oscar held Menteith's gaze as he tightened the noose and rotated the knot to the notch behind his left earlobe. Opening the black hood, he explained what was going to happen once the condemned man stepped onto the trap: He would hear the tinkling of the pin coming loose, the clunk and then the slapping of water as the platform collapsed beneath the upper bucket and its burden was transferred to the lower, the squeaking of the pulleys as the lower bucket dropped to release the trap. He told him what the band would be playing, asked him if he was familiar with the tune, repeated the question before getting a jerky nod and a hoarse "Yes," and made him aware that the final note of the first chorus would be followed immediately by the trap dumping open. When Menteith's curly brows turned up quizzically at the term *chorus*, Oscar demonstrated, humming the opening bars. They came out tonelessly, but Menteith seemed to understand. He nodded again. His throat worked, but this time no sound issued. Oscar said "Yes" for him and pulled the hood over the Scot's head. He glanced down to make sure his own feet were clear of the trap, then looked at the judge, who removed his hat. Oscar gave Menteith's back a gentle, encouraging prod. Menteith hesitated, then stepped forward and placed both feet side by side on the square of sawn wood.

The pin tinkled. Oscar jerked his chin at Bullock, who was watching from the ground with baton raised. The baton slashed down, and the band played "Listen to the Mockingbird," finishing on the downstroke at the end of the bird's trilling call, coincidental with the bang of the trap.

TWENTY-TWO

Oscar Stone
Helena M. T.
September 11 1872

dear Oscar
well youll be happy to here your Old Freind Rudd is Alive and Kicking and that dont mean kicking Clouds under the Galows as hes still on the Right End of that Rope tho not for Long as youll see Presently I got your wire its good to know your Out There spreding the Good Hemp Gospel in Wild Country where the Right Honorabel Judge Lynch had his Hooks in til recent I read about you in the Papers stretching Rope in Abileen Tuson Cheyene etc and think to Myself theres one more Place can use its Trees for Lumber and not Strangling thanks to Profesor Rudds star Puple here at the Acadamy of Knots I cudn't be Prouder if I "got" you Myself I herd from your Man Pilot I inclose a Paket he sent I dont know as I agree you go on looking for your Wife but I hope it all Works Out maybe youll let Old Rudd know it does or dont just so you can reach me by the time you read this Ill be retired from Army Service and

will be Saving Soles at the First Unitarian Church of Carbon City Kansas yes I made good on my Thret and have doned a Colar its truly the First Unitarian as theres no other betwixt Masachusets and California theres only six famblys in the congregassion at present but thats enuf to keep me in chiken diners and maybe the ocassional pig til I convert some more so writ me there and when you come thru stop and see a Man of the Cloth

your Pard the Reverend Fabian T. Rudd Esq

The letter, and the packet that accompanied it, didn't catch up with Oscar until January 1873, when he was in North Platte, Nebraska, waiting out a snowstorm that had postponed the hanging of one Richard Round Oak, a half-breed Sioux convicted of slaughtering a family in Ogallala; it had come in on the Union Pacific just ahead of the blizzard. Hesitant at first to know what information the packet contained, he read Rudd's letter more slowly and carefully than it warranted, even with its crude spellings and absence of punctuation. He felt the sadness of loss. Uncouth as Rudd was, he had been Oscar's teacher, patient and wise, dedicated to the ennoblement of his profession. That wisdom was blunted by his inability to express himself in writing. The elementary errors and shaky scrawl, blotched and spattered where the nib caught on the coarse paper fiber, might have belonged to a backwoods cannibal or the moronic child of an illiterate stablehand. He had experienced the same sensation the day he caught his father masturbating in the outhouse.

However, one thing about the letter made him smile: Rudd had left the life. The pleasantness of the revelation made him pause before he refilled his glass from the bottle of Old Gideon he'd bought in the saloon next to the hotel, and ponder its nature. Why should he feel happy for a hangman who no longer hanged? He emptied the glass again, filled it again, and reread the letter. He topped off the glass one more time and opened the packet.

The cyclops eye of the Pinkerton National Detective Agency glared at him from the letterhead. After the initial encounter he avoided its gaze, and was relieved when he'd read far enough down in John Audubon Pilot's summarizing text to allow the folded top third to flop over and out of sight. The letter had been composed upon a typewriting machine, the first such he had ever received. Pilot reported that railroad personnel aboard the 9:17 train to Chicago on the night in question could not recall seeing a woman traveling alone with a small boy, and that ticket clerks questioned in Springfield, Peoria, and other stops along the route had no recollection of selling a ticket to anyone answering that description from that night to the time they were interrogated. A confidential letter of inquiry sent out to Agency offices in New York, Philadelphia, Detroit, Cleveland, Baltimore, and the headquarters in Chicago had as yet yielded no results from agents in the field. Although the director of the St. Louis office had hopes that something might yet turn up, he confided to his client that Mr. Stone's original assumption might have been wrong, and Mrs. Stone might have taken the 8:58 to Denver instead. Since redirecting the investigation was tantamount to starting over from scratch, an additional expenditure was required. Had he Mr. Stone's permission to alert the offices in Denver and points beyond? A wire draught in the amount of two hundred dollars would be sufficient to commence western operations.

Oscar postponed his decision until he had read the typewritten report, which covered ten pages. Then he got off the bed, sat down at the little writing desk, and used the hotel pen and watery ink to scribble his response on the back of the letter: "O.K. Cash draught to follow. Oscar Stone." The Overland wasn't moving and the telegraph lines were down. He hoped that when the storm blew over and he sent his authorization the trail wouldn't be too cold. It was already five months old.

That done, and the notation made in his pocket passbook to withdraw the requested amount from his account in the Colorado

National Bank in Denver, he had nothing more that required his attention until the snow stopped accumulating upon the gallows. He returned to the bed and put himself to sleep with the help of Old Gideon.

The storm blew for a week. For days afterward, nothing moved but the Platte. The snow lay heaped roof-high against the sides of barns, obliterated frozen creeks, and filled buffalo wallows with lakes of white, as still as meringue. Then city employees and volunteers dug out the streets, cleared wells, and shoveled and swept the snow in clouds from the scaffold next to the city jail. The new day set for the hanging was iron-cold, with a wind that razored ears and faces and erected fresh drifts against the jail's north wall, but the sky was as bright as glass. Oscar, rising, could not face all that head-clobbering white with the hangover he knew awaited him when the effects of another night of drinking began to wear off; he drank a tumbler of Old Gideon for breakfast and filled a flask he had bought in St. Louis—a handsome one of hammered silver with the *U.S.S. Constitution* chased on the side that curved out—to maintain the pleasant furred edge. He had three hours to measure and stretch the rope before the execution.

He had difficulty reading some of the figures he'd written in his notebook during Richard Round Oak's examination; he'd been drinking that day as well, and although alcohol never affected the precision of his measurements, his penmanship always suffered. He decided that what looked at first like a nine was in fact a seven, made a quick calculation, and used a piece of tailor's chalk to mark the rope. Quality hemp was difficult to find, and instead of cutting, he'd taken to marking off the desired length and looping the excess around the crossbeam, preserving footage for use with lighter men. He coiled the rope and put it in his carpetbag.

The mercury was stuck below zero, too cold to stand on sartorial ceremony. He pulled on two pairs of thick socks, waterproof boots, a woolen lumberman's cap with earflaps that buckled beneath his chin, and the buffalo coat he'd acquired in Julesburg that made people mistake him for a doctor when he wore it with a bowler. Leaving the hotel lobby, he pulled his chin into his chest and hurried along the shoveled boardwalk against a stiff wind lethal with ice crystals. Henceforth, he would add a fifty percent surcharge to his fee whenever his work called him to Nebraska, a place of three seasons only: just before a blizzard, in the middle of a blizzard, and just after a blizzard. He thought of Rudd, snug in his parsonage reading Revelations with a blanket over his lap, and adjusted the surcharge ten percent upward.

The gallows was made of box elder, a wood of which he did not approve, but the treeless plain made a luxury of hardwoods that was outside the budget of a small town. Moisture had saturated the porous material and frozen as hard as iron. There would be no bounce in the crossbeam, he would have to be careful not to stretch all the life out of the rope. The rope at least was pliant, and molded itself to the beam when he stood atop the stepladder and coiled it around; in Salt Lake City, where gun oil was scarce, he had substituted sewing machine lubricant, and upon learning that it did not evaporate as easily nor freeze even in extreme cold, decided to use it exclusively. He aligned the top of the chalk mark with the bottom of the beam, allowing the calculated length to dangle above the platform. He had to take off his spectacles and rub the lenses vigorously on his coat to remove frost so that he could see the mark. With Round Oak's height figured in, the drop would be seven feet, three inches, rather long for a man of his girth, but he was not as heavy as he appeared, and the muscles about his neck required a strong jolt to snap the vertebra. Just to be sure, he excavated his notebook and peered again at his scribbled figures through a fresh layer of frost: Yes, he was certain it was a seven, not a nine.

The work was intense and physically demanding, and he was actually sweating when he finished. Conversely, his fingers were bluish and cramped. Gloves impaired his dexterity, and mittens, which were the most practical thing for warmth in that climate, were useless when it came to tying knots. He warmed his hands beneath his armpits and when life tingled back into them he unstopped his flask and warmed his insides.

The trap was controlled by a sliding block which he manipulated with his foot, primitive but effective, and the least likely to malfunction of all the mechanisms with which he had worked. He secured the noose to the neck of the hundredweight sandbag, set the bag atop the trap, and kicked the block. A dozen times the bag plummeted through the opening; a dozen times the trap opened without a shudder or a hesitation. Not wanting to stretch the rope overmuch—the frozen crossbeam resisted the dull *thwang* of the rope without so much as a creak, a dead thing indeed, like a body in the final stages of rigor—he hauled up the bag, released it from the noose, and opened the loop so that it would fit comfortably over the head of a man. For a moment he contemplated the sandbag slouched on the corner of the platform. He always had them removed from sight before a hanging, as their presence detracted from the dignity of the event, but he was tired and unsteady on his feet, and the cold had prevented the usual volunteers from coming out to assist him. He took a thoughtful swig from the flask, took another, returned it to his pocket, then placed the sole of his boot against the shoulder of the bag, and in the act of turning away gave it a firm shove. The bag tumbled over the edge and buried itself in a fresh drift at the base of the scaffold.

When Richard Round Oak was escorted from the jail by the city marshal, two deputies, and a young, gray-faced minister suffering from the cold, Oscar wondered if the seven wasn't a nine after all. The half-breed, long-haired and squat, with a strawberry mark or perhaps an old burn scar puckering the left half of his face, appeared bulkier in a coat of thin ragged canvas than he had in his cell; the steps groaned beneath his weight. While adjusting the noose, the hangman probed again the sinews and tendons at the base of the man's neck and was satisfied that his assessment of their strength was correct. In such cases it was better not to err on the side of conservatism when calculating the drop, to avoid strangulation. Oscar still had bad dreams about South Georgia Crossing, of the boy jerking and twitching at the end of the rope. He seated the knot and tugged down the hood, ignoring the final flash of hatred in the whites of the man's eyes, looked to the marshal for the nod, and used the side of his boot to push the block to the other end of its slot.

The instant that followed would replace the nightmare of South Georgia Crossing in Oscar's sleep for the rest of his life.

The bang when the prisoner's weight came to the end of the rope was flat and without resonance. The rope went taut without quivering, then sprang upward, accordioning upon itself. Oscar's first horrified thought was that it had broken. He then experienced a multiple awareness involving all five of his senses: the thud of a body striking the frozen ground beneath the platform, the sight of something dark and round going up and up with the coiling rope, the shock of hot liquid splashing his face and darkening the lenses of his spectacles, the taste of salt and iron in his mouth, and the murky fetid iodine smell he remembered so vividly from the war, the stench of blood exposed suddenly to the air.

He stepped back involuntarily, stopping abruptly when he felt the railing across his back. He tore off his glasses, shook them violently, and dragged the lenses across the front of his coat. He hooked them back on in time to see the handful of diehard spectators on the ground turning their faces away from the sight of Richard Round Oak's hooded head swinging at the end of the snug noose.

"I wouldn't lose any sleep over it, Mr. Stone. There's plenty of folks hereabouts'll raise a whoop and a holler when they hear how that breed son of a bitch died. I expect he'll be more famous for it than for what he done to earn it in the first place."

"Me, too," Oscar told the marshal. He hoped the man would

leave before the meal he'd ordered came to the table. He wasn't hungry. He only wanted the food to absorb the whiskey he'd drunk before the hanging. He couldn't see himself eating it at all as long as the fellow was sitting across from him, reminding him of what had taken place on the scaffold. He'd chosen a table in the darkest corner of the hotel dining room, but the marshal had spotted him anyway and joined him without being invited. He was one of those frontier specimens who fashioned themselves after the men they read about in New York dime novels, with fleurs-de-lis on his vest and red silk garters gathering the material of his shirtsleeves. In a few short years, Oscar had seen the West begin to parody itself.

"I doubt that, Mr. Stone. Nobody remembers who hung John Brown."

"Ezekiel French." Oscar allowed himself a bitter smile at the other's reaction. "The man under whom I apprenticed was in the way of a historian of his profession."

"Be that as it may, there are a lot of bad hats out here who will think twice about what happened to Richard Round Oak before they do murder."

"That's your concern, not mine."

The waiter came with his meal and a bottle of claret. When Oscar informed him he had not ordered wine, the waiter said, "Compliments of the manager, sir. He was acquainted with the massacred family."

"Please thank him and tell him I'm giving up alcohol."

The waiter left with the bottle and a worried expression.

"He'll probably tear up the bill for your meal," said the marshal.

"Then I will leave the identical amount as a tip. I won't profit from today's business." Oscar picked up his fork, hoping the other would take the hint and leave. "I will ask you not to pay me for my work here. I promised an efficient, orderly hanging. Those soft box elder planks will bear the evidence until they rot."

"An executed murderer was what was requested. As far as I'm

concerned, you gave full satisfaction. It's a generous gesture, Mr. Stone, but speaking on behalf of the citizens of North Platte, I can't accept it."

"It isn't a gesture. I am asking a favor."

The marshal made a final inarticulate noise of protest, but the avaricious glimmer in his eye told Oscar that the fee would be pocketed. Well, let the fellow have his graft. Sufficient blood had been spilled to stain them both.

The marshal rose. "At least allow the city to pay for your accommodations, as agreed. Even if Round Oak had kept his head, you would have had to eat and sleep."

Oscar was too exhausted emotionally, and weary of the company, to protest. When the marshal offered his hand, he pretended not to notice it and picked up his knife. Hand and peace officer withdrew.

When Oscar cut his meat, a trickle of red juice escaped and slid into a pool on his plate. Revolted, he pushed it away and took a gulp of water to settle his stomach. He never ate flesh again.

TWENTY-THREE

"One ninety-five, and one, two, three, four, two hundred dollars. And how long will you be staying in Denver, Mr."—the bank clerk glanced down at the draught Oscar had filled out—"Stone?"

The fellow was young, with only the golden downy beginnings on his cheeks of the burnsides that were the uniform of his trade. He would have been a child at the time six men were hanged just ten blocks from where they stood, if he'd even been living here then. The customer's name meant nothing to him.

"Quite some time," Oscar replied. "I intend to retire here."

"So young? You must be a railroad investor."

"I've been putting money into them for years."

He checked into the King's Rest, but since he'd given up hard liquor he found his own company distasteful after half an hour and went down to the lobby to finish reading his newspaper. He sat in one of the leather club chairs at the base of the railed vestibules that lay stacked one atop another like letter baskets, smoking a cigar and eavesdropping on conversations. It was July 1876: most of the talk was about the massacre at the Little Big Horn, and whether Sitting Bull's victorious Sioux were massing again to attack the great cities of the West. It amused Oscar to imagine hordes of painted savages pouring through the stained-glass doors of the hotel, fanning out across the Brussels carpet, and scaling the brass-trimmed balconies with tomahawks in hand. Then he returned his attention to the account of the battle in the *Rocky Mountain News* and grew sad when his eyes rested once again upon the byline of the last dispatch sent back by the correspondent who had accompanied Custer. Mark Kellogg's narrative of the Seventh Cavalry's march to destiny had been published by the *Bismarck Tribune*, then gone out over the wire to every major newspaper in the country. Oscar remembered the eager and pleasant journalist who had helped him out with the French hotel manager in St. Louis, and didn't want to think of his mutilated corpse lying on some lonely plain in Montana. If Oscar had refused Kellogg his interview, he might still be alive, a disappointed telegrapher in Missouri, but there was no use pursuing that line of thought. If Oscar had decided to accept the job Smollett had offered him in York, he'd be living there with Gretchen, and perhaps with two or three children besides. Would he have regretted not following his dream to Kansas? And would that regret be any more bitter than his failures, his broken marriage, the memory of Richard Round Oak's blood fountaining from his beheaded corpse, his hooded head swinging at the end of the rope like the pendulum of a clock? If the war had taught him anything, it was the uselessness of contemplating a life not lived.

He turned to the business pages, pretending to interest himself in cattle prices while mapping out for himself the life he was living. He would be in need of a source of income before long. He'd spent far too much money on his search for Gretchen, and he hadn't accepted an assignment for more than a year. John Audubon Pilot had written him at length to advise him that if the Pinkertons had failed to pick up any trace of his wife after the first year, the trail was too cold, and any attempt to warm it up would be a waste of the Agency's time and Oscar's money. Oscar had ignored the advice and wired another five hundred dollars to continue the investigation. In the meantime, he'd hanged a parricide in Joplin, the rapist-murderer of a six-year-old girl in Albuquerque, and an out-of-work cowboy in Wichita who had shot to death a clerk in a freight office when he was too slow to open a safe. All three executions had come off efficiently, but each had been delayed several days because Oscar had insisted upon confirming all his measurements a second and third time and tested all the ropes he'd brought, not wanting to trust his own first judgment.

In Portland, Oregon, in 1875, he had finally hanged a woman. There was little controversy over the sentence. The condemned, one Elizabeth Maxson, having convinced herself that her husband, a brakeman with the Oregon & California Railroad, was unfaithful, had cut his throat with a butcher knife as he slept, stabbed to death her seven-year-old son and infant daughter, then cut her own wrists in an attempt at suicide that had convinced no one of her remorse. After her recovery, she had further weakened the case for her defense by declaring on the stand that because the seeds of infidelity had been sown in her children she had spared some future wife and husband the pain of treachery. The jury had deliberated just under ten minutes, and the judge had quoted at length from Exodus before pronouncing sentence. Mrs. Maxson was a tiny, wrenlike woman, and at Oscar's direction a house jack was employed and four square concrete blocks inserted beneath the feet of the gallows to create clearance for a sufficient drop. In his prestage jitters, he overestimated the amount of oil the rope required, tried winding it in bedsheets to soak up the excess, and finally discarded it as hopeless and started all over again with a fresh rope. He measured the woman carefully, apologizing for his ungentlemanly interest in her weight, and after giving long thought to asking a woman to probe the muscles of her neck decided he could trust this chore to none other. They were well developed for her tiny frame—she had been a dedicated housekeeper and had taken in washing besides to supplement her husband's income—and he calculated the drop at eight feet. He found her well-mannered and curious about details. Reticent at first, his answers to her questions became more specific as she pursued certain points, until she had more information than he'd shared with most of his subjects, yet she never once paled or gave any other indication that she was discussing breaking the neck of anyone even remotely familiar to her. She appeared, in fact, to possess none of the empathetic qualities that society had come to expect of her sex. He forbore to think what horrific courses her life might have taken had she been born male.

She was Catholic, and when she knelt upon the scaffold for a quiet prayer with the priest, she made rather a charming sight, dressed in the white lace-trimmed gown she had worn for her wedding, with her auburn hair pinned atop her head and her small white hands clasped in front of her breasts. When it was over, the chief of police helped her to her feet and manacled her hands behind her; adjusting the knot into the delicate depression below her left ear, Oscar noticed she had scented her skin lightly with lemon verbena. Her pulse throbbed evenly in the blue vein in her neck, but he remained in doubt whether women were calmer in the face of death than men, or if *this* woman was an anomaly. He applied the hood gently, hesitated with his hand on the lever perhaps a second longer than normal, then sprang the trap. Her neck broke with a hollow plop, like a reed. Afterward, the slender white-sheathed body hung with a kind of elegance, marred abruptly by the tilted head clad in black. He wished he'd used an ordinary white pillowcase.

He'd accepted an assignment to hang a daylight robber convicted of the murder of a bank clerk in Dodge City, but he sent a wire from his train asking the mayor to appoint a replacement. He then bought a ticket to San Francisco, expecting to rest there for a month. He'd stayed eight. He registered at the Parker House under the name O. Stein, but as he settled into the city's urbane routine of fine restaurants, European-class theater, and discreet bordellos, he realized those things that were spoken of with lascivious enthusiasm on the plains, and denounced ferociously in the East, were almost never a subject of interest in the city that had outgrown its frontier period a generation before. A place that played host to Russian grand dukes, British literary lions, and robber barons from Fifth Avenue scarcely raised a lorgnette to peer at a celebrated hangman. When, following the recommendation of a man he'd played billiards with in a club, Oscar moved his baggage to the opulent new Palace Hotel, he signed his own name in the register. The clerk read the name without recognition and handed him his key with a courteous impersonal smile.

San Francisco offered many distractions, including the bizarre daily spectacle of a seedy local character in brass buttons and epaulets who styled himself Emperor of the United States and Protector of Mexico, who eked out his deranged living from the generosity of merchants and bankers who would have scorned to place a nickel in the hat of a Civil War amputee panhandling on a street corner. Oscar found Emperor Norton I tiresome and repellent, and took to crossing the street to avoid His Imperial Majesty's unwashed flatulence when he saw him approaching. The beggar only served to remind him that if he were to extend his own holiday indefinitely, he had better adjust his tastes in entertainment and living arrangements downward. It was an expensive city.

His determination to give up drinking proved harder to maintain than his sudden distaste for meat. Although the yearning was not physical, he found that wines, liqueurs, tawny ports, imported beers, and a bewildering assortment of brandies and cognacs were as much a part of an evening on the town as tailcoats and silk hats, and he had positively to turn his glass upside down to prevent waiters and aggressive hosts from filling it. The Bay fog seemed to include an alcoholic haze; matrons and mining tycoons alike pursued their daily rounds with flasks in their handbags and waistcoat pockets, their noses as red as any stevedore's. The champions of temperance and women's suffrage—a connection he could never quite understand—were an annoyingly visible drab thread in the city's glittering tapestry, thumping their tambourines on corners and hoisting their Romanesque standards Sundays in Union Square; in social situations, one was well advised to downplay his abstinence or be counted among the cranks. The rules of comportment and behavior were as inviolate as York's stoic Lutheranism and the practice of keeping one's word under threat of assassination on the frontier.

He could not bring himself to think of returning to work with his old enthusiasm. He was filled with self-loathing over the hideous debacle of the Richard Round Oak hanging, but he did not fear another such failure. Perversely, the very possibility of repeating such a disaster would only add seasoning to a meal that had become demoralizingly bland through repetition. He had improved upon Rudd's own formula, refined the old hangman's methods, and had only to use the mixture as before to remove the slightest likelihood of an unsatisfactory result. He had lain to rest the century-old question of which placement was best: the subaural with its natural anchor behind the corner of the jaw as opposed to the occipital with its propensity to slip off the rounded surface at the base of the skull and the submental with its clumsy location of the coils in front of the prisoner's face. He had studied anatomical charts, attended postmortems, and exhausted surgeons of their knowledge of the human spinal cord to identify the second cervical vertebra as the capstone that supported life; snap it clean and the structure collapsed in an instant. Even the variables—height, weight, muscular development and tension—were a matter of simple arithmetic. He knew more about the specialized area of his vocation than any man living. There was no place else to go except where he'd been, over and again, ad infinitum, world without end. Put simply, he was as bored as hell.

When he left San Francisco, bored with that place as well, retirement was not on his mind. He'd selected Denver, the site of the celebrated hanging that had brought him to the attention of a justice-challenged West, in search of inspiration, a pilgrimage to the fountain of his youthful faith. He arranged to have his bags taken to his hotel, then took a two-wheeler to the federal prison, but he was told there by a helpful young turnkey that Marshal Townsend Phelps had lost his federal appointment two years before and had moved on to a deputy's post in Yuma, Arizona Territory. The Denver facility, he added, was seldom used to shelter capital prisoners anymore, the prison in Canon City being better equipped for that purpose. The gallows Oscar had helped design had been dismantled as an impediment to immigration from the East. Condemned men were now hanged one at a time in Canon City. The room where six prisoners had been executed at once was now furnished with cots and a card table for the turnkeys to rest between shifts. Oscar had thanked the young man and gone on to the Colorado First National Bank, where the polite teller became the first to learn of his decision to retire.

But the decision had not brought satisfaction.

Sitting there now in the hotel lobby, drawing on the last inch of his cigar, reluctant to finish it but lacking the will to light another, he could not summon up the energy even to worry about what would become of him when his money ran out. He felt benumbed, just as he had when reading Pilot's wire, with its admission that Pinkerton had failed. He'd been unable even to despair. It was as if the ennui of continuing as he had been had spread to life itself. Caring required more effort than he had in reserve. *That* frightened him, but even the fear was a remote thing, as dull as a blow heard under water—or, more specifically, as unrelated to him as the fear of the many men and the one woman his work had called upon him to dispatch. He was not yet thirty, yet he felt as empty and used up as the old men he saw in every train station between St. Louis and the Barbary Coast, refusing to budge from the middle of the wooden benches where they sat to make room for others, because that seat was more home to them than the furnished rooms or the galvanized iron shacks they went to when forced to move by a deputy. An overstuffed chair in an over-decorated lobby was no different from a hard bench in a depot. He could sit there on a cushion worn to corrugated lumps and hollows by a thousand backsides until his heart stopped beating if no one took the trouble to notice.

He dropped his smoldering stub into the tall spitoon next to his chair and got up to tell the desk clerk he was checking out of the room in which he'd spent just thirty minutes. He asked to borrow a train schedule. He was going to Leavenworth to ask if anyone knew how he could get to a place called Carbon City.

TWENTY-FOUR

He found the city of Leavenworth nearly unrecognizable. Streets had been laid out in proper grids, made possible by the demolition of most of the landmark buildings Oscar remembered. Fabian Rudd's shack—indeed, the rutted path that had led past it—no longer existed, and he could not be certain where it had stood. The fort, too, had grown, and a masonry wall erected around it to contain the influx of inmates since it had officially been declared a federal military prison; a regular business district stood outside the wall where harnesses, carved statuary, and household implements manufactured by prisoners could be purchased in shops managed by former penitents. A sentry installed in a little hut next to the gate stopped Oscar in his hired trap and told him he could not be admitted without a pass signed by the commander.

"Colonel Janning?"

"No, sir. Colonel Owens is CO." The stern young soldier's expression told Oscar the name Janning meant nothing to him.

"I don't need to go in, Corporal. I'm trying to locate an old friend who used to work here, a civilian named Rudd."

"I'm sorry, sir. I don't know the gentleman."

"Before your time, I suppose. Do you know of a town called Carbon City?"

"There's a Carbondale south of Topeka. It's on the A. T. and S. F."

"No, Carbon City was the name. Is there someone inside you could ask?"

"I'm sorry, sir. I can't leave my post. You might try asking in one of the shops. Your pardon, sir, but some of those boys've whored around in a lot of places."

In the second shop Oscar visited, a kind of clearinghouse of handmade picture frames, whittled angels, mailboxes fashioned from artillery shells, and chess sets carved from soapstone, yellow pine, and buffalo chips—the last confirmed by sniffing the bishop—a one-eyed brigand in a green visor with tattoos on his forearms bit down on the silver dollar Oscar gave him and drew a complicated map with a black crayon on a square of white wrapping paper, starting at Emporia. "At least, that was how you got there when they caught me selling my army horse in Abilene in 'seventy-three," he added. "For all I know they pulled up stakes and moved downtrack by now. It wasn't such of a much even then."

"Did you happen to know the minister of the Unitarian church there?"

"Mister, I didn't stop long enough to meet the bartender in the saloon. I had a patrol breathing hellfire down the back of my neck."

Oscar returned to Leavenworth and bought a ticket on the Atchison, Topeka, & Santa Fe for Emporia. After resting there overnight, he hired a stout buckboard, refreshed his directions with the help of the livery operator, and found himself at dusk approaching a scatter of wooden buildings along a street as wide as a pasture, with a sign at one end reading:

CARBON CITY
ELEV. 1,472
POP. 612

The painted letters had faded almost entirely into the weathered gray wood and a spray of shotgun pellets had punched holes in the left side. Time, ill fortune, and drought had dealt even more ruthlessly with the number of structures required to shelter 612 people. Of most of them no trace remained.

He hardly needed a steeple to tell him he'd reached his destination. Located on a low hill at the end of the street, the church was the only building in town with a fresh coat of whitewash and all its shutters and windowpanes intact. The construction itself, with its peaked roof and center gable pointing upward like a finger toward heaven, was sturdy, unoriginal, and no-nonsensically functional, like the Old Woman of Fort Leavenworth, and so had Rudd's stamp all over it. A double row of whitewashed stones flanked the path leading to the front steps, and a professionally painted sign mounted above the door informed the visitor that he had arrived at the FIRST UNITARIAN CHURCH OF CARBON CITY, with the smaller legend, "F. T. Rudd, Pastor," painted beneath and to the right. Inserted in the corner of the panel next to the door handle was a small pasteboard card, sun-faded and rain-streaked, reading, "Knok then enter" in Rudd's spidery scrawl. Oscar rapped three times and pulled open the door.

The interior, lit by the sun through plain windows that sparkled from a recent cleaning, smelled of ammonia and old paper, the latter reminiscent of the old hangman's private library in Leavenworth. An aisle of bare scrubbed plank floor stretched between rows of handmade wooden benches, planed smooth but unvarnished, with racks behind the backrests in which rested hymnals bound in freckled paper, their covers curled like last year's leaves; it was obvious that most of them had not been moved since they were first placed there. The aisle ended at the base of a two-foot platform that ran the width of the building, supporting a lectern in the middle. Behind the lectern, attached to the wall, was a plain cross built of four-by-four timbers six feet high and four feet wide, which had been left unpainted. It put Oscar in mind of the Fort

Leavenworth gibbet, but only because Rudd was standing in front of it with his hands folded behind his back.

The ascetic life did not appear to have affected him physically. He was still built narrow but for his low rounded belly, and although his posture was stooped now, with his high thin shoulders up around his ears, his face—and especially the knob of nose—retained their high color; Oscar suspected that Rudd's pledge to give up drinking was unfulfilled. His hair was longer, particularly above the ears, where wispy tendrils crawled like feelers in the air stirred by the opening and closing of the door, and had gone white to match the stubble on his chin. He was balding on top, but since Oscar had seldom seen him without his old caved-in silk hat, he could not decide whether this was a new development. Incredibly, he had on the old gray vest, shabby frock coat, and striped trousers gone baggy in the knees that he'd worn all through their earlier acquaintance, stained in all the old places and a few that were new. Oscar had known anvils to wear out quicker.

"How can I help you, son?" greeted Rudd. He was squinting, and Oscar guessed he'd grown shortsighted. His own appearance had not changed that much since their last meeting.

He realized he was still wearing his hat and took it off. "Your pardon, Reverend. I've an army deserter outside who needs hanging and I wonder if you could make the necessary arrangements."

"I'm sorry, son. I'm retired from that business. If your soul's in suspension, I'll cut it down."

"Rudd, it's Oscar Stone."

Rudd grinned; eight years slid away like sand from a bank. "Well, lad, I knowed that from your knock. I've lost my old sinful ways, but not my mind. You look to prosper. That's the first new suit to come in here since I buried old Doc Walnut. The town took up a collection on account of he hadn't anything decent."

"I'm retired as well, I think. Where's your congregation? You're in position for a sermon."

"None of it. I do most of my tall thinking right here on this spot. Just now I was wondering if the old barn will stand another winter without new shingles. Church roofs wear out twice as often as any other; they get the rain from above and the praying from below. We surely could use a master carpenter."

"I'm not here to ask for a job."

"I know that, lad. You have your glasses on and I don't figure you got stupid. Anyone with eyes and a brain can see the town's used up. I can't even pay for the wood."

"What happened?"

"Farms played out. Three years of drought, one year of grasshoppers. I'm expecting plague and frogs any time. The bank in Emporia foreclosed. Everybody moved on, even the damn Methodists. My fault, I'm thinking. I brung too much God with me and it burned out the soil. I'm thinking maybe you got to rotate faith like potatoes; one season of sin and depravity for every three of pious good works. Something on that order. Topsoil's too shallow to hold the roots of the Word."

"I'm sorry."

"No reason. Preaching's like hanging; you don't just pick up a rope or a Bible and set to it without science. What I need is a chart."

"What will you do until then?"

"Teach Sunday school, I reckon. I calculate there's plenty of Unitarians in Kansas City don't know they're Unitarians just yet. I'll educate them first. When the field's laid fallow long enough I'll get to the converting. What about you?"

"I don't know," Oscar said. "That's why I came here. You always seem to have most of the answers."

He thought the compliment would bring back Rudd's grin, or at least some deprecating remark that would clear away the stiffness he felt between them. Instead the old hangman looked as grave as he ever had when standing upon the scaffold. He took his hands from behind him and stepped down to the floor. "Let's go to my shack."

This structure, built behind the church at the end of a flagstone walk, did not belong to the same architectural world as Rudd's old shack in Leavenworth. It was a proper house, tiny but equipped with windows and shutters and whitewashed, a miniature version of the church, lacking only a steeple. Inside, however, was the familiar disarray of a place intended for eating and sleeping only, to sustain a life lived for work. Stacks of cheaply bound Bibles occupied every table in the little parlor as well as the top of the upended crate in which they'd been shipped. Evidently there had been many more Bibles than parishioners to accept them. There were bales of religious pamphlets as well, bearing the imprint of a publishing firm in Chicago, cigar butts decomposing in china saucers, and mousetraps placed in strategic spots, some of them sprung but containing no carcasses; Oscar set one off by accident while clearing a pile of pamphlets from an armchair in order to sit. The walls were plastered and papered, decorated with hand-tinted steelpoint engravings of the Annunciation, the Crucifixion, the Sermon on the Mount, and—oddly—George Washington's farewell to his troops, cut out of periodicals and mounted in cheap frames. Two doors opened off the parlor, one to a room containing a cookstove, the other to a bedroom, the mattress littered with more pamphlets, Bibles, and at least one empty bottle. Substitute books on hanging and beheading for the theological literature and they might never have left Leavenworth.

Rudd went into the kitchen and came out carrying a bottle of Old Pepper and two thick barrel glasses. Oscar declined, and asked him what had become of his intention to abstain once he became a minister.

"When I read past Revelations, I found Scripture weren't as clear as I thought on the wickedness of a little snort now and then. There's more goatskin bags than sheep in the Bible. It finally come to me that if our Savior didn't see nothing wrong with making wine out of water, who was I to set myself too good for a little sour grain? Also it's the one thing I've found that's good with the rheumatism. It ain't a cure, mind; only the Lord Hisownself could work that. A swig or two makes the misery worth the having. After nine or ten I'm thinking I'll take up the piano."

As Rudd filled his glass, Oscar noticed the red, swollen knuckles he'd hidden behind his back earlier. It occurred to him that the old hangman was incapable any longer of kneading a rope or tying a proper knot. Had that something to do with his call to the cloth? He had to ask.

"Rudd, why did you leave the life?"

The old man transferred some Bibles from an old wicker chair to the top of an already precarious stack and sat down, cupping his hands around his glass as if to warm them. His eyes were as bright as dimes.

"I could spread a little of that oil I do on Sunday and say I heard the trumpet, but that's just for passing the plate. The pure truth is, short of taking a hitch around their ankles and dangling 'em topside down, there wasn't a way I could hang a man that I hadn't already done twenty times and change. One day there I was, feeling of the neck of this coward of a lieutenant named McQuelty that shot a courier off his horse so he could climb aboard and put distance betwixt himself and a bunch of ornery Arapaho, my hands around this lily-livered jacksnipe's throat, and wondering if they're serving fresh turnips in the mess. I got my mind back on the business at hand and gave Janning my resignation five minutes after McQuelty went through the trap."

"That was it? Turnips?"

"I don't even like 'em, but that ain't the point. When you catch yourself at that moment thinking about anything but how much rope you'll need to do the job neat, it's time to find some other work. I ain't fixed to strangle a man or worse for turnips. Not even a yellow pisspot like Lieutenant McQuelty."

"*I* did worse," Oscar said.

Rudd drank. He said nothing.

Oscar leaned forward and rubbed his palms against each other between his knees. The calluses rasped. "I underestimated the drop and took off a man's head in Nebraska. I was drunk when I examined him, and I was still drunk when I measured the rope. And when I sobered up I was too cowardly to quit."

"I read about it. It looks worse and it's messier'n turd stew, but it beats strangling. Ask a man who's strangled."

"That doesn't change the fact I went against everything you taught me."

"You gave up whiskey?"

"I haven't touched a drop since that day. I swore off meat as well. They always did serve it too bloody out here for my taste. Now I can't even look at it without thinking about Richard Round Oak."

"Still and all, you was drunk. It ain't the same thing as bored."

"I was drunk."

"You fixed that."

"I didn't go far enough. I should have quit hanging when I quit drinking. Instead I went on two more years. I didn't have the courage of your convictions. In my mind that makes me no better than your Lieutenant McQuelty."

Rudd sipped in silence. Along with choosing glasses over straight-from-the-bottle, he'd changed his rate of intake. Finally he leaned over, set the glass on the floor, and settled back with his swollen fingers laced across his belly.

"I still wear my collars frontwise," he said. "I don't burn wax except to read and write and I don't hear confessions. If you come all this way to get a chit from God, you bet the wrong horse."

"I could have done that in San Francisco, where there's a cathedral on every corner. I came here because you're the only friend I have. There's no one else I can talk to about this."

"My advice? Give up liquor or give up stretching rope. I don't see where it makes any sense to give up both."

"I never really liked drinking. I don't miss it, so I don't guess I needed it either. It was just something to pass the time when I wasn't working. There's no reason to go back to it. There's every reason in the world not to go back to work. There's no challenge in it anymore. Unless I take a hitch around their ankles and hang them topside down." He started a smile, but it wasn't worth the effort.

Rudd pulled his hands apart; a spasm of pain swept across his features, disappearing when he held up his hands in front of them. "You see these? There's weeks when I can't hardly pull out my pickle to drain it on account of it hurts like the pit. Even when they was working and I still had the spirit, I couldn't of done what you done that day in Denver, not if I kept the cork in the bottle and studied the books and my chart back to front for a month. I figured the odds of dropping the trap out from under six men shaped six different ways and cracking their necks all at once; the numbers don't go that low. That's why I never writ that book, and it's why I gave you all them wires offering work instead of answering 'em myself, which you being my apprentice I had the right to do. I hadn't the gift."

"Everything I know I learned from you."

"Know-how ain't talent. Talent's what makes the difference betwixt a handyman and an artist. I told you before any ape with a rope can string a man up. All right, you measured too long once and snapped the top off a prisoner. If you hadn't been around to take that job, it might of went to one of the apes, and the half-breed might of dropped six inches and flopped around for three minutes and shit his pants. You can lynch a man from a gallows just the same as a tree, and that's just what they'll go back to if you give up just because you made one more mistake than God Almighty. You want absolution? Here." He snatched a Bible off the stack next to his chair and swept it around in a wide arc, cuffing the side of Oscar's head just above the left ear. Oscar yelled and clapped a hand to his head.

Rudd returned the Bible gently to the stack. "Now you been smote by the Good Book. That's your Hail Mary. Get back to work and quit wasting my time. I got a sermon to write and three people to read it to."

"You could have made your point without that." Oscar rubbed his temple.

"I'm a Unitarian, not a Quaker. I near forgot. This come for you last Christmas. They sent it here from Leavenworth. You ain't been in touch, so I didn't know where to send it." He held out a thick envelope, scuffed all over and bearing a number of postmarks.

Oscar took it carefully, as if it were made of thin crystal. It bore no return address, but he recognized Gretchen's handwriting.

TWENTY-FIVE

Mr. Oscar Stone
% Mr. Rudd
Leavenworth, Kansas
30 November 1875

Dear Oscar,

My father has written to inform me that he has been visited by detectives in your employ requesting my present address. Since I do not trust my father to keep this information in confidence (he is inclined to take your part), I have asked him to send all communications in care of General Delivery in a town where I do not live, to be called for by an acquaintance there and sent on to me in a separate packet. Its eventual destination is not my home either. In the place where I live, I am known by neither Stone nor Smollett, and the people with whom I associate are not aware of the real circumstances of my past. It is quite useless to attempt to locate me. I say this not merely to discourage you from continuing the quest, but also to impress upon you the length to which I am prepared to go in order to avoid contact. Should you succeed in finding me, your attention will not only be unwelcome, but absolutely abhorrent.

You have discovered that I am traveling with a small boy, which I suspect is the reason why you are pressing the search, as you are laboring under the misapprehension that he is your son. He is not. Abraham is the issue of a brief and ill-advised union into which I entered in the midst of my grief and desolation after I left Topeka. His father and I parted company once he learned I was with child. This was a blessing (although I assure you it did not seem so at the time), because he was in no wise a suitable mate, and because his desertion drove me into the shelter of an association with a group of women whose familiarity with the oppressive realities of life in the West led them to abandon the conventions and pious social assumptions of civilization in favor of earthly *salvation. They do not judge, they do not dictate, rather, they are like the compassionate stranger who, upon observing a fellow mortal fallen through the ice of a deep pond and struggling, does not pause to ask if his brother's misfortune is the result of his own foolhardiness in venturing out despite signs warning of the danger, but crawls out to the broken edge and extends a branch for the fellow to grasp. This samaritan sisterhood is not an organization of church women, although some of them attend church. They are wives and widows, unmarried mothers and mothers of children miscarried and stillborn, soiled doves, both retired and still practicing, women who have been raped and daughters who have fled homes where unspeakable crimes occurred—women, in short, who in the East might never have met except in circumstances of hostility, but who on the frontier have learned that to band together is to survive against enemies common to them all.*

I realize that to have been so specific about this unique

sorority is to narrow your field of search, but such is their empathy with those whom they have rescued that I am confident they will not betray me even if you manage to seek them out. Again, however, I entreat you not to try, as many of them are sufficiently placed in their communities to arrange for the arrest or even the physical harm of you or your representative if they suspect I am in danger. You of all people should be aware that violence is the court of final appeal in this place where we live.

If it is not the boy in whom you're interested, but myself, I am compelled to say that there is no possibility of a reconciliation between us. Do you still have nightmares, Oscar, about South Georgia Crossing, or have the many hangings over which you have presided (for I read about you everywhere) provided you with others? If neither of these things is true, and you no longer awake in the night, drenched and choking for air, then I ask you to remember the sensation. It is how I awake from the dream of you standing in that congratulatory crowd at Fort Leavenworth, with the glow of satisfaction upon your face and the grain of the wooden lever with which you dispatched a man still impressed upon your palm—that same dear palm I kissed and caressed when you started from sleep with the picture of that murdered twelve-year-old still twitching in your memory. I saw it again when our eyes met in St. Louis; that is why I ran from you, and why I am still running. I ask you now to let me stop, for Abraham if not for myself. For some time now he has been old enough to take notice of things around him. I fear for the manhood of a boy who has become accustomed to the fugitive life. I have no love for you. Should I come to hate you, it would be like losing you all over again.

If it is not me you are looking for, but forgiveness, this letter is evidence that you have it. I will not betray the sisters and hold a victim to blame for weaknesses over which he has no command. Although I will never understand why you made the choice you made, I will not add guilt of me to the burden you must carry daily in the pursuit of your living. I will always remember with affection the serious young carpenter who courted me against my father's opposition to the adventurous life you had planned, and who rescued our pilgrim train from savages by speaking with them in your father's tongue and sacrificing your spectacles to their chief. Someday, when he is old enough to understand, I shall tell Abraham that story, as a substitute for anything uplifting I could share with him about his real father.

Do not be concerned with my security or my state of mind. I have found decent employment, a number of friendships, and the regard of neighbors who believe I am the widow of a carpenter dead of the cholera, of which there are many victims here. My quarters are clean and I am earning enough to feed and dress myself and my son and to bow our heads for the charity of none. I do not believe I would have been better served if I'd remained in York. Certainly I would not have my dear little Abraham.

In closing, I hope you will read these passages in the spirit in which they were composed, and remember that she who wrote them wishes you comfort and safety, if for no other reason than that she has found these things at last and knows their worth.

Sincerely,
Gretchen Stone
nee *Smollett*

Part Six

THE MASTER EXECUTIONER

A noose is a circle.
—OSCAR STONE

Columbus, Ohio, September 1897

It was a coincidence he could just as well have done without.

Seated in Esmond Broadbent's office awaiting the lawyer's return, the hangman had a clear view through the window of the railroad station across the street, where a pair of teamsters was loading an electric chair into the bed of a stout wagon with iron-reinforced wheels.

The crowd that had gathered on the sidewalk to witness the event was probably disappointed. The device resembled nothing so much as an ordinary wooden chair, ugly and uncomfortable-looking, with straight arms and a ladder back; the chief unconventional fixture, apart from the tangle of thick leather straps designed to pinion the condemned man's wrists, ankles, and torso, looked almost comical. In appearance it was a plain oak plank with two rows of incandescent bulbs running up the outside edges, bolted behind the seat and extending two feet above the back. One wondered if, when the switch was thrown, the bulbs would light up in sequence from bottom to top, like one of those test-your-strength contraptions featured at carnivals equipped with portable generators—ending, not with a bell, but with a man's death. The reality was still amusing, but grimmer still: The bulbs, which worked in unison, glowed dimly at first, then more fiercely as the current increased, and existed merely to demonstrate that the electricity was working—as if the spectacle of a man writhing in its embrace, with smoke and occasionally blue flames pouring out from under the gleaming metal skullcap, were not evidence enough. In fact, the bulbs were fed by current that had already passed through the wretch's body, with his arteries, nervous system, and reservoir of natural fluids performing as the conductor. The effect was that of a ghastly scientific demonstration intended to awe the ignorant. It was nothing more than a late-nineteenth-century variation on the medieval practice of lifting stake-burning victims out of the flames momentarily to be ogled at after their clothes had burned away. Was the twentieth century to resemble so closely the fourteenth?

The coincidence, that both the abominable apparatus and the notorious western hangman should arrive in the same city on the same train, had drawn that proliferating pestilence of straw-hatted reporters for an impromptu press conference on the station platform, to which he'd submitted with his usual show of equanimity, while inwardly his blood simmered. No, he was in Columbus on personal business, not to operate or witness the operation of the electric chair. Yes, it was an interesting circumstance that executioner and instrument of execution should be traveling together, but it was just that; the railroads these days carried everything from baby bottles to dynamite. No, he preferred not to disclose the purpose of his visit, and, no, he would not attend when the People of the State of Ohio electrocuted Rudolph Wenceslaus, Bohemian cobbler, for the bludgeoning death of his uncle with an iron last; furthermore, he had not been invited, and if such an invitation were to come to pass, he would decline. He'd seen a similar machine in action in San Francisco in '95 and did not care to repeat the experience.

He'd hoped to place distance between himself and the station before the chair made its appearance, but as it happened, Esmond Broadbent was not one of the fashionable legal hawks who offered their services in the neighborhood of the courthouse downtown.

This office, with its lumpy upholstery, old scratched desk, and obsolete law books leaking expired statutes from their sagging shelves, required the low rental rates in the shuddering near proximity of the Baltimore & Ohio to survive. Every rumble of a passing express and shrieking whistle of a local slowing to a stop made the glass stopper jingle in the inkstand on the desk and dislodged a fresh dribble of pulverized plaster from the crack in the ceiling, and the accumulated soot on the window created a chiaroscuro effect that did not quite succeed in making the scene outside look like a detail from a painting by Caravaggio. A cinder the size of a butterfly edged in past the sash and floated to a rest on Stone's coatsleeve. He wished he hadn't sent his travel duster on ahead to the hotel with his baggage.

Broadbent entered from the outer office and pushed the door shut against the chatter of a typewriter. He was short and very fat, with bright cunning eyes punched like snaps into the moist pink flesh of his face, and wore a vest too tight, with white shirt billowing out around the bottom like whipped cream. His shirt cuffs were turned back—Stone suspected to conceal frayed edges—and his necktie hung free of the vest, describing a greasy black *Y* whose tail appeared to have dipped itself into every course of his luncheon. The hangman forgave him the untidiness but disapproved of his leaving his suitcoat draped over the back of his chair when he went out to request something from his female secretary. Rape and murder he forgave, since those who committed them had already been judged and sentenced when he came into their association. Impropriety offended him deeply, particularly here on the fringe of what was once the frontier, where people were supposed to know better.

The lawyer apologized for the delay and lowered his bulk into his chair to study the sheet he had excused himself to retrieve. "I'm afraid we've become lax in our filing since the building was condemned."

"How long has that been?" Stone didn't care. He'd run out of small talk five minutes after meeting Broadbent.

"Six years. The city wanted to put in a park, with a statue of Columbus, in time for the four hundredth; you'd think he landed in Ohio. Obviously, they got bogged down. Us, too. If you'd wired us you were coming, we'd have been better prepared. We weren't sure any of our letters reached you."

The "we" of Broadbent & Co., Title Searches and Civil Services, seemed to consist of the attorney and the woman in the shirtwaist typing outside. "I'm in semiretirement," Stone said. "My permanent residence is in Topeka. I found them all waiting for me when I returned from Idaho."

He was barely listening to his own words. The teamsters were struggling with the chair, which evidently was heavier than it looked. They'd shattered one of the bulbs when the chair slipped and banged against a sideboard. He hoped they'd damaged the mechanism. *We begin, Mr. Stone, with a single phase of sixty-cycle alternating current at two thousand volts for fifty-seven seconds, followed by a second shock of the same voltage and duration. The second jolt is just for insurance. Death is instantaneous.*

Stone had told the technician he'd never felt the need to hang a man more than once.

One jolt had certainly been sufficient for the man in the chair, a San Francisco fisherman who'd murdered his partner for his half of the business. He'd lunged forward as if to throw himself to his feet, the straps creaking, while the dynamo that supplied the current hummed for what seemed much longer than fifty-seven seconds, then cut off with a clunk of silence. The body collapsed into the chair, the hooded head tipped forward. Smoke curled up from the contact points. Then came the second jolt. Again the body hurled itself against its constraints, animated entirely now by electrical impulse. This time, just before the humming stopped, a jet of flame shot through the top of the skullcap. One of the turnkeys who had helped strap down the prisoner stepped forward with a fire extinguisher and put out the flames that had sprouted on the oak plank. The stench of scorched flesh and carbon tetrachloride had remained with Stone for days afterward.

"Fabian T. Rudd," Broadbent said.

"I beg your pardon?" The hangman rubbed his nose; the memory of the odor was nearly as strong as the odor itself.

The lawyer repeated the name, reading it from the sheet, as if the typewritten characters were his first encounter. "I never met the good reverend, unfortunately. We represented the original title holder when he bought the lot where he built his church. I suppose he remembered the name from the transaction all those years later when it came time to make his bequest."

"He left the clergy twenty years ago. I doubt anyone still addressed him as reverend." Rudd had written him last in 1885, from a post office box in Des Moines. The letter was barely legible. Manipulating a pencil must have been agony.

"He operated a business that sold Bibles by mail order. I don't suppose he prospered. The Gideons pretty much destroyed the market. I'm afraid it isn't much of an estate, just a few old books and some odd clothing. If you'll sign here, I'll see it's delivered to your hotel." He slid the sheet across the desk.

Stone read the itemized list, smiling thinly when he came to the long title in Latin, which whoever had transposed it had misspelled. It belonged to the hefty ancient history of execution and torture with which Rudd had begun Stone's education. He accepted the pen the lawyer had dipped for him and wrote his name at the bottom. "Was there any personal message?"

"No. I understand he dictated the will from his deathbed. He'd been in a bad way for some time, apparently. The woman who ran the boardinghouse witnessed it and sent it to us along with a crate containing the items." He cleared his throat. "It was cash on delivery."

"How much do you need, Mr. Broadbent?" He took out his checkbook.

The lawyer appeared relieved, and said fifty dollars would cover the firm's services and expenses. Stone gave him a check and pocketed the receipt. When the pair rose to shake hands, he asked Broadbent about Rudd's remains.

"Potter's Field, I'm afraid. Whatever funds Mr. Rudd possessed were claimed by his landlady in return for his accommodations."

"He wouldn't care. He wasn't a material man."

"A man of the spirit."

"More than one, Mr. Broadbent."

A bellman brought Rudd's legacy to Stone's room on a hand cart. The books and clothing were packed in the same oblong wooden crate that had held the old hangman's cheap Bibles. He tipped the young man generously for prying the lid off with a pinch bar, took off his coat, and sat on the floor to sort through the contents. He was surprised to learn that Rudd had owned not one but two black frock coats, identically worn and in need of brushing and pressing—the same bottle sag was evident in the two outside right pockets—and that he'd replaced the old-fashioned high-topped shoes with elastic-sided boots, probably to accommodate arthritic toes. The greasy and battered hat had not traveled well, and after examining it inside and out with a smile he chucked it into the wastebasket. He had spent too much time in hotels and railroad stations to form the habit of collecting sentimental objects. Most of the Leavenworth library was not present, but Rudd had been unable or unwilling to part with the book full of ghastly woodcuts said to have been bound in human skin, and a number of other volumes whose broken spines had poured out their knowledge. There was a grubby memorandum book in which the pastor of the First Unitarian Church of Carbon City had kept the monthly expenses in his crabbed hand, Rudd's prized hangman's chart, yellow, creased, and outdated, and, wedged between slats at the bottom, a black rubber ball as hard as a petrified peach. This he thought he'd keep.

He wasn't sure what to do with the rest. The coats were too

shabby even to give to a veterans' home, and would probably be thrown out. The Latin tome was no doubt valuable, to a collector of arcana if no one else, and he might donate the others to a library, where they would go out with the trash unless someone thought them worth rebinding. He didn't know why the drunken old fool had wanted him to have these things.

Yes, he did. Because a life that left nothing behind for someone else to claim was of no more substance than wind on water. Stone had known before he left Topeka that the estate would be valueless; he'd come because it was Rudd's wish that he come. Who was he to pity a penniless failure decomposing in a nameless grave? At least Rudd had had someone who would make the trip. Who had he?

He didn't dwell upon the point. It had nearly cost him his livelihood two decades before, when the prospect of dispatching yet another stranger for a fee and traveling expenses had seemed harder to bear than the burden of his loneliness. Rudd's answer, that he had a gift and it was his duty to use it regardless of his personal wishes, had been inadequate, but he had acted upon it. Gretchen's letter had helped him come to the decision, effectively sealing off his only passage to a private life that did not involve answering telegrams and arranging for the transportation of his luggage. He had crossed and recrossed his own trail many times in the years since, witnessed at firsthand the evolution of the railroads from a herky-jerky means of excursion through buffalo herds and Indian country, departing parlor cars in the middle of the night for the dubious expedients of smoky coaches stinking of spitoons and unwashed miners, to through Pullmans complete with brocade and Turkish coffee served from silver urns. He hadn't been forced to put up with the torture of a stagecoach ride since Tombstone in 1881, and could scarcely remember when was the last time he'd heard a shot fired close to his hotel room. In that time, his business had fallen off fifty percent, thanks to creeping civilization and the increasing sophistication of law enforcement in places where the peace was once kept by men who were themselves wanted for crimes in other places, but he had invested his money wisely, in cattle futures and railroads, and once the infernal sparking torture chair supplanted the rope, he could retire without ever having to make the choice between a fine meal and an evening at the theater. He could enjoy both night after night, leaving only the days to be gotten through.

Knuckles tapped his door. He asked who it was and got a muffled female voice in response. Assuming it was the maid come to turn down the bed, he got up with a grunt, dusted off his trousers, put on his coat, and opened the door.

"Good evening, Oscar. You've gotten gray. It suits you."

He who had always the right words to say to a terrified condemned prisoner was struck for a reply. Gretchen's hair was still pale blonde. She wore it pinned up now, drawing the eye away from the lines in her face, which had fleshed out though not to disadvantage. She was still a young woman, not yet fifty. Her eyes were as blue as Delft. She wore a gray dress, simple but of good quality, clasped at the throat with an inexpensive brooch, and a matching wrap of light flannel. He had the impression they were the best things in her wardrobe.

"May I come in?" she asked. "It's quite appropriate, you know. We're still married."

He managed to say, "Please," and stepped aside. She stopped before the empty crate and its contents heaped untidily on the carpet. "Are you packing to leave?"

"It's my inheritance. Rudd died."

"Recently? I thought he was an old man in 1866."

"He was about the age I am now." He helped her out of her wrap and hung it in the clothespress. She still wore the verbena scent of her youth. "How did you know I was here?"

"I read the paper. Between the electric chair and Oscar Stone there was little room for anything else. I live in Columbus now. I came here when Father died. He lost Mother nine years ago. I was with him in York the last year."

"He was a good man."

"He thought I should not have left you. He said it shouldn't matter what a man does as long as it's legal and decent, only that he provide for his family. We could not agree on the definition of *decent.* That's why I didn't go home to have my child. All the arguing would not have been good for him."

"Abraham was four or five in 1872. That would make him—"

"Thirty. I still observe his birthday." Her gaze took in the mahogany bed and Tiffany lamps. "I see your work still pays well."

"I only accept one or two assignments a year. I'm not offered many more than that. All the states and most of the remaining territories have permanent prisons and full-time personnel, including executioners. It's rare now to see a town with its own gallows. They send their condemned to the capitals."

"That must be a hardship."

"I have no one to spend money on but myself." He paused. "I wish you'd have let me help out. You were entitled. The boy—"

"The boy is dead. It happened just before his twenty-fifth birthday."

His face felt numb. He drew the Chippendale chair away from the writing desk and held it for her. She thanked him and sat down without touching the back. For the first time in years he wished he had brandy to offer. The deep wing chair was too soft for this conversation. He sat on the edge of the cushion. "How?"

"He went bad. It was my fault. A growing boy needs a man in the house; someone in the house, in any case. I had to work to support us both. He was alone too much. He left when he was fourteen. I came home and he was gone, his clothes too, without a note. I didn't hear anything from him until he sent me a letter from his jail cell. I'd moved several times by then; it took months to reach me. By then he was dead."

"Hanged?" He mouthed the word. His voice was gone. The numbness had spread to his larynx.

"Don't worry, you didn't hang him. You were in Seattle at the time; a mail train robber named Case. I read about it. Abraham's career was even less successful. He shot a faro dealer in a place called Leadville and the bartender stopped him at the door with a shotgun."

He searched his memory for the details; but there had been so many men, and he had never asked. He knew he'd never been to Leadville. "You're certain?"

"He confessed everything in his letter. He'd killed in cold blood, but he didn't want to die a liar to his mother. I will never understand men. Not my father, not my husband, not even the son to whom I gave birth." A silvery trickle glittered on her cheek.

"I'm sorry." There was a terrible inadequacy in the words. He fumbled for his handkerchief. She took it and dabbed at her eyes. "How are you living?" he asked.

"I inherited some money. It wasn't as much as I'd hoped—the Panic of 'seventy-three was hard on all the family investments—but after I sold the house I had enough to support me while I attended secretarial school. I'm an efficient typewriter." She blew her nose gently, then smiled. "Sixty-two words per minute. I've applied for a job with a paper plant here."

"Do you need money?"

She shook her head and gave him back the handkerchief. "I wanted to come see you, Oscar, and to tell you I have no harsh feelings toward you."

"You said that in your letter."

"I don't think I said it well. I wanted you to stop looking for me, for your sake as well as mine. I was young. I thought I had to be cold."

He said nothing to that. It was a cold letter. There was an awkward silence, which he broke. "Will you give me your address?"

"It wouldn't be good for long. I expect to move soon, if I am hired."

"I'd like to give you mine. You might want to write." He took out his leather card case. It was empty. "I'll write it down for you." There was stationery and an inkstand on the desk. He started to rise. She discouraged him with a gesture.

"I'd just throw it away. I don't want to correspond with you; there would be no point, and it would just remind me of some things."

"Was Abraham my son?"

She looked away, at the books on the floor. She turned her head from them quickly, as if she'd guessed their nature. She looked at him. "Yes."

He nodded, and went on nodding. Stopping was more difficult. He wanted to close his eyes, show some expression other than the blank professional face he presented to peace officers and prisoners. He'd forgotten how.

"There was no man," she said. "If I'd told you he was yours, you'd never have stopped looking for me. I told him the same story I told others, that his father died of cholera. My lie with you was more successful. I don't think he believed me. I think he thought he was born out of wedlock. I'd rather he thought that than the truth."

"It wasn't successful," he said. "I always thought he was mine. Your letter gave me a reason not to confirm it."

"We failed Abraham. Both of us did."

He looked at the books, a malevolent mess on the deep figured carpet. "I wish I'd never met Rudd."

"It wasn't Rudd. It would have been someone else if not Rudd."

"It's simpler to think that," he said.

She gathered her skirts and stood. "Thank you for seeing me, Oscar. I was afraid you'd turn me away at the door."

He wished he had. He got up and helped her on with her wrap. "Good-bye, Gretchen."

"Good-bye." She waited for him to open the door. He paused with his hand on the knob.

"I had another hanging right after Seattle," he said. "It was in Canon City. Most of the Colorado executions take place there now."

Her eyes were cast down. "I'm sure it was Leadville. In any case, both hangings happened the same week. You couldn't have gotten there in time to do both. Not from Washington."

"By then it was a three-day trip. The damn trains cut travel in half every couple of years. What name was he using?"

"I don't remember."

"Another unsuccessful lie."

She raised her eyes. They were cool and dry. "Are you certain you want to know?"

He hesitated. "Yes."

She shook her head; whether because she didn't believe him or truly couldn't remember, he could not be sure. She said good-bye again.

He opened the door.

And she was gone.

The doctor whom the hotel clerk had recommended was white-haired, narrow and lean, and as he sat on his turning-stool reading his notations, his bony knees came up almost to his chin. The wall behind him was a solid nest of cubbyholes containing white apothecary jars and evil-looking brown bottles with rubber eyedroppers set into the lids. The room smelled brown as well.

"You're a healthy specimen, Mr. Stone. If I were forced to suggest a change, I'd advise you to lose some weight and reduce your cigar consumption. Apart from that, I don't see any reason why you won't live to see ninety."

The patient slid off the end of the leather-upholstered examining table and reattached his collar without comment. The doctor had weighed him, measured his height, told him to strip, and conducted the standard assortment of outrages upon his person. Stone had put up with the last part in return for the first two figures. He'd gained six pounds since his last examination and lost a quarter inch off his stature.

"I wish I had more patients like you. Most people don't come to me unless they're pregnant or sick. I can't remember the last time I examined someone just to see how he was doing."

"Perhaps it will catch on. I was always a bit before my time, until recently." He thanked the doctor and paid the nurse-receptionist on the way out.

The weather had changed overnight; not in that sudden harsh way that heaped yards of snow on top of wildflowers in the plains, but in the click of a ratchet. Warm moist air became cool and bracing, the nostril-crinkling odor of burning leaves replaced the buttery smell from popcorn wagons, straw boaters went into storage and bowlers came out. It all reminded him of his youth in Pennsylvania. He leaned forward and asked the driver of his two-wheeler to stop.

"Eight more blocks to the hotel, sir." The fellow's German accent had a gritty eastern edge. They were contemporaries, and had likely been neighbors.

"I'll walk."

"Can't blame you, sir. Enjoy it while you can. These old bones feel a bad winter coming on."

He gave the driver a modest tip and got out, carrying his Gladstone bag. Walking, he turned a corner, and caught the stench from a pulp plant on the river. He wondered if it was the same one where Gretchen had applied for work. Then the wind changed directions and he smelled manure. He went that way, holding down his hat. Stiff breezes lifted his coattails when he crossed the spaces between brick buildings. Columbus seemed to be built entirely of brick—chimneys, bridges, even the streets were paved with rows of terra-cotta rectangles glazed with dirt, the last with the manufacturers' names pressed into them in neat sunken capitals—like York, and now just like Denver, where he'd hanged six men at once back when there wasn't a brick to be found in ten blocks. The second half of the century would endure. The first had already gone to fires and termites.

He came at length to the source of the odor: a squat carriage house—brick, of course—behind a three-story house of turrets and gables on a two-acre corner lot. Nothing more than a hook-and-eye secured the iron-banded wooden doors. He opened them, and drew them shut behind him swiftly to avoid attracting attention from anyone who happened to glance out a window in the house. Inside, he waited, but no sound of approaching footsteps came from without. The perfect crime.

He was in a well-kept enclosure, open to the rafters, with two stalls on either side and a handsome black carriage with yellow wheels and wicker inserts taking up half the passage in between. Two of the stalls were occupied, by a black and a blaze-faced sorrel, who raised their heads and blew shuddering snorts in wary greeting. Sunlight shafted grainily through a single-paned window at the rear. The air was sweet with green hay and fresh manure; a brown smell, but different from the one in the doctor's office, friendlier. It all reminded him of the barn he had helped his father and brother build.

A stepladder leaned against the wall next to the doors. He set it up in the middle of the earthen floor, packed hard as granite, opened his bag, and drew out the rope he'd spent most of last night oiling after Gretchen had left his room, coiled into a supple figure eight. It was a good one of Indian hemp that he'd found quite unexpectedly in the back room of a hardware store in Duluth and had been saving. Although he'd made use of a gallows in Albuquerque to stretch it, he had not used it once in a hanging. The candidates had all seemed undeserving for one reason or another, and he hadn't known if he'd ever find another like it. Quickly he fashioned a noose. Using his dressmaker's tape, he measured seven feet, six inches back from the thirteenth coil, then, marking the spot with his thumb, climbed the ladder and tied the rope around the four-by-four beam that extended horizontally across the space at the base of the roof, using a square hitch. He wrapped the excess around the beam and tied off the end in a slipknot. He grasped the rope in two hands and tugged hard twice. The beam was solid, giving up not so much as a creak. He climbed back down.

He found a three-legged stool that was probably used by whoever took care of the horses to sit on while paring hooves, and drew it out of its corner. He took off his coat, folded it neatly, and placed it on the seat. Atop it he laid his vest, his watch and chain, his collar, and his hat, squaring it carefully to avoid warping the brim. He unhooked his spectacles and folded the legs and leaned them against the crown. He hoped the clothes weren't there so long they smelled like manure.

He removed some money from his wallet and laid the notes on top of the pile: compensation for the owner of the building.

He moved the stepladder a foot and started climbing, then descended with a mild oath and burrowed among the clothes on the stool until he found the black hood in his coat pocket. Then he climbed to the top step, put his head through the noose, and spent some time adjusting the knot so that it fit snugly into the hollow below his left ear. The fibers scratched his skin. He wondered if he'd used enough oil. Lately he'd been wondering about Vaseline, but that was what they used on the contact points of the electric chair, to avoid burning the prisoner's skin.

He looked around slowly, although the details of his surroundings were blurred, then tugged the hood over his head.

Breathing through the porous cotton was surprisingly easy. The quickened pants of all the others when their vision was cut off had misled him. He took a deep breath and let it out; had any of them done that? He thought it odd that he couldn't remember, but then he couldn't remember the features of the young man he had dispatched in Canon City in 1892. He'd spent all night trying. He'd been too busy with his measurements and getting the knot in the right place. *If you take your time with a thing, you can't help but do it well.* And now he'd hesitated too long, and had to breathe again. He hadn't made the others wait.

"Well—" he said, and stepped off.